SEASCAPE

STEPHANIE BURKE

ELLORA'S CAVE
ROMANTICA PUBLISHING

An Ellora's Cave Romantica Publication

www.ellorascave.com

Seascape

ISBN 9781419951169
ALL RIGHTS RESERVED.
Seascape Copyright © 2003 Stephanie Burke
Edited by Martha Punches
Cover art by Syneca

Electronic Book Publication June 2003
Trade paperback Publication February 2007

With the exception of quotes used in reviews, this book may not be reproduced or used in whole or in part by any means existing without written permission from the publisher, Ellora's Cave Publishing, Inc.® 1056 Home Avenue, Akron OH 44310-3502.

This book is a work of fiction and any resemblance to persons, living or dead, or places, events or locales is purely coincidental. The characters are productions of the authors' imagination and used fictitiously.

Content Advisory:

S – ENSUOUS
E – ROTIC
X – TREME

Ellora's Cave Publishing offers three levels of Romantica™ reading entertainment: S (S-ensuous), E (E-rotic), and X (X-treme).

The following material contains graphic sexual content meant for mature readers. This story has been rated E–rotic.

S-*ensuous* love scenes are explicit and leave nothing to the imagination.

E-*rotic* love scenes are explicit, leave nothing to the imagination, and are high in volume per the overall word count. E-rated titles might contain material that some readers find objectionable—in other words, almost anything goes, sexually. E-rated titles are the most graphic titles we carry in terms of both sexual language and descriptiveness in these works of literature.

X-*treme* titles differ from E-rated titles only in plot premise and storyline execution. Stories designated with the letter X tend to contain difficult or controversial subject matter not for the faint of heart.

Also by Stephanie Burke

☙

Hidden Passions Vol. 1
Hidden Passions Vol. 2
Lucavarious
Merlin's Kiss
More Than Skin Deep *(anthology)*
Reaver of Souls
Testrios 1: Keeper of the Flames
Testrios 2: Dangerous Heat
The Slayer
Things That Go Bump In The Night III *(anthology)*
Wicked Wishes *(anthology)*

About the Author

ಐ

Stephanie is married to the most wonderfully maddening Irish Viking ever created and has given birth to two children, affectionately known as The Viking kittens. Stephanie's main support in her writing career has been her wonderful parents who are always willing to take her spawns, uh, children for a weekend so that she can work, her older sister Teresa, the stuffed chicken, and of course, her Irish Viking, Dennis. Stephanie loves to write paranormal and fantasy characters with a lot of humor, because there is no such thing as enough laughter in the world. She also loves to write erotica, just to shock people, but in her heart she is a romance fanatic...

Stephanie welcomes comments from readers. You can find her website and email address on her author bio page at www.ellorascave.com.

SEASCAPE

ఐ

Chapter One

"I'll kill her, I swear I will!"

The gunman's hand shook as he made his declaration to the silent passengers onboard Pacifica Airline Flight 769. His eyes were wide with unholy delight and more than a hint of fanaticism.

"I want this plane to take me to the Hawaiian International Airport and then I want a plane, gassed and ready to take me to Iran. Hurry it up, 'cause I am just itching to make an example out of someone!"

He jerked the frightened young woman closer to his sweating body, his eyes twitching nervously as he swung his head from side to side watching the cowering hostages.

"Please," the young woman pleaded as she sobbed quietly in the grasp of the madman. Her face was pale as her fingers gripped the forearm that encircled her neck.

"Shut up!" he screamed, his forearm tightening around her neck. "You just shut up!"

A few of the women let loose frightened squeaks of panic as they saw the young woman's face pale further.

Iran was the general thought that flowed through the plane. These men were crazy.

"We don't negotiate with terrorists!" a small mechanical-sounding voice said over the radio. A second terrorist held the cockpit crew at bay with a submachine gun and exhibited an even more threatening demeanor. Equally sweaty and nervous, the man's wild eyes jerked to his compatriot.

"Waste her!" a third urged. "That's the only way these bastards will know we mean business." There was no compassion in his eyes as he viewed the frightened young woman, only a cold determination to have his own way.

"Please," she begged, but the arm tightening around her throat cut off her words and well as the flow of oxygen. She subsided with a small whimper.

"I will make a better hostage."

Everyone froze at the cool, calm voice that made this announcement.

"Well, someone has balls!" the third gunman sneered as he eyed the elegant woman who stood before him. "Cute, too."

Dressed in a red business suit and matching leather pumps, the woman exuded wealth and power. Her smooth brown hair was pulled neatly into a bun at her nape and her dark brown eyes looked serious. Her café au lait complexion was flawless, and the gold-framed glasses covering her eyes gave her a studious appearance. This was a woman of means.

"And why are you so anxious to die, chickie?" he sneered as he looked her up and down with grim disdain.

"She is worth nothing to you—a pawn that serves no purpose. I, on the other hand, am worth quite a lot to the government."

The young woman looked at the woman, tears of fear filling her eyes as she frantically shook her head no.

"Well, exactly who are you, bitch?" he growled, ignoring his captive's nervous pleas.

"I am Dr. Elanna Richfield."

Several people on the plane gasped at her name. Elanna Richfield was synonymous with God! She alone was responsible for cracking a genetic code that caused cancer. Her research, groundbreaking as it was, was just the tip of the Richfield iceberg. Rumor had it she had actually taken the information she discovered and found a cure! Already there were rumors of her adapting that cure for AIDS and several other deadly diseases around the world. Elanna Richfield was literally worth her weight in gold.

"A celebrity!" the man cried, his eyes lighting up with his good fortune. "All right, young one, you can go! I have bigger bait in her!"

With a careless movement of his arm, he pulled the hostage from his partner and literally threw her across the aisle, then motioned to Elanna to approach him. "Slowly, if you would, doctor. I get nervous really easy and I just can't seem to make my finger move off this trigger!"

Elanna nodded to him, but first stopped to check the young woman who had been sitting beside her when the attack first started.

"Elanna, no!" she whispered, shooting furtive glances at the waiting gunman.

"You are more important than I am, honey," Elanna returned as she knelt by her side.

"Move it, lady!" the man growled, but she turned her serious, piercing brown eyes upon him.

"I am just checking her pulse. It's a little high and you don't want to lose any of your precious hostages. The government's reaction would not be favorable."

Ignoring his sputtering, Elanna again turned to the young woman.

"You know that the cure is coursing through your body right now, reversing the cancer in your system. You are a miracle child!" she whispered as she stared into the teen's large, scared eyes. "A few treatments have dissolved that brain tumor and have already stopped the disease from shutting down your liver and kidneys. You are what's important! In your body lies the secret to it all! I am just the messenger, honey. This trip to Pacifica just finalized your treatments."

"But what if something happens to you?" the young one sobbed. "What about the doctors waiting for us on the mainland? What about the hospitals and the scientists? Elanna, I'm scared." Tears ran down her face, and her whole body shook as she pleaded with the woman.

"Any doctor can read my notes, honey. Any scientist worth his salt can decipher my work. But no one can replace you. Please be brave for me."

"Elanna!" the girl sobbed as she stood to make her way to waiting death.

"Tell no one who you are. Dr. Sandstone will meet you when this is over and the plane finally lands. We made those arrangements before we left the States. We don't need to give them any more leverage than what they have right now."

Turning, she quietly walked over to the gunman and stared her death right in the face.

Twenty minutes later, after the pilot was forced to make the radio announcement that they had the famous doctor as a hostage, they were given the same reply. "We do not negotiate with terrorists!"

"Say good-bye to the doctor!" the man growled as he grabbed Elanna by the collar of her crisp red jacket.

"You're gonna shoot her?" his partner asked, glee ringing through in his voice. "Can I do it?"

Everyone collectively sucked in a deep breath. Elanna paled a little, but kept her head up.

"No, I have a better idea!" he announced.

Sure that they were about to witness a rape scene or a bloodbath, a few of the passengers began to beg and plead for her life.

"Shut up!" he screamed, his eyes wide and his expression deadly, as he dragged Elanna over to the door of the plane.

"Know how to swim, bitch?" he growled as he cracked the door open.

The plane was small and was used to give tours of the South Sea Islands, so there was no real loss in cabin pressure. The plane continued to move steadily over the blue waters despite the small alarm that sounded as the door was pushed open.

"Is that their final answer?" he called to his friend.

"Yeah, man. Go on and waste her."

"Good-bye, good doctor," the man said as he jerked her around to face him. "I hope you have your affairs in order."

There were shouts of surprise from the passengers as the gunman calmly shoved the doctor from the plane. Dispassionately, he watched as the red suit twirled and rotated in the clear skies. There was no sound—he probably would not be able to hear it anyway—but her arms and legs began to flail wildly as she plummeted faster and faster to her watery grave. Soon, she disappeared from view and the plane continued on its journey with its now sobbing and hysterical hostages.

"What do they say now?" the man demanded. He calmly closed the door as if he hadn't just taken a life and consigned future generations to the bottom of the sea with the brilliant doctor.

There was a moment of silence, then the radio voice sounded loud and clear. "We will cooperate with you. Your demands will be met when you land the plane in Hawaii."

"Damn, I love democracy!" the gunman crowed. "It's so much fun being the bad guy. Who gives a shit if you break a few eggs getting what you want? It's all part of the job description."

His grinning companion added his comments. "Damn straight!" They both laughed as the plane moved onward.

*****

Elanna was too frightened to move. Her eyes grew wider as the crystal blue waters of the ocean loomed close and closer. Unlike what she'd expected, her life didn't flash before her eyes. Instead, she thought of all she had yet to accomplish, all that she would never do. She would never experience good sex or have babies. She would never see *Phantom of the Opera* in New York. She would never sample sashimi or get a tattoo! Her flower garden would never have that pond she had meant to buy and she would never see another sunset. Most of all, she would never see that young woman she had treated cry tears of joy as the cancer was expunged from her body. She would never again…be.

She closed her burning eyes, dried from the air, as she felt the mist from the waters and heard the roar of the wind as it tore her hair free from its bun. Then she slammed face first into a brick wall.

Chapter Two

೫

Storm was doing what he loved best! All by himself, he lay completely still and let the waves ripple over his bare skin.

He stifled a groan as heat suffused him, turning his muscles into mush and causing his brain to shut down.

Nothing had ever felt as good as this! He could see himself staying here, just lying, relaxed, as he felt his tensions melt away. This was better than diving off the cliffs near his home. This was better than roasting in the hot sun. This was better than sex—well, *almost* better than sex.

Nothing could get to him now! At this moment in life, everything was perfection. He looked up at the bright blue sky, inhaled deeply of the fresh air, and smiled. And then it hit him.

Not some grand plan to spend the rest of the day loafing, or some great idea to increase his fighting potential, but a hard, plummeting body.

"Shit!" he bubbled before he went under. Instinctively, he grabbed on to the body that hit him, wondering if it was still alive. But then he slowed their headlong plunge into the depths of his waters by spinning and then flipping himself onto his back.

Gradually his momentum slowed and he began to kick to the surface of the water again. The body had knocked him straight out of the jets of warm water that flowed freely from the volcanic rock and plummeted them a few hundred feet below the surface. If the body was still alive, it would need fresh air, and need it soon.

Knowing that the time for this human was dwindling, he decided to act. Tightening the muscles of his abdomen, he began to spin and twirl, forcing his body to undulate out of the downward plunge, slowly propelling him and the human to the surface. Too fast would be just as deadly as drowning.

He tightened his hold on the body, struggling to maintain his grip as the sea threatened to snatch his find away from him.

Closer and closer to the surface he spiraled, feeling the water temperature increase even as the sun began to cast its watery light around him.

He could detect no movement from the human—no struggles, nor panic—and that frightened him enough to force him to increase his pace.

With an uncommonly loud splash, his head broke through the surface of the water. He flung his sodden hair behind him, paying no attention to the droplets of water that flew like diamonds around his head.

With another gigantic effort, he tightened his hold on the human and forced its head to the surface. But that was not enough! He needed to get to some type of land!

Noting that the lava formations he had scouted out weeks ago were only a few yards in the distance, he gave one mighty flip, and in seconds he propelled them towards the floating mass of rock.

Was this human alive, or would there be another body to feed to the scavengers on the bottom? He held the human closer.

Moving quickly, he soon came to the rock mass and hefted the human onto the stone, using the incredible strength of his arms and careful to protect the head and back.

Still half submerged in the water, he impatiently brushed his turquoise hair behind his shell-shaped ears, and began to examine the body—the female, he amended as he noted her body beneath the tattered red cloth she wore.

Closing his eyes, he rested his hands, with their long nails, an inch above her form and began to seek.

Using the power flowing through his body like the waters of the sea, he began an intimate search of her body, categorizing her injuries, making ready to repair what he could.

Her right arm was broken, but that was a common problem and easily remedied. He made a note to set it, then continued with the search.

Her pelvic bone was crushed—a bit more difficult, but could be repaired. Three of her ribs were broken, one puncturing her lung. Because she was human and didn't have a backup set to breathe with—or even gills for that matter—the puncture was his first priority. Putting his diagnosis on hold, he moved his attention to her ribs and her damaged lung.

Reaching into a sealskin pouch hanging at his waist, he produced a small bag of herbs, smiling as the sun caused the normally bright colors to dull. It may not be human medicine, but it was effective, nevertheless. Taking a pinch of the powder into his mouth, he tilted her head to the side, draining it of water, before clapping his warm firm lips over her cold, blue ones.

Taking a deep breath, he forced the powder into her body, mentally directing it to her lungs. In a matter of seconds, the color began to flood back into her face as the powder latched onto the lining of her lungs, repairing the tear even as he rested his hands upon her chest, repairing the damaged ribs.

In minutes, she took a deep breath, gurgling a bit at the water still left inside her body.

"Gills would have been so much simpler," he sighed as he lifted his head and placed both hands upon her shoulders.

He turned her to her side easily, patting her back as her unconscious body forced the water from the newly repaired lung, allowing her blood to be oxygenated and saving her from suffocation.

He gently placed her onto her back again, and began to repair the rest of her battered body.

"Humans are so stupid," he said to the woman as he worked, expecting no answer and receiving none. "To throw a perfectly good female away, you had to be stupid or crazy."

With a sigh of disgust at the peculiarities of humans, he slid the woman back into the water and carefully began towing her to a place of safety.

The small island he had in mind was big enough to hold her until he could find a way to get rid of her. He did not need this complication in his life, but as a Master Healer, he had no choice but to help her. Sometimes, his morals got him into trouble. As he looked down at her caramel-brown skin, he felt that warning tingle start deep in his stomach.

So much for loafing the day away.

* * * * *

Elanna heard a voice speaking softly to her, calling her back to wakefulness, bringing her back from the world of darkness she had floated in, safe and blessedly pain-free.

But as she opened her eyes, a blinding light almost made her pray for that dark void again.

"No, female. Open your eyes. Let me see if your mind is damaged."

Mind damaged? Who was this person talking to her? She was Elanna Richfield, one of the greatest minds in the free world! She was the person heads of state and politicians turned to for answers! She was up for the Nobel Peace Prize! She was…about to hurl!

"Sick," she struggled to say as her saliva grew thick in her mouth. Waves of nausea rushed through her, making the world spin and her eyes water.

"Oh, dear," the voice muttered and she found herself being lifted and tilted to the side.

In an embarrassingly loud evacuation, the meager contents of her stomach were expelled from her body, leaving her weak and shaking.

"I'm sorry," she managed, but the voice just sighed.

"It would have happened sooner or later. The powder had to find a way out of your system now that its work is done, and my dear, you just don't have the same physical make-up as my people do."

"Umm," she grunted in reply, closing her eyes and sinking again into misery.

She must be in a waterbed, because the gentle movements of the bed were part of her problem. She could get seasick while lying on a water bottle. She and water just didn't mix. So what bozo would put her onto a waterbed when she was ill?

But the warm breeze blowing was nice, almost calming. Now if they turned down that blasted light, she might be able to open her eyes for more than a few seconds!

"Don't go to sleep," the voice interrupted. "Dead weight is so hard to tug, even when you are floating on the surface."

"Surface," she mumbled. "Right."

Surface?

She opened her eyes, just a peek this time, and almost gave in to the urge to upchuck again!

She was floating in water! A hell of a lot of water! With no land in sight!

"What!" she squeaked, it was all she could muster in her weakened condition. But awareness of her surroundings also brought awareness of her own physical state.

Her right arm throbbed, her head was pounding and it felt as if she had been beaten with a big stick. No, a log, she decided as the pounding in her head picked up tempo and cadence. Had a rock band taken up residence in her head?

"Exactly," the voice answered. "What happened to you? Are humans now throwing out their surplus women?"

The voice was not sarcastic, or even amused. He was dead serious.

"Look, mister...whoever you are. Where am I and who are you?" She strained to keep her eyes open in order to look back over her shoulders to see who was pulling her so efficiently through the water. Had there been a plane crash? Were they the only survivors?

"I am Storm," he replied.

His calm voice gave her the strength to tilt her head back, and she gasped at what she saw.

The man had blue hair! Well, blue-green, though she couldn't ever remember seeing him on the plane.

He looked down at her and she almost struggled to break his hold on her.

His eyes! The pupils were a glowing, pale amethyst—almost white. It wasn't natural! Even his eyebrows were blue-green.

"Who are you?" she asked as she stiffened in his arms. And she was definitely lying in his arms. One arm was wrapped around her waist, while her head rested against his chest as she was towed through the water. "What are you?"

"I am the male that has saved your life, female." He smiled, his parted lips revealing razor-sharp teeth.

Before she could comment on his need for good orthodontics, she felt something flip at her bare feet. Looking down, she saw that she wore the remains of her power suit, but the clothes were in tatters. That wasn't what held her horrified gaze.

It was the wide mother-of-pearl flipper waving at her that held her attention. It was a large fin that beautifully reflected the sun. But the fact that it continued up underneath her, to the hips that were attached to the body with the arms that held her against his chest, destroyed the mental fortress Elanna had built.

"You're not human!" she screamed as her gaze snapped up to his.

"Thank the Creator!" he retorted with a laugh.

"I think I'm gonna be sick," she replied again as the waves of nausea returned with a vengeance.

"Just like a human, polluting the sea," he sighed even as he lifted and tilted her again.

It wasn't that Elanna was speechless. She was too busy retching her guts out to comment.

Chapter Three

"Human females are quite peculiar," Storm commented as he watched the woman mumble to herself. She kept stuttering things like, "This is not happening to me! I am a scientist, damn it!" and "I must have lost my mind! I am dead and this is hell!"

Finally, she was starting to give him a headache! Enough was enough!

"Female." He shook her a little, splashing her to grab her attention.

"Excuse me." She stopped muttering and clutching her hands to look over her shoulder and glare at him. "I am having a nervous breakdown! It is my right and I earned it! And I refuse to have a figment of my imagination take the joy out of it! I suggest you finish swimming me to Bedlam. Otherwise, be quiet!"

Storm blinked large opaque eyes at her. For once, he was at a loss for words. Swimming figment?

"Ah."

"I said hush! Going insane is a single-person project! I don't need any more help getting there!"

"But…"

"*Hush!*"

He hushed. What else could he do?

Wait a minute! *He* could do a lot! *He* was a warrior and a healer! He was The Storm!

"You can't tell *me* to hush!" he huffed after contemplating his choices for a moment. "I am The Storm!"

"And storms break!" she all but growled, never even turning her head to address him properly.

That did it! There was one thing he could do to garner a little respect from this...this...magic-less creature! He simply let her go!

She sank beneath the surface without a bubble or a sound, gone like so many unpleasant memories.

"Gone!" he crowed, as he symbolically dusted his hands of these pesky human affairs.

Then the guilt hit him. But it was only one human female, and she was even thrown away by her people! He looked down at the smooth water, still arguing ethics with himself. Yeah, she was mouthy and rude, but females could be trained. Right? And her body would pollute his waters.

He sighed deeply, defeated by morals. Rolling his eyes skyward, he positioned his body and dove, his long mother-of-pearl flipper flinging glittering drops of water into the air, before silently sinking below the surface of the water.

She was easy to spot.

She was slowly sinking under water, not struggling, just slowly floating downwards.

He was impressed. Most humans would be terrified and fighting to the surface by no. But his discarded female was calmly accepting her fate. That bothered him.

With a powerful flip of his tail, he shot like a torpedo in her direction, circling in front of her to grab her attention.

Elanna was calm. She was serene. She was sinking into the ocean to her watery grave! Her figment, that lovely creature decked out in sea colors, had released her to end her suffering. Too bad he had a fish tail. A little pre-death sex would have been a welcome tension-breaker.

Then she shook her head at her own foolishness. Pre-death sex, indeed! It would probably be lousy and last seconds. That's the way her luck went! Instead of a barely clothed hunk, she got Fish Boy.

And speaking of Fish Boy, there he was now!

Storm smiled at the female, noting her resigned expression before he took a grip on her arms and began to tug her upright.

She offered no resistance, so it was quite easy to get her to the surface. Though she did shoot him an evil look when he had her settled once more against his chest and began to tug her towards the island he had targeted. By his calculations, it was quite close.

"You tried to kill me," Elanna said as she felt herself being tugged again. "You are real and you just dropped me into the ocean like so much dead weight!"

She had come to the startling conclusion that she was sane and alive when the sun began to sear into her saltwater-affected eyes. If she were insane, she would probably enjoy the stinging sensation, and if she were dead, she wouldn't feel it enough to care. Therefore, she was alive and this Mercreature was tugging her somewhere.

"If I wanted you dead," Storm answered, "I would have never healed you."

"But you dropped me!" she insisted. "You just let me go!"

"You told me to hush!" he snapped, feeling guilty about his childish actions. But he had never come across such disrespect. Well, from anyone but the queen. She was a real bitch.

"I tell you to hush and you try to kill me?" She was still trying to clarify this point.

"Actually," he drawled. "I was trying to punish you for your disrespect and to knock you out of your shock. That muttering can get to be annoying."

"Oh," she replied quietly. "I see."

Then she balled up her neat little fist and sent it soaring over her shoulder and into his left eye.

"Great Creator!" Storm cried out as he turned and took that unexpected fist right into his face. His hands tensed and he almost let her go, but he managed to keep his grip on her.

"If you ever try to teach me a lesson again, Fish Boy, I will gut and fillet your ass!" Her words were given in a calm manner, no temper or anger showing.

He liked it!

"Brave words, female," he said, a grin tugging at his lips. In one move, she managed to alleviate any guilt that he was feeling, because retribution had been served. He would wear the bruise with honor, if it did indeed mark.

"Serious words," she returned, as she peered over her shoulder to get a good look at him, this time a look not clouded by shock or nausea.

He was kind of cute, in a weird *Little Mermaid* kind of way. His hair, wet and clinging to his powerful shoulders, was still the wonderful colors of the sea, and those eyes were an interesting change from what she was used to. Well, seeing that she was used to bloodshot eyes peering out over wire frames, this was a pleasant surprise. His teeth were actually the most fascinating thing about him. They looked even and sharp at the same time. She remembered… What did she remember?

"Ah, Storm, is it?" she asked.

"That is correct, female."

"How did I wind up here?"

"You don't remember?" he asked, his voice doctor-calm.

"No."

"You fell from the sky. I assume this is the way humans now deal with overpopulation in this age. It is a waste, if you ask me."

"What?"

Before she got to question him further, he called out, "Land ahead."

Well, it was land.

It actually was a small tropical island.

Swaying palm trees were set a distance back from the white sands of the beach. Tropical flowers exploded in a profusion of color, brilliant reds and yellows lighting up the deep green grass that carpeted the ground. Small tropical birds flew through the blue sky, their trilling songs filling the air with music. It was truly an island paradise.

"Is this where you live?" she breathed, a touch of awe in her voice.

"No, this is where *you* live."

"Me?" she squeaked, suddenly frightened for the first time. All thoughts of regaining the rest of her memory were shut down by a stab of fear.

"You!" he confirmed.

"Why can't I stay with you?"

"Because you lack the necessary equipment."

She blinked at him, feeling the water grow warmer and shallower as he moved closer towards the island.

"Equipment?" she asked, struggling to remain calm.

"Equipment! Gills, fins, cold blood able to maintain heat in the lower depths. The necessary equipment."

"So you will stay with me?" she asked, trying to keep the fear from her voice.

"No, female. I have work to do and I lack the necessary equipment to stay on dry land."

"My name is Elanna, and don't you grow legs when you dry out or something?" she asked, remembering all of her old folklore she learned as a kid, and from old Disney movie classics.

"I have never tried," came the droll reply. "Can you grow gills if you stay in the water long enough?"

"Got a few hundred years?" she asked, using a bit of humor to hide her terror. He was going to leave her on that island? All alone? Wait! Maybe there were some people there! "Are there any inhabitants?"

"Just you and the birds!" he replied as he felt his fins brush sand. "And now it's time for us to part."

"Wait!" she called out as he maneuvered her around onto her stomach, helping her float in the water.

"Can you swim?" he asked as he watched her panicked gaze focused on the island.

"Yes," she managed. "I don't like to… But you…"

"Well then, this is good-bye, Elanna! Have a nice life!"

"Wait!" she called, but with the merest motion of his arms, she was propelled towards the island.

Her sudden lack of buoyancy left her floundering for a moment. She regained her balance and struck out in a swimmer's crawl, keeping her head above the shallow water.

As soon as her knees touched ground, she turned back to see where Storm had gone, but there was no trace of him, not even a ripple in the water.

"Storm!" she called out as she climbed shakily to her feet. "Storm! You can't leave me here! I don't know how to survive!"

Silence was her answer.

She stood there a moment, shoulders drooped in exhaustion and dejection, before she began to rally.

Well, Fish Boy had saved her life, now it was up to her to maintain it. Besides, she held several PhDs! How hard could survival living be?

Chapter Four

"I have two PhDs," Elanna muttered. "I have two PhDs and three Masters. I have two PhDs, three Masters and a damn certificate from Betty Crocker. Two PhDs, three Masters, a certificate from Betty Crocker and a Girl Scout badge for selling the most Girl Scout cookies, and I can't make the damn thing stand!"

In frustration, she lashed out at the stick-and-grass structure with a bare foot, a mistake she recognized immediately as needles of pain shot through her toes.

"Drowning would have been easier!"

She looked at the pile of palm tree branches that was supposed to be shelter, and almost gave in to the urge to weep. But hopping around on one foot took precedence over a few shed tears.

Since that afternoon when Fish Boy almost literally threw her to this tiny island, she had explored it as best as she could and found it to be totally void of human life.

There was a freshwater spring somewhat inland, but it was too cool and filled with biting insects to consider remaining there for the night.

So she had kicked off the tatters of her stockings, tied what was left of her shirt around her waist, hiked up her sensible skirt and got to work.

She first attempted to climb the rough bark trunks of the palm trees, but decided she needed a degree in physical education to manage it. So she settled for finding a sharp stone near the water's edge and slashing through the lower-hanging branches. She had building materials.

Next, she tried to strip thin pieces of palm to lash together to make a crude teepee-shaped structure, but for some strange reason, her plans started to fail her, and she learned a few valuable lessons.

Green palm leaves could cut if you tightened them enough, sand is not a stable foundation and palms refuse to stand without major support.

So here she was, hopping around on one foot after her fifth and latest attempt at a stable structure failed. She had finally given in to the temptation to kick the blasted thing straight to hell where it belonged.

"Kill me!" she finally screamed into the darkening sky. "Kill me now and get it over with!"

As she uttered those words, a strange picture flashed in the back of her mind. A plane? Had she been on a plane? And there was a little girl. What was she doing with a little girl?

"Human ingenuity at work," a sarcastic voice chimed in from behind her, making her lose the images forming in the back of her mind.

Sighing in defeat, she turned to see no one other than the Fish Boy himself, all blue-green hair and pale eyes, lying in the surf, just observing her.

"Miss me?" he asked as he took in her bedraggled condition and the pile of palm fronds that lay on the ground around her. "Oh! I see we have been decorating."

"What do you want?" she asked, barely civil. This thing left her here and she felt no need to be polite.

"Just to see if you were making out all right."

He actually felt a bit guilty for abandoning her like he did, but she belonged on land and he belonged in the sea. She had her place and he had his. He just delivered her to her place a little quicker than she wanted, was all.

"And I brought you some fish."

With that, he tossed a few sea bass to the sand near her feet, smiling as if he had done her a great service.

"You can thank me now," he said, waiting smugly, anticipating her warm gratitude.

The first fish caught him in the center of his chest, the second right across his smug lips.

"Hey!" he protested as he dodged the third and last fish. This female was crazy! No wonder the other humans tossed her out.

"Thank you?" she snarled, her deep eyes flashing angrily at him. "Thank you for stranding me on this spit of land? For abandoning me here?"

"I didn't exactly abandon you," he protested.

"For leaving me here with no tools and no way to survive?"

"Humans live off the land!" he stuttered, but her next words cut into him like a blade.

"For leaving me here all alone?"

"Well, you were not exactly alone," he sighed as he fluttered his fin to moisten his iridescent skin as he reclined on his stomach near the shore.

"Alone as in no one else here!" she clarified, just in case that had two different definitions of the word.

"I was kind of keeping watch over you," he sighed as he ran his hands through his hair, frowning as he noticed his hair drying out.

"Well, I am still here and you can leave," she retorted. "Don't you have some fisherwomen to lure to their unsuspecting deaths or something?" All that was missing was a huge rock for him to perch on, and then he could be right out of *The Little Mermaid*. Now all she needed was a talking crab and an evil octopus to make her day complete.

"That old story?" he sighed. "First off, it was the Mermaids who were accused of doing such things. Mermen are supposed to just hover, I guess. And secondly, if I could lure people to death with my song, there would be none of those monstrously huge ships dumping all kinds of poisons into my part of the ocean. Besides, I much prefer wrapping humans up in our hair and carrying them below to secret caves and keeping them as love slaves," he laughed.

"Forget about it!" she snorted. "You aren't equipped and I am not in the mood."

For a second, he looked at her stunned, then exploded in laughter.

"Elanna, I think I am beginning to like you."

"Storm," she said, as she plopped on her bottom in the sand and stared at him. "I'm beginning to wish that you would go to hell."

He laughed even harder.

"I give up!" She ran one hand across her forehead, and for the first time she noticed her hair.

"*Eeeek*!" she squeaked as she felt the short tangled mass spring out in stiff corkscrews all over her head. She had had a natural style like this in the past, but that look was achieved with conditioners and careful styling. This wiry mess on top of her head was sand- and salt-encrusted and probably made her look like a demented scarecrow.

"I kind of like it," Storm offered, as he noticed her hands patting and feeling the top of her hair. "It's so different from the long straight locks I am used to. Can you get my hair to do that?" He was actually serious.

He had never seen skin quite so dark or eyes that deep shade of brown or hair that did that marvelous whirlpool curl. He wanted to touch it, but he was too far out in the water, drying out, and she was on land, where she belonged. With a flip of his tail, he showered himself with water, cooling off his heated skin and wetting himself thoroughly.

"My hair does this because I am black," she sighed. "And until I can get some conditioner here, I'm afraid that I will be able to pick it up off of the ground and hand it to you." She let her hands drop into her lap in defeat. What was hair when you were going to be eliminated by the elements anyway?

"Conditioner?" he asked, looking confused. "I have no idea what conditioner is, but some of the women I know use heavy oils in their hair. To make it shine and glisten."

"Oils, yeah," she muttered. "I have no food or shelter, and he offers me hair oils."

"I offered you food, good food," he retorted. "But you threw it back at me."

"Have you noticed, Einstein," Elanna snorted, "I lack those sharp, pointy little teeth that you have in your mouth? Let alone the tools to clean and cook fish! Why not hand me an oyster and tell me to get to chewing!"

Storm eased his hand from his pouch because he was indeed about to offer her an oyster to nibble on.

"I see your point," he sighed, then looked almost as defeated as she did, but only for a second. He hid his emotions well.

"So now I guess it's a race to see if I'll starve to death, or if I will die from exposure." She looked up at the sun, dropping rapidly in the sky, and shook her head in defeat.

"I would not let you die, Elanna," Storm sighed. "I am the one who saved you. Therefore, I am the one to see to your needs, at least until someone comes along to help you get back to where you belong."

"And where is that?" she asked. She could remember the dumbest things. For instance, she remembered all about her education and that she loved tomatoes, but she couldn't remember where home was, or how she'd landed in this predicament. How *had* she ended up here?

"Don't you know?" he asked, looking a bit confused.

"If I knew, I wouldn't have asked!" She laughed. And laughed.

Anything to keep from crying.

"All I know is that you fell out of the sky and landed almost on top of me." He felt a strange emotion for her, not exactly pity, but something close to it.

"And landed in paradise," she quipped as she shook her head sadly. "There is nothing you can do to help me, Storm, unless you have a ready supply of human food on hand and the things I need to make fire." Fire? Was that the answer?

Elanna hopped up on her feet and ran around gathering stones.

"What are you doing?" Storm asked. One moment the woman was near tears in her misery, the next second she was up and tearing around the island.

"Stones, rocks! Flint and iron pyrite! All that I need to start a fire, Storm! A real fire!"

Storm watched as she discarded stone after stone, finally selecting two that seemed right.

"Now they need to be dried." And having neither towel nor cloth to do the trick, she ripped off a piece of her skirt—hey, it was ruined anyway—and quickly checked the stones for moisture. They were dry, having been near the water, but not close enough to get splashed.

"Tinder! I need tinder! Where is there dry wood on a tropical island?" But the few dried pieces of grass and the torn bit material in her hand would be perfect.

Gathering her collection together on the beach, she dropped to her knees and laid out the kindling on a relatively smooth bit of sand, tinder first, then began to strike the stones together.

Storm watched curiously as she banged two rocks together—a futile effort if you asked him—but he never missed a detail as she labored.

"Come on!" she muttered as several sparks flew, but none strong enough to ignite the materials. "Come on!"

Finally she was rewarded when a large spark flew and landed on the edge of her tinder.

Bending low, her bottom straight up in the air, she blew gently on the spark, just like in science lab.

"Yes!" she hissed as the spark flared and the dried grasses caught fire. "Success!"

She sat up, and Storm gasped, amazed at what she had accomplished with two rocks and some grass. She had made fire! It was enough to draw his attention away from the round curves of her butt he had been enjoying!

"See?" she crowed to Storm. "I may not die! I might just live to see tomorrow!"

"But that was so hard!" Storm said as he watched her face light up in pleasure at her accomplishment before she gathered more tinder.

"Nothing worth doing is ever easy!" she quipped as she ran to add a bit more dried grass to her small fire.

"But the powder is much easier," he insisted.

"Powder?" she asked absently as she tried to decide what to cook first. Hmm, that could be a bit of a problem, seeing that she had nothing to cook. What would she eat now that she had a fire? Well, she would just have to put in a few requests with her fishtailed friend.

"Yes, powder," he said and he reached into his waist pouch and withdrew a small bit of powder. Easing closer to the shore, he sighted a palm frond that she had abandoned earlier. Now taking a pinch of the purple powder, he dropped it in his palm and blew, his gentle breath becoming something much closer to a finely controlled gust of wind. That thin, strong stream of air carried the power to the palm frond, where it immediately exploded into a ball of white light!

Elanna gasped, falling on her bottom, as the flash caught her attention. She watched in shocked horror as the green palm frond exploded into a strong, steadily burning flame.

She turned wide eyes to her Fish Boy, noticing the calm look on his face.

"You did that?" she asked.

"Powder," he replied as he again flicked his tail to wet his skin.

"Well, then, why in the hell didn't you tell me you could do that?" she cried, disgusted with him for not telling her sooner and with herself for that bit of bragging that she had indulged in. He was obviously more intelligent than she gave him credit for.

"You never asked," he responded as he sighed in pleasure, the water drenching him once again as he splashed.

"Argh!" she screamed, then took a few deep breaths to calm herself.

"Elanna?" he asked, wondering what was bothering her now.

"Go," she gritted out. "Go and get my fish. And this time, clean them. You probably have fish-scaling powder in that bag!"

Seascape

"Clean them?" he asked, smiling that he still had the upper hand in making her react. For a moment she had scared him with her smug routine, but now she was back to her old prickly self.

"Go get my fish, clean them and bring them back here, please, so that I may eat and forget that this day ever happened!"

"Your wish," he replied before smartly turning around and diving beneath the surface of the water. No, he wouldn't leave Elanna just yet. She was too entertaining. His day of rest was turning out to be fun after all!

"I wish," she sighed as she looked between her small fire and the blazing inferno he had made with his powder. "I wish I knew where I was, where I belonged and how to get back."

Then dropping to her knees to add more grass to her fire, she closed her eyes for a moment and let the waves of fear thread through her. "I wish I could remember."

* * * * *

"I wish I could remember why I decided to save that female," Storm sighed as he took a deep breath and dove to the darker depths of the sea. He sighed with pleasure, as the water became cooler and his body temperature dropped. It was hard being of the sea and trying to exist on land too. Although he and his people were capable, it was draining and something not often done. There were too many horror stories passed around to Merchildren when they were young to make them not wish to go to land often.

"I gave her fish in the first place," he said, then chuckled as he remembered her face when he used fire powder to ignite that palm frond. That was definitely worth spending a few moments baking in the hot sun.

A few large sea bass swam past, and in a blinding flash of speed, he reached out and caught the hapless fish by the front gills.

"Sorry," he grimaced as he held the struggling fish, then saying a small prayer to the Creator, he quickly snapped its back, painlessly ending its life.

"And she wanted it cleaned too," he sighed as he pulled a small blade from his pouch and began to gut the fish, leaving the entrails to float to the bottom to feed the scavengers. There was no fear of sharks, because he had issued a death warning to any that trespassed into his waters, and they were smart enough to know he meant what he said.

So the scavengers were fed, the sharks steered clear, there was no waste, and all was right with the world.

The summons caught him just as he turned to swim back to the private island. It was delivered on the waves, carried like so many whale songs, but set to a frequency that he understood.

The bitch queen had awakened and wanted him. He was being royally paged.

"And I thought I had the day off," he sighed as he placed the fish into his pouch beside the oysters he still had. After checking to be sure the expandable material could hold its load, he made a swift decision then continued on his way to the island. The queen could wait a bit longer.

Chapter Five

"Where is that blue-haired idiot?" Amadala raged as she floated in her private cavern.

Who needed grand palaces when the sea provided a wealth of hidden caverns of such beauty they boggled the mind?

Her chambers were studded with crystal and shells that picked up the color of her pink scales and hair and reflected that hue a thousand times over in the small room.

She paid no attention to this beauty, as she angrily swished her lower fins back and forth.

Her hair floated on a soft cloud around her bare upper body, exposing and hiding her well-developed arms and her full breasts crowned with matching coral nipples. Her eyes were a shade lighter, and she took pains to show off her perfect coloring.

But then, she was the queen, by right of blood and muscle…and the ravings of a madman.

When the mantle of leadership first passed to her years ago, every Merperson in the sea had a right to challenge her. At the end of the seven-day battle, she had stood alone, victorious. She also became the chosen of the people when she let the maidens who fought her go free, without any harassment from the new queen. It showed she had compassion and brains. After all, who would want to follow a queen who would do away or punish her best warriors out of spite? That would be too human!

"Where is that man?" she continued to rage out loud. "I sent for him hours ago!"

"With all due respect, Lady," a deep voice said from the entrance of the cavern. "Maybe he is busy."

Amadala turned to face the man who had spoken to her so harshly, then sucked in a deep swallow of water as she viewed the Merman swimming towards her. She resisted the urge to bite her knuckles and groan as she caught sight of him. And there was a lot to see.

Physically, he had to be the largest man she had ever seen, larger even than Storm, and that was saying a lot!

His hair was black with just a hint of deep midnight-blue swimming in its depths. His chest was miles wide. His muscular arms were crossed as he lazily swam in her direction. And his tail! Mercy!

His tail fin was solid black and shiny, absorbing and reflecting the colors of her own pink hues and separating them into a thousand rainbows. It was wide and full, complete with a delicate-looking clear fringe, though she knew it to contain several sharp spines. Storm had also been born with such an adornment, yet he exposed it only when necessary, the modest idiot.

"And who are you to enter my cavern unannounced?" she demanded, trying to remain regal and in control.

"I go where I please, Amadala. And I choose to be here."

"Well, who are you?" she asked. She had no fear that he would harm her. One cry from her lips would bring armies to her rescue. But she was curious.

"You may consider me the master of all I survey, and I am seeing you right now, woman."

As she moved closer, she saw one of his eyes was heavy-lidded and sensual, the other covered by a small dark shell. His lips were full and his teeth sharp as he gave her a small smile. There was also an intriguing cleft in his chin. Very sexy.

"No one masters me," she said, returning the smirk. "I am queen of all that I see here, and no one can take that away."

"I'm not after your title, woman. It is of no consequence to me. I am after something more substantial." His one eye examined her from flowing hair to delicate fin with its matching pink hues.

This did not look good at all, Amadala decided, before she spoke again.

"Then I'm afraid there is nothing here for you," she said, trying not to nibble on her lip as she attempted to figure out the hunk of muscle's intentions.

"Oh, I wouldn't say that," he said as he moved within touching range. "I wouldn't say that at all."

"Of all the—" Amadala began, but was cut off.

"I am Sting, woman. And I have come to collect my bride."

"Bride?" she asked.

"You!"

"*Storm*!" Amadala closed her eyes and screamed as loud as she could, on that idiot's frequency!

"Scream all you like," he snorted. "It will avail you naught!"

And he was right!

The council that gave them their powers, which oversaw all of the legalities within the Merpeople, had finally decided.

They were ready for her to produce the next queen. They had chosen her a mate!

* * * * *

Storm ignored the loud wailing in his ear and smiled.

This would really get the old girl's fins up. He laughed as he made his way to the island and Elanna.

He would answer her, he was loyal, but it was his off day and he needed a break from her royal bitchiness.

Not that Amadala was a bad queen, she just needed to work on her Merpeople skills.

One sure way to get your main advisors to avoid you was to keep bothering them with inconsequential matters.

In one week, she had him chase a pod of dolphins to get their latest gossip, and a pod on the move was fast. Then she had him collect the oil of anemones, to make her fin shimmer. After that, he had to wait on her as a host for her challenge day, when all the Merfolk came to complain about unfair practices and air grievances.

He was not her mate, so why was he always called upon to be an ornament on her arm? But he knew the answer.

His coloring set off hers the best.

So instead of seeing to his patients or the warriors under him, he spent a lot of time just swimming around and looking cute.

He would be glad when the council decided on a mate for her and got her out of his hair! It was time for her to start breeding the next ruler, and he just felt sorry for the man who was tricked into taking her on. She was almost too much for words.

And now, with having to deal with Elanna, how much was a man supposed to take? He needed a vacation, especially now, since his one-day rest period had been interrupted.

Surfacing near the island, he slowly swam near the beach where she had been last, hoping to sneak up on her again and make her angry.

It was fascinating the way a little red had leached into her brown skin. And her hair! It was beautiful and soft-looking, and so different from what he was used to. He hoped to get close enough to her to touch it, just to see how it felt.

He knew her human legs were no match for the beauty of a well-turned fin, but they were shapely and seemed to fit her body.

"I wonder what she looks like naked?" he asked himself as he drew close to the site where they both had started the fires.

Oh, that was cute, too! Seeing her run around, her skirt rising up as she bent low to pick up rocks.

Rocks! Who would have believed it? It was a story for him to tell his children too, if he ever got free long enough of crazy women to actually find a mate.

It would be nice to see her naked, he thought. For medical purposes only. If the people he treated thought he wasted time on something as perverted as human couplings, then he would lose all…

She was naked.

Well, almost.

She was wearing some thin kind of garment over her female reproductive organs and more white cloth over her breasts, but that was about it.

And her skin was brown all over, a perfect golden brown that seemed to shimmer in the sun.

She was on her knees, apparently washing her torn garments, even though he could fathom no reason why!

It was a warm day, and humans needed warmth. The cloth coverings were just a hindrance against her and the sun. Why did they cover up their skin as if they were ashamed?

Well, if he had no tail fin and had those funny-looking...feet...at the ends, he would cover them up too, but legs and feet were normal for her kind.

But then, humans were never considered all that bright to begin with.

She reached around her back and the material hiding her breasts fell off.

For the first time in his life, Storm breathed in seawater and choked!

Her breasts were full and round. They had dark coral-colored nipples that seemed to draw his attention. Never had he seen a Mermaid with such a delightful coloring. Or bouncy breasts!

They bounced!

His eyes almost popped out of his head as he saw her jerk her head up at his cough. Her breasts bobbed as she squeaked and reached for that abandoned piece of material.

"Who do you think you are?" she screamed as she scrambled back from the water's edge, leaving her garment to float away with the next passing wave. "What do you think you are doing?"

"I am The Storm!" he called indignantly, trying in vain not to watch as her muscled body scrambled back from him. She felt safe, apparently, on dry land. "And I brought fish!"

"Fish?"

"As you ordered, female. Caught and cleaned."

"And what were you doing staring at me?"

"Staring? I was just observing...humans in their element!" he defended.

"You were peeping!" she replied, with a sniff.

"I was not! I was just... *What*?" he roared as his name came hurtling out at him on a wave.

"I'm asking the questions here, Fish Boy!" she said, her eyes narrowing dangerously.

"Not you, her!" he retorted as he turned his gaze back to the water.

"Her?"

"I have to go, Elanna," he said on a sigh. "I am being summoned."

"By who?"

"I am sorry, Elanna. I will return when I can."

How to get the fish to her without getting them covered in sand? There was no hope for it.

He removed his pouch from around his waist and tossed it on the sand by her feet.

"Don't mess with my powders."

"You're going to leave me again?" she called, exasperated and a bit frightened. The sun was beginning to wane and she knew that night would soon be upon her.

"I have to," he said, looking down into the waters again. "Just leave my powders alone, and I will be back soon."

"Storm!" she called as he turned and flipped neatly back into the water. His tail flapped the surface once, a reassurance she assumed. "Don't leave me alone!"

But he was gone.

With a sigh, she bent to pick up the pouch after fastening her bra again. Any thoughts of rinsing off the sweat of the day were gone now, and again she was all alone.

"Powders?" she asked out loud as she examined the pouch.

It seemed to be made out of sealskin.

There was a simple flap opening, and she discovered inside several other sealskin pouches, a few oysters and a neatly cleaned fillet of fish. At least he had kept his word.

She carried her treasures over to her fire, and quickly devised a way to cook her fish by laying it over a few green palm fronds.

His fire still burned brightly, so she decided to spend the night next to it, just in case hers burnt out and there were some strange animals on the island.

She tried to forget not remembering by poking through his powders.

What could it hurt? And her curiosity was purely scientific. His species had never been recorded before, and any insights to them should be studied.

Her thinking justified, she again opened the pouch and pulled out the first powder sack. It had a few bumps on the surface, but it looked like the others.

She fumbled with it until she noticed an opening just at the top.

Curiosity piqued, she opened the bag and leaned in close to see what she had found.

Unfortunately for her, just at that moment a gust of wind passed, kicking the powdery substance contained within up and around her face.

Reflexively, she inhaled, coughing as the powder filled her nostrils and raced to her lungs.

"Bad idea," she gasped as, still coughing, she placed the bag back in the pouch.

Then suddenly, the world began to look very strange.

She looked up, and the fire seemed to be dancing, swaying back and forth.

That looked like fun!

She giggled a bit—*was that her?*—and rose suddenly to her feet. She wanted to dance too!

But the sand was sucking her down, bad sand!

And the water looked inviting!

"Look!" she called. "The waves are calling to me!"

She took one step forward, the dancing forgotten. She wanted to get closer to the beautiful water!

"Wait for me! I am coming!"

She took another step and another, delighting in the way the sands seemed to be pushing her towards the beckoning water.

She looked down at her hands and damn if they didn't glow!

She waved them in front of her face, and smiled as the colors gold, red, brown, green and purple melded and swayed before her eyes.

But the water was calling again. It was leaving her, like everyone else.

She had to catch it! She didn't want to be alone anymore.

"Wait!" she called. "I want to go with you! Don't leave me!"

Racing now, she dragged her feet, stumbling and tripping as she raced to catch up with the water.

She would not be left alone again. She would not be tossed aside or left behind! She could go to the water, just as it asked. And then she wouldn't be alone anymore.

Chapter Six

෩

Storm dove deep into the waters surrounding his home territory. He loved the feel of the tepid waters, high enough to benefit from the heating rays of the sun, but deep enough to remain undetected by the humans above.

He looked around and marveled at the beauty he saw, a beauty never seen on the surface.

There were the multicolored coral reefs and their iridescent inhabitants who darted and dove in schools of rainbow hues.

There were myriad tropical underwater plants waving softly in the light currents.

The sun cast yellow shadows on the dark rocks, creating an abstract picture of undersea life, and all of it touched a deep part of his heart.

He could never consider giving up his home territory, even to get away from his queen!

Storm! she bellowed again, this time with real fear in her tones.

Maybe this wasn't another oil-gathering expedition after all. Maybe she needed her healer. Then again, legs may sprout from his fins.

Knowing Amadala, she wanted another amusement before she had to face the council. More's the pity!

As he dove low to enter the chamber way to her private cavern, he felt the presence of another Merman, a presence unknown to him.

His thoughts turning serious, he raced through the narrow stone ways to her main chamber.

He exploded onto the scene, a massive form racing through air bubbles of distress, and didn't stop until he was in a defensive position in front of his queen, his spines rising to their fullest.

The other Merman, a dark-scaled man, just stood there, arms crossed, looking almost bored with the sudden activity, even as Amadala latched onto his upper arm.

"What?" he finally gritted out, keeping his attention on the stranger in their midst.

"Get him!" the shaken queen demanded. "Show him that I am the ruler here, and answer to no one!"

The dark stranger just raised an eyebrow, his intense eye still on Amadala.

"Why?" Storm asked, letting a bit of his agitation show.

He raced here, away from the semi-nude human, to get caught in between a contest of wills between these two? Who was he, anyway? He didn't seem to be dangerous, just observant and focused on his queen.

"Because… Just because! I am the queen and I command!" She nervously looked over her shoulder at Sting, waiting and reading his reactions.

"What?" Storm snarled, losing all patience.

"Because I am the queen!"

"I heard you, and darling, you are going to have to come up with something better than that!" He narrowed his eyes and glared at her, forgetting the stranger, focusing his ire on Amadala.

"He wants to take me away!" she said, trying her best to hide her nervousness.

"You want to take her away?" he asked, turning his light-colored eyes to the stranger's dark ones. "Is that correct?"

"Yes, it is!" the man declared, uncrossing his arms and moving into a defensive position.

"Well then, good luck! I wish you well! You'll need it!" he said, suddenly all smiles and sunshine. He even stuck out a hand to be shaken by the dark stranger.

"Storm!" Amadala wailed, looking at her master healer and first warrior in dismay.

"I don't believe I have your name," he went on, ignoring his queen's glower.

"Sting," the man replied, looked searchingly at the light-colored warrior before him.

He knew better than to judge a man at first glance, and this man was deceptive.

His light coloring may give him the appearance of a tame, calm man, but his inner spirit told the truth. This man was a formidable enemy and had the look of a master fighter. No healer he ever knew developed the musculature of a warrior by making powders and using the healing energy. This man was a double threat, someone who knew where to inflict the most damage, and had the ability to see that damage done.

"Sting, I don't believe I have heard that name before, but since you're after the queen here, I wish you well of her!"

"Storm!" Amadala snapped, dropping the helpless female routine. "You are supposed to be my defender!"

"It's my day off," he retorted, turning his eyes back to her. "And he has the council written all over him!"

Sting blinked in surprise. How did this warrior know that?

"How did you know that?" Amadala asked, her eyes widening in shock.

"I didn't," Storm replied, his face breaking into a smile. "But you just confirmed what I thought. Besides, no Merman in his right mind would try to take you on. No Merman, that is, from this territory."

"I am a good queen!" Amadala snarled as she looked at Storm, her pink eyes turning almost red in her anger.

"I never said you weren't," he replied. "But you are a little bitch when you are not wearing your crown!"

Sting stiffened at Storm's words, but wisely held his tongue. This place was too enclosed for serious fighting, and the man had only confirmed what the council had warned him about.

"But I was going to mate with you!" she wailed, getting desperate now.

Her main defense had just eluded her, and now she was clutching at seaweed.

Sting stiffened, but relaxed as the turquoise-scaled Merman burst into laughter.

"If you'll excuse me, I have some business to attend to. Don't call me again, Amadala. It's my day off!"

"But you can't refuse!" she cried out, trying to think of some loophole that could free her from this unwanted mating. "I enact the order of first choice!"

"Oh hell," Storm sighed, his shoulders drooping a bit at her words.

"Yes! The order of first choice! The only way you can't mate with me is if you already have a chosen mate"

"What is this?" Sting asked, looking as dangerous as his name. "What games do you play, Amadala?"

"No games!" she crowed. "I have made my first choice, and until Storm produces an intended mate, which he can't do, I am spoken for!"

Sting began to lazily circle the devastated-looking man and the gleeful woman.

He had no doubts that the man, Storm, did not want this match, but his rightful mate was using him to get her way.

That was very *unqueen*-like behavior, but she had him trapped.

He had forgotten about the ancient law that protected the queen from disagreeable matches. But this was not the case. She was abusing her power and one of her most trusted subjects, just to have her way. There had to be a way out of this.

"There has to be a way out of this!" Storm nearly wailed, upset at the prospect of being shackled with Amadala for the rest of his natural life.

"Well, unless you produce a woman, there isn't a way," she laughed, lifting an eyebrow mockingly at the angry circling male.

All I want to do is see to the human and get some rest, Storm thought as his mind reeled. He had to get back and check on her and retrieve his medicine pouch. He didn't have time for Amadala and her intrigue. If the council had chosen this man, then she should be his problem. Where was good fate when he needed it? Just look at that human! Fate was kind enough to drop her in his lap and... The human!

"I can do that!" Storm said suddenly, brightening dramatically, pulling his shoulders up to their full extension. "I can produce a woman!"

"What?" Amadala shrieked, losing the air that had puffed up her chest in her victory against Sting. "You have no woman, Storm! I scared that first one away nearly two years ago. And I know for a fact you have been too busy to go and meet one! You are trying to get out of mating with me, and I won't have it!"

She narrowed her eyes at her first-in-command, ready to strangle him for not playing along with the game.

"Oh, but I can produce a woman, my queen," he said and nodded at the suddenly relieved-looking Sting. "And I was on my way to retrieve my medicine pouch when you called."

Amadala gasped and her eyes grew wide. Leaving his pouch with a woman—his main source of power and protection—was tantamount to already having the mating ceremony! When did this happen? And more importantly, what was she going to do now?

"I want to meet her!" she rasped out, her voice sounding dull and scared on the wavelength that she sent it on. "I want to meet her now!"

"As would I," Sting added with a big grin. "Just to stand witness, you understand."

Storm silently cursed his runaway mouth, while keeping his features pleasant.

"Of course," he replied.

I hope Elanna is in a better mood, he thought as he turned and swam from the cavern. Maybe she would play along, because there sure wasn't time to warn her.

* * * * *

The warm waters rushed up to greet her, to welcome her, to end her loneliness.

Elanna smiled as she spread her arms out wide, welcoming the invading moisture that rose higher and higher with each step.

It was almost like being safe and warm again in her mother's womb. The gentle birth waters of the sea protecting her, offering her solace from the strange mess her world had become.

Another step and more warmth flooded through her.

Nothing else mattered right now. Just the warmth and the feeling of love!

She looked up and the stars danced, leaving a glowing trail upon the darkening night sky. They smiled down at her, telling her she was doing the right thing.

Another step and the waves lapped gently at her thighs, making her shiver as her nerves were awakening to the teasing sensation of the retreating water.

"Wait for me," she gasped, stepping out farther and farther, wanting to float away and be one with the comforting sea. "I am coming!"

The water rushed past her breasts, droplets of the clear, salty fluid touching her cheeks in delight.

She tossed her head back and giggled, feeling special and cherished.

"Almost there," she breathed. The water kissed her chin, enveloping her in a wet warm embrace. This felt so good, she almost cried. "Almost there!"

* * * * *

"Who is this woman, Storm?" Amadala asked as they hurriedly swam towards the island, Sting trailing beside her, making her aware of his presence.

"She is...well, a bit different," he hedged. "But her beauty is like none other."

That tweaked her vanity a bit. Storm never called her beautiful! He just looked at her like she was an annoying kid sister.

"No one is as beautiful as you think," she snorted. "Beauty is a matter of opinion."

"And in my opinion, I have never seen a more lovely…female!"

That should shut her up, he thought, detecting a hint of humor from the quiet Sting.

"Are we there yet?" she snapped. "And why are we traveling so close to the surface?"

"Not far now," Storm answered, wondering if his lady fair would play this game to the end. But he was not lying, though. She was the most unique creature he had ever run into! She was so different, that he…kind of…craved looking at her. Especially after seeing her partially nude. Her breasts and hair alone were enough to give him, well, wet dreams.

"I can't wait to meet this paragon," Amadala snapped, rolling her eyes.

Sting began to chuckle. He was really beginning to enjoy himself! And he thought being sent out here to the queen's home territory would be a step down from the excitement of council life. But he could not have been more mistaken! Already he was enthralled in conflict, and, he hoped, had found an ally.

This Storm seemed to want him to mate with Amadala!

He sensed no jealousy coming from the man, just an intense need to be away.

But if she used him in his duties as she tried to use him to get out of her obligations, he could understand the urgency. But he hoped there really was a woman waiting for him at the end of this trip.

Otherwise, the only way to keep his word to the council was to kill Storm. And he didn't look easy to kill!

* * * * *

Elanna took another step, and suddenly the sea was not so warm and comforting.

The heat was still there, and the waves pulling her along were just as strong, but suddenly, she couldn't breathe!

She tried to inhale as a wave washed over her, but the blinding pain to her brain caused her to fight to push the waters away.

This wasn't supposed to happen! The very seas were turning against her now!

What was wrong with her that so many rejected her? Even the sea no longer found her pleasing.

But she had no time for further thoughts, as another wave hit her, knocking her feet from under her, forcing her under and upside down.

This isn't right, she thought frantically, her arms and legs flailing.

Some forgotten instinct urged her to hold her breath, but she found it hard to find the way up. Up was where the air was. Up was safe, but she could only spin and fight and the now angry waters battled her struggling body.

She had to breathe! She inhaled again, the stinging water making her eyes burn, and pressure built up in her chest as the liquid began to fill her lungs.

She again struggled, and opened her mouth in a silent cry, but more water rushed in to add to the pressure in her chest.

Her head began to spin and the pain began to whirl around her, making her arms and legs leaden.

Why fight it any more?

But she again opened her mouth in a scream. She would fight! The sea rejected her, so she would reject it!

She renewed her struggles, slapping and beating at the now angry waters, trying to fight her way free.

* * * * *

"Did you hear something?" Sting asked suddenly.

The three Merpeople froze, and Storm opened his senses, struggling to hear what had disturbed the dark Merman.

Storm swam in place, his face scrunched up in concern. Something was wrong.

Then he heard it, faint and not tuned to any frequency.

It was an angry scream, a cry of pain and fear.

Elanna!

It was Elanna!

Forgetting the others, he turned and extended his fins and opened his mouth, sucking in water and expelling it through a special opening in his back, pouring on an incredible speed.

Leaving the others behind, he torpedoed towards the sound, the slight cry for help!

Elanna was in danger, and it was up to him to save her.

Chapter Seven

Not again, Storm frantically thought as he raced to where he was picking up signs of Elanna and her distress. *This can't be happening again!*

He streaked forward, fighting against the waves that suddenly seemed less hospitable, fighting against his own physical limitations that wouldn't allow him to move swiftly enough, fighting against time.

Dark thoughts and memories flooded his brain, caused his body to shiver as he undulated through the waters, leaving his queen and the stranger behind.

He remembered, how he remembered.

The bright red billows had floated up through the water. The acrid taste of it had filled his mouth and blinded his eyes.

How far one single drop of blood could taint the water red, blot out the sun and kill the warmth of the living seas.

* * * * *

Keep fighting, Elanna's mind screamed, but her limbs refused to get the message.

Slowly, so slowly they jerked, barely fighting at all. And then movement slowed.

A great weight was pushing against her chest, her mind was starting to grow hazy. What was the use in fighting anyway? It was so much easier to rest.

Tiny bubbles began to flow from her mouth, her nose, the corners of her eyes. Tiny little bubbles flowed like those in champagne. They flowed upwards, softly, merging to form one celebratory line.

Why not celebrate? The sea had her wish, had her way. One less human to destroy it, one less person to pollute it.

Now her dead body would feed the fish, give the creatures life.

Not a bad exchange, Elanna thought with the last of her functioning mind. Too bad she had to die to be of help, though. She just liked life so much.

Then she was falling, drifting, slowly sinking downward. Funny, but this felt so familiar. But before, there had been a flash of greenish-blue hair and very light eyes.

She blinked.

Oh, there they were.

* * * * *

Storm reached Elanna just as her body began a death spiral.

How did she get out this far? was his second thought. His first was, *Oh my God! I can't live through this again!*

But as he reached her, her eyelids blinked at him. There was still time.

Clamping his mouth onto hers, he began to pull with all of the strength in his lungs.

She had no gills or openings to force the water through, so he pulled it from her body, through his, and back out to the sea, returning it to its rightful place.

Then with one mighty heave, he forced in as much oxygen as her lungs could hold.

Careful of his sharp teeth, he clamped her mouth tighter, and wrapped his strong arms around her.

It may not work, but he had to try.

Then he felt it, the healing powder filling her body. He felt it start to work on her, oxygenating the suffocating cells, turning her pale blood rich and vibrant again. He felt it repairing the damage to her lungs, and nostrils. He prayed it was not too late to protect her brain.

If those cells were lost, nothing would be able to save her.

So intent on keeping her alive was he that he never noticed when first Sting and then Amadala appeared at his side.

"*Ish!*" the queen shuddered as she saw what Storm held in his arms. "It's a human!"

Sting remained quiet, but he observed the other man's actions.

The way he had taken off earlier at the first hint of this female's troubles made him think. What was this woman to him?

"Storm!" Amadala cried. "Storm! Stop that at once! You have no idea where it has been!"

Storm paid them both no heed, he just kept breathing into her mouth, praying her eyes would blink, praying he would not have to see another woman he cared for perish!

"Well, if you won't stop this foolishness, I will put an end to it!" Amadala growled as she raised her hands in preparation to yank the human female out of her chosen mate's arms.

"Stop!" Sting commanded softly.

His calm words did more to stop Amadala than any yelling would.

"This is obscene!" she countered, glaring at him with her pink eyes, her long hair flowing gently around her. "My chosen should not be toying with a human female, and a dead one at that!"

Seascape

But before any answers could be called out, Elanna began to jerk.

Yes, Storm thought as he felt life return to her limbs.

There is somebody kissing me, Elanna thought. *And he needs lessons*!

Having her mouth mashed like this was most unpleasant. And what was he trying to do? Make her boobs bigger by blowing them up from her mouth?

She opened her eyes and immediately the sharp sting of saltwater forced them closed again.

Then she felt the pressure. It was all around her, surrounding her like a blanket. Where was she?

She lifted her arms and pressed them against cool male flesh, trying to force him away from her, but the arms held her fast.

What was happening?

She began to struggle, to fight against the arms holding her, and then she felt the upward movements.

Water! She was in water! Its liquid warmth flowed from her head to her feet, dragging at her as she was moved towards the surface.

But what had happened?

"Follow him!" Amadala ordered Sting, as she took off after Storm.

Sting followed without argument, because he intended to anyway.

Storm sighed in pleasure as he felt Elanna come to life in his arms.

He was not too late! She was alive, and apparently functioning, he decided as he felt her start to struggle.

He could almost hear her words of complaint as he decided to move her upwards so he could see if she could breathe on her own.

As they broke the surface, Storm disconnected his mouth from Elanna's, laughing at the pop that was heard, so tight was the seal.

He never realized how desperate he was to save her until that moment. And a lot of it had to do with that incident, but mainly it was because he didn't want to see this human female die.

Elanna sucked in a deep breath, the sound of her breathing loud and forced as she tried to gulp in air—sweet air!

She blinked rapidly, trying to get her hands up to wipe at her eyes, but then realized that she was still in a tight clench.

"Don't!" a voice said and she looked up into a pair of almost white, glowing eyes.

"Fish Boy?" she gasped, still blinking rapidly to dispel the sting. "Storm?"

His name came to her like a bolt out of the blue. He had saved her before! He was not totally human, and he had saved her again.

Storm threw back his head and began to laugh. His deep boisterous laugh filled the night sky and rose to the heavens. Elanna was alive and already back to her old prickly self. Thank the Creator!

"Storm," she began, then was cut off by a bout of coughing, her body ridding itself of the few remaining drops of water. "What happened?"

"You tell me," Storm began as he loosened his hold on her, delighting in the feel of the warmth returning to her body and the soft movements of her legs. "I leave you for a few moments and then you decide to go exploring!"

"I…" she began as she closed her eyes to think. "I remember a party? No! Bright lights?"

She broke off again as she coughed up more water, then continued.

"The stars were dancing, Storm! It was so beautiful!"

Storm's eyes narrowed in suspicion.

"Elanna, did you open my pack?"

Elanna's eyebrows crinkled in confusion as she tried to recapture the memory.

"I think I opened a bag, a small bag."

"Oh hell!" Storm groaned. "You can never trust a human!"

"What?" Elanna shrieked. "What do you mean, trust a human? You were the one who left the stuff with me in the first place!"

"I was the one who gave you specific instruction not to touch my pack!" he returned. "Or are you a child that cannot obey simple orders?"

Elanna flushed brightly. It was kind of her responsibility not to go into the pack and to open a substance of unknown origin without proper training. But damn it! She was human! She made mistakes!

"Silence on the defensive front?" Storm added when he saw the look on her face.

"I should not have opened the pack," she finally agreed, glowering at him.

"And I have saved you twice now, is that correct?"

"Yes," she sighed, wondering where he was going with this line of reasoning.

"Then you have to help me out, sort of like a tradeoff?" he asked, slyly.

Looks like he found a woman after all!

"Yeah," she agreed. "I'll help you. But I have no idea how I can be of service," she pouted, poking out her lower lip.

She hated being beholden to anyone, especially half-human fish boys with deadly powders in their packs.

"Great!" Storm crowed, just as the surface exploded in movement and a pink head popped up right beside her.

"What is going on here?" the woman demanded, her pink eyes glowing softly in the night sky. She glared at the human who was wrapped all around her safety net. How dare that…that…female put her arms around her way out?

A second head emerged quietly on her left side, a black eye, inky hair flowing around it, stared intently at her.

She coughed nervously.

Slowly, the man emerged, his size rivaling Storm. He too was all muscle and long hair, but he was frankly more intimidating than her Fish Boy. He had to be, uh, Fish Man?

Her head swiveled from Storm to the dark stranger, and she finally decided on Fish Boy the Second. He had to prove himself to be a man, and the only finned person to even start doing that was Storm.

Instinctively, she gripped Storm tighter, looking for protection from the familiar source. He hadn't let her down yet!

"Queen Amadala," Storm began formally. "I present to you my chosen mate."

"Mate?" Amadala screamed.

"Mate?" Elanna said, before a quick squeeze cleared the confusion off her face. "Oh, yeah! Mate! That's me! I'm the mate!" She smiled sickly at the woman's outraged face.

"This is impossible!" the queen cried out, her face turning crimson in her rage. "You're not even the same species!"

"You know what that means?" Storm said, laughter in his voice as he hugged Elanna tighter, one palm forcing her head into his neck, a cozy pose that gave them the look of intimacy.

Elanna, not wanting to struggle and make a scene, coughed once, then tucked her face deeper into his neck, noting that he smelled like the sea. Besides, it seemed safer to put as many vulnerable points of her body in protective custody, away from those pink slashing eyes.

"Yeah, we are getting mated," a deep voice said to her left, causing all parties to jump in surprise, all but Storm, anyway.

The dark-haired man had spoken yet there was a gleam of triumph on his otherwise calm face.

"*No!*" wailed Amadala, just before the dark one moved faster then a blink, and had his arms around her, like a set of manacles chaining her to a rock!

"Yes," he breathed, a sentiment strangely echoed by Storm as he buried his face in Elanna's hair, trying in vain to stop a chuckle. "Free again!"

Chapter Eight

"As fun as this whole day has been," Storm sighed with oh-so sincere regret, "I feel it is time that my future mate and I take our leave."

"Not so fast!" Amadala snarled, turning bright pink eyes on her so-called right hand.

"Very fast," Storm interrupted. "So fast, in fact, your fins will spin! My female has just been injured and I must see to her needs."

"She looks fine to me!" Amadala screeched as Sting held her closer, his one black eye glinting with delight as he adjusted his patch over the other.

"Looks can be deceiving," Storm replied dramatically as he pulled Elanna closer to his body, noting the actual shiver in her arms and the slightly dazed look in her eyes.

Whatever she had gotten into was leaving her body, but it was taking its own sweet time about it. She was still being affected.

"Exactly," Sting suddenly piped in, rather helpfully. "Appearances are deceiving, and I am sure the queen believes what you are saying about the human."

"Exactly!" Storm said, nodding his agreement.

"That is why we will have your mating ceremony tomorrow so that the queen can no longer deny what is before her."

He glared at his reluctant mate, but the amusement in her face seemed to say check and mate!

"Right! Tomorrow! First thing… Tomorrow?"

Was this guy trying to help or harm?

"Tomorrow!" Sting insisted. "Then my mating will take place and everyone will be happy."

"Tomorrow?" Elanna mumbled, still a bit confused as to what was taking place.

She suddenly felt pounds heavier, even though she was being supported by the buoyant water and Storm's strong arms. This was all a bit too much! Her mind wanted to shut down, but common sense told her to stay awake and find out what was going on!

"Tomorrow!" Sting insisted. "I'm sure the council will approve."

"Approve? Of all the stupidity!" Amadala snarled, turning her piercing anger towards Elanna, who was still trying to stay up to speed.

"Tomorrow?" she mumbled again. Tomorrow suddenly seemed very important. *Wake up*, she mentally yelled at her brain. *We need to follow this.*

"Why stupidity?" Storm asked, his voice suddenly deep and angered.

"Because she is human!" Amadala pointed out, as if that one obvious fact escaped everyone.

"She is also my choice!" Storm snarled. "The council once deprived me of my choice, only to face disastrous consequences."

As he spoke, the formerly calm seas began to stir and churn. Sudden fat waves crashed against them, lifting them and lowering them in such a way that both Sting and Amadala had to make an effort to stay afloat.

For once, Amadala's pink eyes showed a hint of fear and she instinctively reached for Sting.

"I don't think that this is the time—" she began, but was cut off.

"Then when is a good time, Amadala? When shall we discuss what the council has cost me, what I have lost and what I willingly gave up, but can just as easily take away again?"

Elanna tightened her grip on Storm, the rocking waves turning her stomach, and tried to latch onto what he was saying. Who had taken something from him? It was getting harder and harder to concentrate.

"I don't think—" Amadala began again, partially using Sting as a shield, but again Storm ignored her.

"That is the problem with you royals," he snarled. "You never think!"

Lightning crashed and thunder boomed in the clear skies as he gave vent to his frustrations.

There was a lot running through Storm's head right now. The pressure Amadala applied to him, her attempt at manipulation, his manipulation of the situation, and foremost, the near loss of Elanna.

He would not lose another one!

The council would not interfere in his life again!

The reason he stepped down from his position was because...

"Storm? I don't feel so well."

It was Elanna's calm voice that snapped his attention from the pit of rage where his mind had been sinking.

She sounded so weak and lost, so unlike the woman who he had sparred with all day.

He turned to look at her, noting the pale skin and the dazed eyes.

"I have to get you to safety," he said, once again sounding like a doctor, calm and levelheaded.

As the sudden fury that engulfed them just as quickly disappeared, Amadala took a deep breath and noticed who she was clinging to.

"Ugh!" she groaned as she quickly released Sting's arm and looked around to see if anyone saw the breach.

She had no idea why she had clung to the dark-haired man while fear made her blood thick, but she had. And looking at him, she saw he had noticed as well.

"What do you need?" Sting suddenly asked, turning away from his pink-haired minx to watch the Merman pull his fury within and focus on his mate. "How can I help?"

"I need to take her below," he said finally, tearing his eyes away from the small figure Elanna made huddled against him. "I need to find out what she inhaled and I can't do that here."

"How?" Sting asked, still keeping his distance from the man.

He had no idea what went on between Storm and the council, but he felt the man's sincerity when it came to the human. His brief flash of temper had shaken the seas, and Sting wondered if, like him, Storm was a Child of Triton.

"I'll breathe for her, but I need my pouch from the beach." He nodded his head in the direction of the small island where he had left Elanna earlier.

"I can get it," Sting said and took off towards the shore.

"How can he grab it when he can't go on land?" Amadala asked as she watched Sting take off, her fear of Storm forgotten as he suddenly took on his old personality. "I'd better go and see what that man is up to."

What he was capable of was more like it. If Sting possessed half of the powers that Storm suspected, he would be a very dangerous man, indeed.

And her scrutiny was in no way because his muscular frame easily cut through water, the inky dark hair sensuously moving around his body, or the thickness of his tail fin! She was reconnoitering the enemy! Yes, she was just seeing what she was up against. Well, at least that's what she told herself.

Storm looked down at Elanna, noticed her watching him and tried to smile.

"Elanna, I am taking you home with me," he said finally, moving her around so she faced him.

"You live under the sea!" she sang softly, losing her train of thought. "Under the sea! Where the... Where the... I forget the words."

"Elanna!" Storm sighed. She was kind of cute as she looked up at him with big innocent eyes. This was not the same woman who had christened him Fish Boy, but this side was fun to watch, too.

"Elanna, I need you to listen carefully to what I am saying."

"Your eyes are glowing," she informed him.

"That happens when I am angry," he returned. "Now listen to what I am saying."

"Pinkie wasn't wearing a bra," she again added. "But I guess she won't sag because the water holds them up."

She nodded as if she had just made an important discovery.

Storm sighed. The drug was taking effect again. He supposed her adrenaline rush had countered some of what she had ingested, but now the drug was taking over again.

"I am going to take you home with me, Elanna. And to do that, I must place my mouth over yours."

"No way!" she giggled. "You have shark teeth, and I want to keep my tongue, thank you very much! I'll breathe on my own!"

"Elanna, you are not equipped to breathe under water."

"Neither are you, Fish Boy!" she giggled. "If you were, you would have gills!"

"I have a filter in my nose," he sighed.

"Oh good! Get me one too, and then we can go under the sea together! Under the sea!"

She released her grip on him to clap her hands and sank like a brick.

Shaking his head, Storm reached below the water and got a handful of her wonderfully different hair. With a small tug, she again popped to the surface, her eyes wide open and staring.

"I was born with my filter, Elanna. We will have to share."

She blinked rapidly, getting the stinging saltwater out of her eyes, but nodded solemnly.

"I like to share," she said. "I would like to share a lot with you, but you don't have a dick!"

"A what?" he asked, his face scrunched up in confusion.

"A dick, a schlong, a pecker, a woody, a stiffy, a rod, a staff, a one-eyed monster, tube steak, trouser snake, a booty love stick!"

"A what?" he asked, his voice rising in astonishment. She didn't mean what he thought she meant, did she?

"A penis! A male reproductive organ! I would share, but you don't have one. Does this mean I have a fish fetish?"

She actually looked worried for a moment.

"Uh, Elanna, you are intoxicated!"

It was all he could think of to say. The woman was out of her mind! Why would she want to share…intimacies with a Merman? She didn't know anything about him. She had no idea what Merfolk reproduction entailed.

And suddenly she was the sexiest bundle of flesh he had ever held in his arms.

Damn, the idea of educating her was so tempting, but he had to see what damage she had done to herself first.

"I am stoned!" she whispered rather loudly in his ear. "And I am going to go home with you. That's okay, though. I don't have a home and I can share with you."

She gave him a lopsided grin as she blinked up at him.

"Okay, Elanna," he said as he tried to tear his eyes away from the sensuality expressed in her eyes, the set of her lips, the positioning of her body. "I'm going to take you home with me, and to do that I must place my mouth over yours."

"You won't bite?" she asked in all seriousness.

"No, I won't bite." *Not until you are sober and ask me to*, he added silently.

Sex with a human was looking more intriguing all of the time.

"Okay. I trust you, Storm," she sighed as she wrapped both arms around his neck, nestling into him, trusting him to keep her safe.

Storm felt his heart lurch at her words, words so like another's, who had wrapped herself trustingly around him and waited for him to make the world right. Someone he had let down and ultimately lost.

"Close your eyes, Elanna," he quietly instructed, his thoughts sobering him. "We are going to dive very deeply and very quickly. You must not struggle. I will keep you safe."

That said, he slowly bent his head towards her, felt the heat wafting up from her body, saw the trust in her beautiful brown eyes before she let her lids drop.

Taking a deep breath, he placed his lips over hers, startled for a moment at the softness of her skin. Then he drew in a breath, making a seal around their mouths.

Again inhaling deeply, testing the connection, he hugged her close to his body and dove.

Chapter Nine

Sting stretched out almost flat in the water, his one black eye piercing and direct as he swiftly and stealthily moved towards the island.

There was a bag to retrieve, probably sealskin, and gray.

His purpose—to remove the bag from the beach, return it to the male, Storm, and force his future mate to agree to a speedy ceremony.

Simple, for a man of his talents.

The two fires on the beach puzzled him, but as he drew closer to the sandy shore, he spent more time avoiding sharp rocks and hidden boulders lying just beneath the surface of the water.

Storm had to be crazy, or very smart, to stash his future mate here.

Even Amadala would not think to search this dangerous shore to intimidate a woman interested in Storm.

Why this was so important to her, he had no idea. But he was determined to find out.

Speaking of the witch, he thought as he heard her moving towards him.

He slowly shook his head, his long black hair waving in the water around him, as he paused for her approach.

Shaking his head in disgust, he noted that she used no stealth, no skill when approaching an unknown area. The Royal Highness just splashed through, expecting nothing to get in her royal way.

"Lady, you need to be more discreet when you travel."

"Why?" she growled as she moved to his side, cursing as she snagged her fins on a particularly sharp rock. "It's not like a boatload of sailors are out looking for a good time!"

Sting sighed and shook his head sadly before turning to face her.

"That is not the issue, lady. You are my queen and my mate, and you must be protected at all costs."

"Let's get one thing straight, buddy," Amadala growled as she tossed her pink hair over her shoulders. "You don't own me! I am still going to mate with Storm, whether he likes it or not! There will never be a time when I pass rulership over to you so I can breed the next generation."

"But Amadala," Sting said quietly, his one eye piercing in its intensity, "the council has decided."

"To the land dwellers with the council!" she hissed. "I am queen! All will obey my dictates."

"You are such a bitch!" Sting said quietly, but with feeling.

Amadala stopped mid-tirade!

"What did you call me?" she hissed, as she narrowed her eyes into tiny pink slits and glared at him with all the frustration contained within her body.

"A bitch," he returned. "A human term that quite fits you."

"I know what a bitch is," she snarled as she moved closer to him.

"Good, then desist in acting like one."

Amadala's mouth opened and closed silently, a testament to her anger, but looked rather like…a fish out of water.

Before she could regroup for the next attack, he again stopped her with his words.

"Storm does not want you. He would mate with a human to be rid of you. He is also very angry with the high council, and I suspect is a Child of Triton, and therefore a dangerous man. I understand your desire for such a man to pass the mantle of leadership to when your time comes to reproduce, but that man is not Storm."

"You do not know what is best for me!" she exclaimed, stung at his words.

"I know it is not in your best interests to pressure a man capable of creating storms with his mere thoughts. And I know if you persist in manipulating him, your health may become an issue."

"Storm would never..."

"Storm is carrying some deep-seated pain, Amadala. And something is bringing it to the surface. Why he played flunky for you all of these years is a matter for him to know. But it is clear that it is a role he no longer desires to possess. Therefore, Queen Amadala, tomorrow, Storm will be matched with his human counterpart, and you and I will become one."

"What makes you think that Storm, even if he mates with this...human, will not rush to my aid? He has been my loyal servant for years! Nothing will change that. He can flick you away as easily as a bottom feeder tosses gravel."

"Well, Amadala," Sting said calmly as he closed the small distance between the two of them. "He did not rush to your aid a few moments ago, before his announcement. And, dear Amadala, I believe the fact that he left me to deal with you proves he no longer wants the job. And lastly, Amadala, my future mate, I am also a Child of Triton, and possess my own brand of magic."

With that, he easily gripped her upper arms in a firm yet gentle grip and began to lower his head towards her.

He's going to kiss me, Amadala thought as her eyes widened in…she didn't know what! They just widened in reaction!

The cool water acted as a conductor, swirling warm water heated by his body, towards her, making her shiver as though the essence of him was surrounding her.

She felt her arms begin to tremble, to test the strength he so easily controlled, as his fingers hit erogenous nerves in her arms.

The sight of his darkly handsome face, coming closer to her, was almost more than her heart could bear.

It beat, pounding in her chest, her breath caught as she inhaled the seawater scent of him, deep within her body, making her senses jump in excitement.

Slowly, his eye closed, the long lashes resting against his cheek, as he came closer, closer, closer!

Then she was flying through the air to land with a splash several feet behind him, clear of the rocks, and yet close enough to reach in an emergency.

Sting spared her not a glance as he slowly lowered his arms, ignoring the curses she spat at his back.

He had a job to do, and he didn't have time for her female foolishness.

With one hand, he flipped the eye patch up, and using the energy from the dual burning fires, he silently aimed his left hand in the direction of the pouch.

Flipping his arm, palm up, he made a come-hither motion with his fingers, and the pouch suddenly lifted and shot in his direction.

Amadala gasped, her curses halted, as she watched the pouch float slowly towards him.

Seconds later, it rested neatly in his hand and he turned to confront his mate.

"How did you do that?" she croaked, shocked by the repercussions this meant.

"I already told you," he said as he lowered the patch again, hiding the silver glint that seemed to sparkle in his perfectly normal-looking eye. "I am a Child of Triton."

"But," she stuttered. "But you are not named for an element!" she wailed almost in despair.

"You never want to know why they call me Sting," he replied as he fastened the pouch around his waist. "And if demonstration hour is over, we must get to Storm and his mate. She may be more seriously injured than we thought."

Still in shock, Amadala followed Sting, not knowing if she should be impressed or frightened.

But she had learned one thing. She had better watch her fins where Sting was concerned. There might be some way to get out of mating with him yet, but there would be no more rash decisions on her part. They only put her in more hot water.

* * * * *

Elanna felt Storm draw the breath from her lungs as he suddenly plunged into the deep dark sea.

She only had time to close her eyes and emit a small squeak of protest, when suddenly the water was rushing over her head, sliding over her body, encompassing her in its almost oily warmth.

Her arms reflexively tightened around Storm, plastering her breasts against his chest, the thin barrier of her torn blouse not enough to protect her from the tingling heat of his body.

She sucked in a scared breath and felt his chest move suddenly with her motion, fresh oxygen flooding her body.

He was breathing for her, with her, she realized in amazement.

Then she noticed his strong arms surrounding her, protecting her as they plunged deeper into the water.

His muscles shifted with his movements, and being pressed so tightly against him, she had no choice but to feel each muscle move and slide under his smooth firm skin.

She sighed and felt his chest expand with her movements.

This is a dream, she thought to herself as she felt the temperature in the water drop, but not alarmingly so. *This is my first kiss from a Merman! And he's not cutting me with his teeth.*

Her fuzzy mind latched onto the one thought that Storm was protecting her, as time began to slip away.

She felt almost detached, awash in a sea of new sensations, of being totally cared for, of having her senses expand in new and different ways.

She resisted the urge to wrap her legs around his…

He didn't have legs!

If he didn't have legs, what was that bulge between their bodies?

That growing bulge between their bodies!

She had no chance to ponder this particular line of questioning, for suddenly they were moving swiftly upwards, hurtling towards the sky.

With a mighty splash, they exploded for the water, sending crystalline droplets all around them.

Storm broke his connection to Elanna with a pop, but still kept his arms around her, supporting her in the water, keeping her safe.

"Where...where...where are...we?" she gasped as her lungs fought to take over the breathing for her body once again.

"In a cave," Storm replied, giving her the short answer.

"Why?" she managed, as she tried to turn her head to see around the cave.

It was pitch-black and quite cool, but the air was fresh and sweet.

Her head was still spinning, and she drunkenly held on to Storm, the only still solid thing in her topsy-turvy world.

"Ah, housekeeping?" he said, as he pulled one arm from around her waist to brush her hair back from her face.

She may have had trouble seeing, but he was perfectly sighted in the dark.

"Housekeeping?" she asked, her breathing still rough and her voice reedy.

"Housekeeping," he affirmed. Then almost as an afterthought, "Ah, welcome home?"

Chapter Ten

ഔ

"I feel sick," Elanna mumbled as she lay shivering against the cold, damp stones of the cavern.

"You ingested something, Elanna, and it will expel itself soon," he said. "Or I'll force it out of you," he mumbled, sure that she didn't want to hear that comment.

"I'm cold." She shivered, teeth rattling as her body sought to warm itself.

"When they return with the pouch, I'll have you warm and dry."

"How?" she giggled, still feeling lightheaded. "You don't have any legs."

"Want me to grow some?" he asked, rolling his eyes at her. All of this cuteness was distracting! He had to figure out a way to get Amadala and Sting mated so he and Elanna could part easily. He'd say they were just too different. *Who could argue with that?* he decided as he watched her long bare legs tremble in the dim light.

"Can you?" she asked, eyes wide, voice filled with innocent wonder. "Can I watch them grow? Is it like, evolution? Wow!"

"No, I can't grow legs!" he snorted, glaring at her now.

"Not even a third one?" she snickered.

"A what?" he asked. Humans had only two legs, right?

"A third leg, a dick, a pecker—"

"I remember!" he cut her off, shaking his head.

"So you have a third leg! Can I see it?"

"No!" he all but shouted, a blush staining the skin of his face. He could blush? *That has never happened to me before*, he thought with disgust.

"But I feel like playing with it!" she moaned as her hormones took a jump at the thought of a muscular Storm. Well, he did have a nice upper body, and there were studies conducted that proved weight training and other strenuous exercises, such as swimming, had a positive and direct impact on male sexual performance!

Damn it, she was curious! She wanted to see!

"Play with yourself!" he all but snarled as he watched her large liquid eyes stare at him.

He cleared his throat nervously and tried to look away from her shivering body, but his mind began to drift.

Would she shiver with passion as he plunged?

"I did, and it wasn't worth it!"

"Excuse me?" he choked, her words drawing him back to the present.

"I got a vibrator 'cause I wanted to see what an orgasm was like. You know, sex is overrated! I mean, he had fun, but I was left with a wet ass and wet spot!"

"What?" he cried, his face scrunched up in a strange almost impossible expression.

"He was bad!" she called out as the subject seemed to warm her body a bit.

"Bad?"

"Rotten! Miserable! NBA—no-balling asshole!"

"Oh." What was he supposed to say now? *What was balling, anyway?*

"And I tried my best, Storm!" she sniffled as her big eyes began to fill with liquid.

She was lying there in the rags of her clothing, her hair a sodden mass on top of her head, shivering as if her skeleton was about to hop out, and he found himself terribly aroused by her.

He needed help.

"It's, uh, not your fault?" he tried to soothe, but it came out more like a question.

"Damn right, it wasn't my fault!" she shouted, her tears suddenly drying up. He found her anger even more appealing.

"I had the things, the garters, motion lotion and the hot oil, but what did I get? A two-minute hump! He was a minuteman! They all are minutemen! And then he fell asleep!"

"Really," he said in shock and disbelief. Shock of all she had gone through, and that a man had left her wanting. Motion lotion? He had to remember to make a note of this and ask around.

"Really. So I decided to be by myself and look at how happy I am?"

Then she burst into tears.

"Female!" Storm wailed as he maneuvered himself over to her stone perch and pulled her into an upright position.

Immediately, she collapsed over him and he had to fight to keep her from flipping over into the water.

"Elanna," he called as he felt her body shake with tears.

"What is wrong with me? I can't remember, Storm! I can't remember! And I feel sick, then happy, then mad, then sad!"

"You ingested some of my powder, Elanna. I won't know how to help until Sting and Amadala get back with the pouch."

"Pinkie hates me," she sniffled as Storm managed to ease her back so he had room to maneuver.

"Amadala hates everybody," he returned easily as he braced his arms on the stone.

With a push off from his tail fin, he was propelled through the air, to twist and land with a wet *splat* on the stone beside her.

"You're sitting!" she cried excitedly as she stared in wonder at Storm.

"What? You thought we swam all of the time? I do have a butt, Elanna," he laughed as he pulled her into his arms.

"Stop it! You are getting me wet!" Did she really say that? She began to giggle.

"What?" he asked, but used her weakening resistance to pull her into his lap.

"Nothing," she managed, covering her face with her hands. "Why do I think of sex around you?"

"Beats me!" he replied, sucking a bit on his sharp teeth as his pale eyes bore into hers.

"I feel safe," she said as she snuggled suddenly into his arms.

"I'll keep you safe," he returned, his mind again clouded by scarlet billows, flowing freely throughout the water.

Her body still shivered, but the convulsions seem to ease a bit. Maybe he was capable of heating her just a bit.

He closed his eyes and began to savor the feel of her in his arms.

She was softer than any other woman he had ever known! Plus, her skin pulsed with a heat of its own, something lacking in some Merfolk. Her heart beat rapidly against his chest. Her warm breaths almost stung his neck as she snuggled in deeper. He sighed as he flipped back his hair with a toss of his head and rested his chin against her head.

"Get your hands off of my man!" a voice hissed as Amadala's head poked through the water in front of them.

She had led Sting, as he had no idea where Storm's private caverns were, so she was the first to see this intimate little scene.

And now she was livid! Storm had to mate with *her*! He couldn't leave her at the mercy of that…that…that dark-haired shark!

"*What*?" Elanna stiffened up in Storm's arms, and he tried to hold her back, but she was having another mood swing—this one vicious!

"You heard me, you filthy human!"

"Kiss ass, you undercooked pink fish stick! Fish Boy is mine!"

Before he could guess what was happening, Elanna launched herself out of Storm arms and flew at Amadala, never mind that she was treading in very deep waters!

Her anger and frustration had found a target. Her body was ready; her mind gave the call! *Attack*!

Amadala gasped as one hundred thirty-five pounds of enraged woman slammed into her.

Elanna wasted no time with hair pulling. She wanted to see blood!

Balling up her hand, she plowed her fist right into Amadala's sharp-toothed mouth, cutting her knuckles, but paying it no attention!

"Bitch!" Amadala shrieked as she grabbed a fistful of Elanna's hair and forced her under the water!

"*Amadala*, *no*!" Storm called up, but just wasted his breath!

One of Elanna's legs flew up, catching Amadala in the stomach, forcing her to let go with a *whoosh*, as the air exploded from her body.

"That's a fighting word!" Elanna shrieked as she laid her elbow across Amadala's face, cracking sharply against her chest and spinning her body in a complete circle.

"Storm is mine!" Elanna shrieked as she felt arms reach around and grip her waist.

"Let me go!" she bellowed as she was swung around to face a black eye patch.

"Cyclops!" she shrieked, then suddenly everything was amazingly funny to her.

She looked over her shoulder to see Storm hefting a shrieking Amadala onto a rock outcrop, holding her away from his body.

She looked pissed but Storm seemed to be holding in laughter.

She turned back to tall, dark and not so dangerous. Who took a man with an eye patch seriously in this day and age anyway? She exploded into laughter again.

"Female, are you hurt?" he asked as she realized she was lying limply in his arms.

"I don't feel so good," she murmured, before she exploded into helpless giggles.

"She inhaled the epimorph!" Storm exclaimed, his eyes crinkling up in concern.

"What is that?" Sting asked, unfamiliar with the powders and practices of healers.

"It's a rebuilder! If a warrior were seriously injured in battle, I would use the epimorph to regenerate the injured parts, external to internal."

"So it is good?" he asked, his one eyebrow rising up in question.

"It is bad! Very bad!" Storm sighed. "She is not of our people, does not have the same organs and parts! This power is trying to create what is not already there!"

"Meaning?"

"Meaning it will soon kill her!"

Storm looked over at the slumbering woman, lying comfortably in Sting's arms, patiently waiting for him to save her.

But this time he could not.

It turned his thoughts to another time, another woman who needed him, who he was not able to save. And his heart bled.

"So," Sting began. "I take it you will be wed first?"

"What?" Storm cried out, turning to face the dark man.

"You will be wed first. If Amadala finds out, she will postpone until your human is dead, then you will have to produce another reason not to mate with her."

"Oh, damn my fins!" Storm sighed, dropping his head into his hands.

He had forgotten all about the pink wonder.

After the fight, Amadala had gone to her own cavern, but promised to be back soon.

He had to protect Elanna from the queen, even if it meant mating with her.

"Tomorrow," he sighed. "Then I'll have to find some way to tell her that she only has a few days to live."

Chapter Eleven

≈

"Storm," Elanna gasped, fighting for each breath. "What's happening to me? And please don't lie."

"Elanna," Storm began running his fingers through his hair, not even caring that being this close to the heat of the perpetual fire was painfully drying out his skin.

What he had to say hurt him more than any torn and ripped flesh ever could.

"Please, Storm. Until now you have been brutally honest," she said, her voice weak with the constant fight to stay focused.

Her hair, a dry mass of tangles on top of her head, perfectly matched her inner self, dry, brittle and twisted. She forced her eyes to look up towards his face, to read the truth of her situation there, and then she had to fight against the urge to laugh hysterically.

"Curiosity does kill the cat!" she crowed as tears of anger, frustration, and amusement filled her eyes to track down her salt-encrusted skin.

"I am so sorry," Storm began, feeling the responsibility of this tragedy.

"You didn't do it, Fish Boy!" she laughed. "I did it to myself. I knew better than to go messing around with chemicals unknown to me. I did it to myself, and that's what hurts the most, or is the funniest, depending on how you look at it."

A small chuckle escaped her lips, before a broken sob exploded from her chest.

"This feels so familiar," she gasped and laughed as she dropped her head back to the hard stone, but grateful she could still experience this discomfort. For her, it was a last-minute pleasure to be savored.

Storm looked at the woman, the human woman who bravely faced her death and felt the urge to slit his wrists.

Again the thought of another woman, a dying woman, filled his mind.

Had it been ten years?

Ten years to mourn, only to be pulled away from his mourning by another woman, only to watch her perish as well.

The council was responsible for his first tragedy, while he alone would bear the burden of this death.

Ten years to mourn, to think, to blame, and now again he was faced with the death of someone he cared about. It was almost too much to bear.

Her name had been Neima, and she was about as plain as a Merwoman could be.

Her hair and eyes were a pale gray that blended with the water, but her spirit was such a beautiful thing to behold.

It was she who led him away from his countless studies as both a warrior and a healer, she who had taught him to trust in his powers, to not be afraid of them. She had also helped him control his temper, the thing that made him such a feared warrior and left him alone most of the time.

"Come play with me!" she would laugh as she tugged at his long hair, ignoring the occasional zing of electricity as he lost his hold on his talent. And laughingly, he had joined her in frolicking in the sea.

This was the strongest and most feared Child of Triton, the future leader of The People. He played like a child in the water, frolicked like a child and loved every minute of it.

The council, on the other hand, felt such frivolity was dangerous and ordered him away from her. And when that didn't have the desired effect, the council turned on her.

She was warned the fate of her family was in peril and the only way to prevent something from happening to them was to no longer see Storm until he was fully grown.

Stricken, she tore herself away from his life, away from the one thing that had brought her joy, and withdrew into a protective shell. A shell that could only be breached by the blue-haired Merman named Storm.

Understanding her predicament, Storm vowed to her that when his training was complete, he would return to her, and that was a promise he kept.

As soon as he was old enough to make a pledge, he vowed his eternal love to Neima, swearing on his life to protect her in all things.

Safe from the council and a man proven in battle and in knowledge and treatment of others, Storm had no reason to deny himself the company of his one true love.

The future king of The People held enough influence to see that her family was safe and nothing would stand in the way of their mating.

But certain members of the council, people who believed in the old way of mating power with power, felt Neima and her quiet beauty and charm not fit to be the mate of the king.

Their plan was simple, and although the other members of the council did not approve, they did nothing to stop the plan being hatched.

On the day of their mating, Neima was sent off to a far quadrant of the civilized territories to fetch some supposed traditional sea flowers to present to her mate and future king.

While she was gone, another was put in her place, in the guise of being the love of Storm's life.

It was a good plan and would have succeeded with no harm to anyone, except a few bruised feelings.

Storm could keep Neima as a plaything, while fulfilling the old traditions of marrying into power. This woman, this replacement, did not possess the powers of Triton, but it existed in her blood, and that was enough for them.

The plan would have worked, but for one thing.

There was no way any amount of cosmetics could transform brightly colored pink tendrils into Neima's long gray locks that escaped from around the long veil hiding the woman's face.

Amadala never knew of this plan and thought she was entering into a willing mating with the future king, but as soon as she saw his stricken face, she asked him if this was not his desire.

"Who are you and where is my Neima?" he asked coldly, stunning the people who had gathered for the ceremony, and frightening the council with his steely-eyed glare.

"My name is Amadala, and I was led to believe you wished this joining," she returned bravely, turning to glare at her parents, who had to have known what was going on.

"You are not my choice," he said, recognizing the truth of her words. "I must know where she is."

Storm felt his stomach lodge itself somewhere in the vicinity of his throat as he thought about his sweet and innocent Neima, off somewhere crying her eyes out for him.

"Where is she?"

After much hemming and hawing, he was told where to find Neima.

Turning without a word, he left the council chambers where the mating rite was to be performed, and raced towards the uncivilized part of their kingdom, Amadala following to offer her apologies for her family in this hateful prank.

He smelled the blood first, heard her low cry abruptly cut off and raced towards his beloved, fear lending him strength.

Storm made it there just in time to see what was left of his beloved being devoured by a pack of sharks.

"No!" he had wailed, rushing in and tearing at the pack, scattering them, trying to kill them with his bare hands.

It was Amadala who managed to pull him away as the hungry predators turned to attack en masse.

"Neima," he had wailed, as Amadala rushed him back to the council.

When he reached their chambers, his fear and anguish turned into hatred and a deep, dark killing anger.

"You did this!" he screamed, stained by the blood of his beloved, covered in scrapes and cuts. "You caused this! Murderers! Murderers, every one of you!"

Then in a feat of strength that had yet to be matched, Storm threw back his head and released his anger, his pain, his torment, into the sea!

"Murderers!"

The sea responded, absorbing his anguish and multiplying it a thousandfold.

The usually calm waters of the deep sea began to churn and swirl as the cave walls began to shake. A low vibrating rumble of thunder could be heard, an impossible thing, but very true as the panic-stricken members rushed to leave the room, to get away from the madman and the power they had always feared.

"Run!" he screamed, the blood from his body swirling around him creating a tubular whirling cave of pale brown that more than showed his caged fury. "Run, you bastards!

Run like she was not able to do! Run, you cowards, deceivers, killers of innocence! Run, or I will kill you in her name!"

The growling thunder increased as the oxygen began to leach from the water, causing a panic never been felt before. The council members struggled to find enough air to breathe and to make their escape, but the enraged Triton gave them no quarter.

"How does it feel to be helpless, to be scared, to know that you are going to die?" he roared as he began to tear the room down with the strength of his powers, the lashing water tearing into the stone as if it were the flesh of some small fish.

"*Neima*," he screamed, his face twisted into the visage of an avenging angel. "Oh Creator…Neima! Why?"

The fury he began erupted as great flashes of lightning exploded from his body, striking without direction or control.

"Storm!" a voice called, tearing him back to the present and away from the screaming council that had begged for forgiveness, something they would never have from him.

"Storm?"

It was Elanna, beautiful, exotic, different Elanna with a fighting spirit which matched his own and whose determination far exceeded his own stubbornness. Beautiful, dying Elanna and again another woman that he was of no use to.

"Yes, human?" he asked, his voice raspy in the silence of the tunnel.

"If we get mated, will that pink-haired monster leave you alone?"

"What?" he asked, surprise deepening his voice.

"I am dead anyway, so it's not like you are going to be stuck with a human mate." She smiled around a sudden wince of pain as if the possibility of her lost future just occurred to her. "Besides, you saved my life, and if you had to mate with that witch, I think that it would kill you inside."

"Are you trying to protect me, human?" he asked.

"Paying back a debt, helping a friend," she said as sudden tears filled her eyes.

"Hmm...Elanna, what you ask is serious."

"Please let me do this, Storm, this one last thing. Then I'll know my life served a purpose. This must be it, as many times as you have saved me."

"Elanna," he began but she cut him off.

"Okay, Fish Boy! Enough of this!" Anger was taking over again. "Tomorrow we will be mated and I will die with some dignity!"

"Oh, Elanna," Storm sighed. "If there was something I could do..."

"There is! This mating! Then I can die in peace."

She closed her eyes again, resting her body on the hard stone, and missed the tears freely falling from his eyes.

Chapter Twelve

ಏ

"It's raining, it's pouring! The mean old man is snoring," Elanna mumbled as she felt water trickle down her face.

It seemed like only yesterday, or was it the day before, she was dragged down to this cave, but after weeks of waiting she was going to be a bride, at last.

Bride?

Who was she going to marry?

Then came the trickling again, forcing her to open her eyes and see what exactly was going on.

Her eyelids felt as if they weighed a metric ton and were gritty besides, but she gathered every ounce of energy at her possession and forced those peepers open and saw...

A black eye patch?

"The Willmar Eye Clinic is down the hall," she mumbled as an equally black eye focused in on her.

"Female, I see you have awakened."

"My name is Dr. Elanna... Who are...? Oh dear!"

She was in a cave. She remembered! She was in a cave and she was about to mate with... Why was she lying in the arms of a strange man — uh, fish?

"I am not a dear! I am Sting, Master of the deadly—"

"Where is my Fish Boy?" she demanded, cutting off his words as she sat up as fast as her weak muscles could work. "Why are you here? Only one mating per lifetime, pal, and you ain't it!"

"Fish Boy?" he asked, a puzzled look creasing his face. "Fish Boy?"

"Storm! Where is my Storm?"

"Readying himself for the ritual," he answered, still not quite sure what to make of this human female.

"Readying himself? We are supposed to be readying ourselves?"

She looked down at her salt-encrusted skin and wrinkled her nose in displeasure.

Then something occurred to her.

Reaching up one hand, she tentatively felt the mass now existing on her head, and bit back a scream.

"My hair," she managed to gasp out, her dismay lending her strength.

"It is the most amazing thing I have ever seen."

Sting didn't actually mean to blurt out that compliment, but he truly had never seen anything like this before.

Her hair was a mass of tiny curls! The shine of the saltwater only made it look as if it held diamonds or sparkled with life and vitality from within. It was a rich creamy color, almost the deep brown of some coral he had once seen, or the enchanting scales on a deadly tigerfish. Her skin was just as enchanting and exotic. All in all, he could see the attraction Storm felt for this human. He had honestly never seen a more exotic creature in his life.

"Needs to be washed!" she retorted as she felt the wiry mess her hair had become.

Elanna was not a vain creature by any stretch of the imagination, but with all of the strange mythical creatures surrounding her, she wanted to look her best. Half drowned and gritty was not part of her ideal beauty.

"If you feel you must," he said, before she was raised gently in his arms, and tossed over his shoulder.

"*Eeeeeekkk!*" Elanna screamed all the way down as she felt her body hurtle over space to land in a warm pool of water.

"You asshole!" she bellowed as she struggled to the surface of the water. "You idiot! You menace to society!"

"I only fulfilled your wishes as expeditiously as possible," he calmly said. "Are you not in the washing chamber?"

Then Elanna took a good hard look around her,

She was no longer in the cave where she had had her conversation with Storm. She was in a larger, warmer, fuller cave.

And by fuller, she meant the three women, coloring running from yellow, to red, to lavender, who smiled at her around masses of long straight hair.

"What's an asshole?" Sting asked as he swam towards her, and she realized that she was in a small pot-shaped crevice floating in a pool of deep-looking water.

"It's…it's… Who are those women?"

"Hello!" the trio sang out, making her flinch with the whole cuteness of the gesture.

"Ella, Bella and Rage."

"Rage?" she asked, eyebrows raised, even as her feet found footing and discovered that she could stand and still be covered by the warm water. "The redhead?"

"No, me!" said the middle Merwoman, who was some odd shade of lavender.

"Rage?" Elanna asked, her disbelief showing on face and in her tone.

"I know! It's my parent's fault! I think they wanted a boy."

"Named Rage?" Elanna asked as she shuddered in growing pleasure. The warm water was beginning to sink into her pores, soaking away what seemed like years of salt and silt.

What was wrong with these people? Who would name a child Rage?

She looked over at Sting, who was flexing his arm fins, spreading the deadly looking spines that eased out of their delicate-looking sheaths.

"Okay, I guess Rage would be a good name for one of you people."

"Rage is an excellent name, for a man," Rage continued with a sigh. "But it sure makes mating hard for a woman! Do you know men actually think that I have a temper?" she gritted out, her face taking on what seemed to be a flush of anger, her eyes narrowing in thought even as her tail swished madly through the water.

"I guess it's not so odd," Elanna allowed while rolling her eyes at the strange but aptly named woman. She would really hate to get on her bad side.

"But that is another story," Sting said with a sigh, turning his attention back to the human in the crevasse. "Are you warm? If so, we must proceed with the preparations."

"Not with you in here," Elanna said cheerfully, looking away from the three girls to the black-haired man.

"My presence is required," he replied. "I must attest to your readiness."

"Readiness to what?" Elanna asked, her voice deepening with her new state of mind, worry mixed with a fair amount of trepidation.

"Readiness to proceed with the ceremony," Sting said. "These three will act as witnesses and will assist you in cleaning up afterwards."

"Cleaning up? Afterwards? What are you talking about, Cyclops?"

"Cyclops?" Sting asked, that one black eyebrow rising in confusion.

"Just what do you think you are going to do to me?" she questioned, more plainly this time.

"Why, test your readiness…"

"Details, one-eye!" she bellowed, finally losing her patience and sighed as the trio of backup singers began to giggle.

"Human, you do try my patience!"

"Details!" Elanna finally shrieked, not caring that she appeared undignified. *She* needed to know what was going on.

"I need to see if you are…receptive," he stumbled, a blush heating his face as the trio giggled again.

"Say what?"

"Well, Merfolk are quite…long," he stuttered, for once losing his cool. "We mate from behind and the male has to be long enough to reach…"

"I get the picture!" Elanna struggled to breathe through her suddenly constricted throat.

"Good!" Sting said, cheering up considerably. "Then you won't mind if I—"

"Hell, no!" she cut him off.

"Pardon me?" he asked trying to gain the understanding of her words.

"No! No, Cyclops. *No!*"

"But how will I—"

"I am human!" she retorted, a bright blush almost sizzling her face with its heat. "We expand and contour to fit," she mumbled as she suddenly took great interest in the water that she was boiling in.

"You what?" Sting asked, suddenly amazed as he gazed at this human.

Well, human reproduction was never covered in school, and if what she said were true, if that got out... Mermen would start actively searching out human castoff women for themselves!

"Humans come in a variety of sizes, and, uh, shapes," Elanna explained. Was it growing hotter in here or was it her? "We can accommodate a male of almost any size."

"That's amazing!" Sting gasped, noticing that the trio went silent. "Are you sure?"

"Of course I'm sure!" she said, exasperated. "I know my own body, pal!"

"Very good," he said. "Very, very good. This means as soon as you are cleaned, the ceremony can begin."

"Ceremony?" she asked again. "But I have no clothes!"

"And hair in strange places," he returned, making her aware that she was totally naked in the water!

"Where are my clothes, you pervert?" she shrieked. "What did you do to them?"

"They fell apart," Sting replied wondering what her problem was now. Humans were strange! They dressed in layers to hide what the Creator had given them. Strange indeed.

"I want clothes!" she bellowed. "I want a covering! I want my Fish Boy! This place is strange! *Storm!*"

Sting blanched as she began to leak water from her eyes and scream out the name of her future mate. What was wrong with her eyes? She was starting to scare him a bit.

"Storm!" he yelled, echoing her cry.

The trio had remained silent and worried as they watched the human seem to…break. What was wrong with her?

"Storm!" Elanna cried again, a shout that was echoed by Sting's cry of "*Storm*!" and the trio screaming, "Storm, Storm, *Storm*!"

"I want my Fish Boy!" Elanna said, her tenacious hold on her emotions breaking as she gave in to her rising fears. She wanted her anchor, and all she had was a group of three screaming mimis and a black-hearted, black-haired…Cyclops! "*Storm*!"

"What?" came the irritated bellow as the water suddenly exploded in front of Elanna's stone cooking pot.

"*Storm*!" they all cried out in relief.

Turning in a full circle and observing the situation before him, Storm said the only thing that made sense to him, being more familiar with the human language and all.

"Hell!"

Chapter Thirteen

ಉ

"Of all the... I have never been... Why is it that...? *Ahh!*"

Storm threw up his arms in frustration and Rage and her sisters, the fearful Sting who had cowed Amadala, and his future mate, the one who gave him the cute name Fish Boy, Elanna, all stared at him in varying degrees of distress and relief.

"He did it!" Elanna cried at the same time Sting stammered, "She's faulty!" The trio called out, "Protect us! They are possessed!"

"*Quiet!*" Storm bellowed, staring at Sting until the shamefaced warrior crossed his arms and glared defiantly at the water surrounding him.

Elanna blinked rapidly, banishing the tears while sighing in relief. Her knight-in-shining-fish-scales had come.

The trio just looked confused, and lavender-haired Rage looked almost angry in her confusion.

"Elanna, what is going on?" he asked, knowing her emotions were still unstable because of the epimorph, but she would give him the most disjointed answer.

"He said he had to test me for readiness! I don't know what that means! And he threw me into this cooking pot like a plucked chicken."

"Chicken?" everyone but Storm exclaimed, looking questioningly at Elanna, as if she was seriously demented.

"And my clothes are gone and they saw me naked. Naked, Storm! And he commented on my hair, my personal hair, and they want to clean me. Keep them away from me!"

Storm blinked at this tirade, then turned to Sting.

"And you?" he asked.

"Well, she is leaking from the eyes, Storm! A most amazing thing! I have never seen the like and feared she was ill."

"I'm dying, you nimrod!" Elanna screamed as she rose to her feet, forgetting for a moment that she was naked. Then with a squeak, she sank back down in the warm water to her chin. She still managed to look frightened, relieved, self-righteous, and angry at the same time.

"Well, more ill. What is this Nimrod?" he asked, turning away from Storm to Elanna, earning a squeak and a splash as she sank in the water up to her nose.

"And you?" Storm asked, turning to the sisters.

And naturally, Rage spoke for all of them.

"There is something wrong with all of them, Storm! And I want out of here!"

"Okay," Storm sighed, turning to face Sting first. Not out of respect, but he wanted the Merman out of the way so that he could reason with Elanna. "Humans cry. It's something I learned in Greece. It is some release of some kind, likened to shedding scales."

"Oh," Sting said, catching on to Storm's meaning. "It is emotional!"

"Yes," Storm agreed, nodding to Sting. "And now, you may leave."

"But the ceremony…"

"I'll handle it," Storm sighed, motioning the black-haired man from the chamber.

"But the testing…"

"She is human. She will adjust to me," he said. "You will see."

"Yeah!" Elanna cried out, justified at last. Then, "What do you mean you'll see?"

"Rage, you and your sisters have brought the cleaning supplies?"

"Yes, but we aren't staying! They are all insane, Storm, including Amadala's mate. I don't think you're safe in here!"

"I am fine. You all may leave. I'll handle everything."

"But you are a man!" Rage protested, her silent sisters nodding behind her.

"Rage," Storm said with growing impatience. "I said that I would handle it."

"As you wish," Rage said, suddenly very meek, bowing before she and her sisters disappeared down into the water. Without a splash, all three women were gone.

"Goodbye, Sting," Storm said, as he arched one eyebrow in his direction.

"I guess, because she is human, but you had better mate her, Storm. I want Amadala to be baited and mated by tomorrow."

"Understood," Storm laughed and Sting let a rare smile crack his stern visage.

"Lady, it's been...something."

Without a sound, he too disappeared and finally Elanna was left alone with Storm.

"Are you ready?" he asked as he lovingly stroked the water and flowed it in her direction.

"What did you learn in Greece?" she asked. "And why were you there?"

Anything to postpone having a cleansing...whatever that was.

"The council thought it was important for me to know the ways of humans," he said with a sneer.

Yes, they wanted the king to be well-versed in the ways of man, since man was increasingly invading their waters. So he had met with a few devout people, knowledgeable in the old ways, and had learned to perfect his human speak. Not to mention a crash course in humanity. Although he thought a lot of what they did was barbaric, he could appreciate the gentler traits of the species.

"You don't like the council much, do you?" she asked, picking up on his dissatisfaction with the whole institution.

"No. They think that they know everything, when in fact, they know nothing but what's before their very own noses."

"Okay," she said, her mood swinging to something more like interest.

Suddenly, she was hanging on the edge of her bath, eyes greedily devouring Storm's well-muscled upper body, and wondering about Sting's statements.

The words "from behind", and all of those hints about size, suddenly flooded her brain.

What was that bulge that she had felt before and how did it work?

All scientific, she assured herself, while the other half of her brain called her a liar.

She tilted her head to the side as she took in his exposed form. He was worth a second glance! Despite the neon hair, the vampire eyes and the shark-man teeth.

"Why are you looking at me like that?" he asked as he moved closer to her.

"No reason," she replied, her voice husky with growing interest.

"Well, you look funny," he said as he turned, and with a flip of his tail fin, propelled himself across the chamber to where the trio had stood.

Once there, he retrieved the pouch they had left floating on the surface and quickly returned to Elanna.

"What's that?" she asked, wondering if this cleansing involved a sponge bath.

"Things that no lady would be mated without."

"Clothes?" she asked again, suddenly not worried about her nudity. Storm could look all he wanted. Her body began to vibrate with need.

"Cleansing sands," he replied, reaching and pulling out a handful of glittery dust.

Automatically, she recoiled. She suddenly had developed a distrust of Merfolk powders. *No wonder why?* she thought as she snorted.

"It is safe," he assured her, as he slowly approached. "It is just for washing."

He reached down into her tub and collected a handful of water. This he added to the powder and it immediately exploded into foam.

"You have soap?" she asked in wonder. "But you are in the water all of the time!"

But then she recalled what fish smelled like when not cooled and out of the water for a few days and had to agree with the discovery.

"We have soap, Elanna. We also find a use for combs and teeth cleaners."

Fish breath, she supposed, but the comb jab hurt.

Her hair was still a tangled mess.

"Give me the soap," she sighed, hoping that it would at least get the salt out of her hair. Her stylist would be livid if he ever saw the mess on her head!

He gave her the pouch and watched as she made a mass of foam, following his motions, then slapped the stuff into her hair.

"Why did you do that?" he asked, suddenly distressed.

He moved closer to the crevasse and hefted his body to sit on the side.

"Your hair is perfect!"

"It's a mess!" she said as she began to work the lather into her tightly curled hair.

"But you will destroy the texture!"

He eyed her head in dismay as the pretty salt crystals that had decorated her hair, melted into nothing, her curls falling down around her shoulders in a straight mass.

"It will pouf back up!" Elanna sighed and wished for a blow dryer. Not that she was distressed about her hair in its natural state, but she was used to having it pulled back into a bun. Her new Afro needed some getting used to.

"I don't believe you!" Storm cried as he reached out to touch her sudsy hair.

Of all the things about Elanna that had appealed to him, her hair was the first! It was so different than anything he had ever seen—so filled with life, so thick and vibrant.

He looked at his own straight locks and sighed. Some people never appreciated their good fortune.

"It will curl like wool in a moment, Storm. Stop worrying." Elanna didn't understand it, but if he thought nappy-tangled hair was beautiful, who was she to argue? "Feel."

She moved closer to him, still keeping her upper body below water, and let him explore.

"Mmm," Storm purred as he ran his fingers through her hair.

It sensuously wrapped around his fingers, surrounding him with her life force, caressing him as he caressed her locks. He could die rather happily playing in her hair.

Elanna closed her eyes and sighed in pleasure as Storm's strong fingers massaged her scalp and tugged gently at her hair.

She had never realized how hair and scalp could be erogenous zones, but her body understood.

Her nipples stiffened in the hot water and her skin tingled with shocking impulses. Her mind drifted and a low moan rolled out of her throat. This was pure bliss!

She moaned as his hands continued their massage, slipping down to her neck, then onward towards her shoulders.

She shuddered gently, her emotions turning from keen interest to lust without her even thinking about the issue.

Her hands moved up to lock on to his wrists and pulled his hands forward until they were almost touching her breasts.

She groaned at the contact, lost in the hot water and his steamy touch.

"Elanna," he said quietly, shifting her forward a bit so that he could slip into the water behind her. "Do you have any idea what you are doing to me?"

"I am saving you," she purred, delighted at the contact. She shuddered at the unfamiliar feel of his lower body nestling against hers.

"You are turning me inside out," he said as his hands moved back to her shoulders to play with the foam that had begun to slip across her body.

She trembled at the feel, arching into Storm and pulling his hand back around her so that she was enveloped in his arms, covered by his sea scent, nestled in the safety he offered.

He moaned, finally voicing his desires as his hand slipped down that extra inch to finally cup her foam-slicked breasts.

"Storm!" Elanna all but sang as thunder boomed within her body. Never had another's touch on her breasts shaken her so.

Her hands snaked down around behind her to grip his waist and pull herself closer to that mysterious bulge between them.

"Elanna," he hissed as he felt her hands slide around him, her move arch forward to explore him, felt his slit begin to part and her hand touching…

"What are you doing?" a voice shrieked as a splash announced an intruder into his oasis of pleasure.

Elanna jumped, her hand moving away from the intriguing orifice while his slit clamped closed, tight as a drum, trapping the bulge within.

"Amadala," Storm growled, a sudden wind blowing in the chamber. "What do you want?"

Chapter Fourteen

"Can I go to sleep now?"

"Just a little longer."

"But I am so tired now!"

"Just a little longer."

"And I am hungry."

"Just a little longer!"

Storm sighed as Elanna sagged in his arms.

It had been an hour since Amadala intruded in on their private moment, and Storm vacillated between anger, relief, amazement and annoyance.

"What are you doing with her?" Amadala shrieked, her skin melting into some strange pale red that almost matched her hair and eyes. "You can't be serious, Storm! She's a human! A human! You don't know where she's been!"

"Yeah?" Elanna retorted, eyes shining like two dark moons of fury. "Well, at least I don't smell like fish!"

"Fish!" Amadala hissed as she narrowed her eyes at Elanna.

Elanna prepared herself to leap at the Merwoman, ready to pull her hair from her head and rip out her eyes. Well, at least that's what she wanted to do.

"If the flounder fits!" Elanna hissed right back, readying herself for action, her Storm-lust turning into bloodlust.

"Amadala!" Storm called as he wrapped his arms around Elanna, holding her back from attack, and realizing how strong she actually was. "You have no business here!"

"But I do!" she cheerfully called out. "The four council members are here to approve your bride!"

"What?"

Storm went as still as death, and strangely, the water in the room did too.

"I... Uh, I..." Amadala stammered as she suddenly mentally cursed herself for drawing the council in. She had misjudged that situation, overplayed her hand for emotional reasons, and now she had to accept the consequences.

"You called that hell-spawned four to me? To judge the woman I have chosen?"

He hunched his shoulders as his eyes began to swirl and glow. He pinned Amadala to the spot with the intensity of his stare, glancing straight into her soul, and finding it lacking.

"I... It is tradition!" she tried to argue, but the winds began to blow softly, swirling around the room. Oddly still waters began to glisten with the rage illuminating his eyes.

"Again, you expect me to put a woman I want under their castigation?"

He slowly released Elanna and shoved her behind him. He was losing himself in his growing rage, but he knew enough to protect his woman.

"They... I..."

"Silence!" he roared suddenly, his loud booming voice just as terrifying as his silent hiss. "You overstep yourself, female!" he growled as he leaned over the lip of the crevasse like some great colorful, poisonous viper.

"I..."

"Remember, Amadala! You rule in my stead! If I so choose, I will bring this kingdom to its knees and hold you responsible for beginning the end!"

"Storm," Amadala pleaded, holding her hands out in supplication. Storm was losing himself in the past, in his memories, and that was dangerous.

"And yet you bring those whom I despise more than anything else in this ocean, to my caves to assess my woman? For that you must pay!"

Suddenly a quiet rumbling was heard, a noise so low and terrifying that Elanna was knocked out of her fury and into sudden fear.

"Storm? What are you doing?" Amadala asked, fright making her voice tight. Her eyes widened as she gazed imploringly at him, then around the room, finally on Elanna. "What is happening?"

There was a sudden wet *whoosh*, the sound of a waterfall roaring its power, of lightning striking the sea, of an underwater volcano erupting! But instead of liquid hot magma, a swirling, turning funnel of pure-white, rough water exploded underneath Amadala, catching her in its grasp, spinning her, twisting her, flipping her until the pink of her flesh had totally disappeared inside this cone of fury!

Frightened almost beyond comprehension, Amadala tried to scream as she felt her body being tossed around and bounced off an impenetrable wall of water.

She grunted and shrieked as she felt her scales, her beautiful iridescent scales, being torn from her body, the rough fingers of water tearing at her hair, the awesome pressure that made her eyes feel as if they would pop from her very head.

With a last desperate gasp of air, she sent out a silent signal to the only person who could help her, the first person who popped into her mind as she felt the seas turn against her.

"*Sting!*" she chirped on a sound wave, sure that he would arrive in time to see her dying at the hands of the man whom she had befriended so many years before.

"Amadala!" Sting called as he erupted into hell!

He had been waiting in another nearby cavern, finalizing his plans for his mating on the morrow, when he had hear that short, frightened squeak, his name being called out in pain and fear. Almost instantly he recognized the voice as Amadala's and knew that she had finally pushed the Child of Triton too far.

But he never expected this!

Storm was a true Child of Triton, controlling the seas with a mere thought, and now these thoughts would kill his chosen mate if he did not act.

"Storm!" he bellowed, falling into a fighting stance while trying to garner the enraged man's attention.

"Away with you!" Storm hissed as he pushed Elanna farther back behind him and concentrated on the battle position the other Merman took, arms extended so that the deadly arm fins shone brightly in the artificial light.

"She is my woman!" he argued, one hand reaching for his eye patch.

"She will be the death of mine!" Storm bellowed.

Never had he felt so out of control! One moment he was cuddly and frisky in his woman's arms, amazed that he could still feel this way, and fearful of what this growing love would do to him. Anger that she was dying, that he could not help her, that he had so short a time with her.

Then Amadala brought in the council.

Those murderous sharks would never lay a hand on Elanna, would never putrefy her air with their presence!

"Don't make me hurt you!" Sting said with true regret. He realized that Storm, though hiding it well, had been pushed to his emotional limit, thanks to Amadala's final plan. Never had a strategy so backfired.

"Try!" Storm hissed.

Then moving quickly to catch him off guard, Sting ripped off his shell eye patch, his one hidden eye glittering and exploding in a rainbow of color. Raising one hand, he sought to lift Storm from the crevasse, thereby breaking his concentration and ending this nightmare.

But Storm was a well-trained Triton.

He easily increased the pressure around the stone bowl, increasing the wind so much that Sting's power was useless.

Hissing, Sting extended his arm and tensed.

Two very sharp needles exploded from his arm fins, flying towards a non-vital part of Storm's body.

But these halted inches from his skin to melt into the water.

"The Creator help me," Sting whispered. "I don't want to kill you!"

He had a few more weapons at his disposal, but they would prove fatal if Storm let his guard drop, and he didn't want to see the other man dead, his blood on his hands because of the actions of his woman.

The whistling of the wind grew, the pressure built, and Sting knew that he had to make a decision between Amadala and Storm.

"Forgive me," he whispered as he raised his arm, his choice made, and focused his rainbow-hued eye on his arm fin.

The end would be quick.

He closed his eyes and then...

"Storm, stop it!"

It was Elanna's voice.

Elanna stood back and watched in amazement as the mild and long-suffering man she knew suddenly became a beast of Clive Barkerian proportions.

She watched as a funnel of water swallowed up Amadəla, and as Sting tried to stop him, her anger quickly melted away to concern.

She couldn't let Storm live with these deaths on his conscience. She was here to save him, so damn it, she would save him. If only from himself.

"Storm!" she called again, and was rewarded when he turned in her direction.

"Elanna," he hissed. "They will not murder you, too!"

"I know!" Elanna soothed as she stepped nearer.

She reached out one trembling hand to caress his face. She was not afraid that he would hurt her. Storm would die before hurting her. This she knew in her heart.

"I know because you are here to protect me."

She caressed his face, felt the unnatural cold, felt his body shiver at the warmth of her touch and moved closer.

"I didn't protect her enough," he said quietly, the swirling of his eyes lessening.

"You protected her the best you could," Elanna improvised, not knowing who or what he was speaking of. "I know you will protect me."

The wind began to die back, though the funnel still spun, but slower so that a glimpse of pink could now be seen.

"I'll protect you," he vowed as he let go of the edge of the stone and clasped her hands to his face. "If it is the last thing I do!"

Just as quickly, Storm closed his eyes and the funnel abruptly collapsed.

It was almost anticlimactic.

"Thank you," Sting said, having opened his eyes when Elanna had begun to speak.

He slowly tied his patch around his eye as he stared at Elanna, cradling Storm's body in her arms.

The Child of Triton seemed to be racked with shivers, emotional as well as physical.

"I didn't do it for her," Elanna said with quiet dignity. "She's an interfering, nosy bitch!"

"Nevertheless, she is my bitch," Sting sighed as he dove deep to find Amadala. He knew she was alive, because he could hear her frightened whimpers.

Surely she had no equilibrium by now, and the fish she had consumed earlier would, by now, be feeding the fish.

He shuddered at the thought, but dove after his maiden...fair?

* * * * *

Several hours later, Elanna had been scrubbed and primped enough to make her forget that she had ever longed for a full day at the health spa.

As soon as Storm recovered himself, he sent a message to the council, his words terse and clear.

Stay away!

Then he proceeded to briskly wash Elanna's body, rather impersonally.

She groaned as she recalled she had ever desired her Fish Boy! He rushed through the cleansing, their earlier intimacies vanished along with Amadala's pretty pink scales.

Well, actually, a few of her scales were still floating in that chamber, but the point was moot.

Now she sat on a stone outcrop, a finger actually—well, scientifically, an archipelago. She was waiting for the Life

Binder, the Merman who would join her with Storm for the rest of her short life.

Now she was so miserable, she wanted to cry.

"I want to get this over with!" she whispered, and again Storm smiled at her with overly calm eyes and a steady demeanor.

"Soon," he whispered, just as a green-haired man emerged from the water carrying a rather large knife.

"Storm?" she asked as the man approached them. "He has a sharp instrument!"

"Relax," he whispered back. "It will all be over soon."

Chapter Fifteen

For the first time since being diagnosed with death that she could recall, Elanna's life flashed before her eyes. Oh, all of the things that she wanted to do, that she never got the chance to do, she could still do if that man wasn't approaching her with that *big-assed knife*!

"Storm," she hissed, gripping his hair as his head rested near her thigh as he treaded water beside her. "I would prefer having the powder kill me than having a knife make an intimate acquaintance with some major organ."

Storm looked up at her and blinked once.

"That man!" she finally screamed, pointing with her free hand. "He has a knife, Storm! And a big one to boot! No marriage I have ever heard of required a knife! A broomstick maybe, but you don't have feet so it's a moot point!"

"Oww!" Storm groaned as he glared up at her.

"Oww! Oww?" She gave his hair another tug, easily moving his body with the buoyancy of the water as she pointed. "He has a knife and you are complaining? Storm, do something!"

Reaching up and gingerly untangling her hand, and a few strands of his hair along with it from his head, he looked up at her as he rubbed his suddenly aching scalp.

"Female, you have problems!"

"I don't have problems!" she nearly screeched as her gaze flew to the man with the knife approaching her and her future husband…mate! "I have issues, boggles and dilemmas! And the major one is holding a knife! *Storm*!"

She wailed the last as the knife-wielding man stopped in front of them.

Sliding back as far as she could go on her stone seat, and that wasn't far, she nearly lifted Storm out of the water in an effort to guard herself. Hey, she was brave, but even bravery had its limits. Storm was a Merperson, he could handle the man. Besides, he could make underwater funnels. He was better equipped!

Rolling his eyes at her, Storm managed to move far enough away from her to extend his forearm.

"What are you doing?" she hissed as she tried to pull his arm back, and having no success at it! *Maybe he was still kind of mental*, she thought, remembering his earlier episode. "You put your arm down now, mister!"

"Are you sure," the armed and dangerous man said, looking from Elanna to Storm, "you want to mate with this creature? Your offspring may prove to be…unstable."

"Unstable!" Elanna suddenly let go of Storm's arm to glare at the man, never noticing that Storm almost went face forward into the drink as she released him. "Who you calling unstable, you jolly green…fish!"

"Female," he started, pulling himself up with great dignity and brandishing the knife like a pointer towards her body. "I'll have you know I am the Life Binder, the one who shall perform ceremonies, both mystical and esoteric, to unite the two of you in—"

"Blah, blah, blah!" Elanna cut him off, her fear swallowed up by her sudden indignation. Who did he think he was speaking to? She was Dr. Elanna Richfield! She was the foremost authority in oncology research and inventor of the…the… Damn! She forgot!

"Blah, blah, blah?" the green-haired man said, looking at Elanna as if she were a creature under a microscope. "Blah, blah, blah? What is this blah, blah, blah?"

"What is a broomstick?" Storm asked, finally pulling himself upright and smoothing down his hair.

"It's a stick, with a broom on the end of it."

The men just stared.

"It's a thingy, used to clean floors."

They glared at her.

"Never mind! What are you going to do with his arm and that knife?"

"I am going to unite you both in a holy binding state. You shall become one flesh, one being, one—"

"Wait, wait, wait." Elanna closed her eyes, shook her head and waved her arms in front of him, sending him to a stuttering halt. "You are not cutting me with that thing."

"Oh, yes, I will!"

"Oh, no, you won't!"

"Why not?"

"It'll hurt! That's why not!"

Storm watched Elanna, this defiant Elanna, and fought the urge to laugh. This was funny, very funny!

"What's a little pain compared with the sanctity of life?"

"A big deal, if you ask me!" she returned. "Life was not meant to be lived in pain! If it were, why would we hope for the better? I like a pain-free life, my friend. Circumstances and environments give us enough pain."

"Interesting philosophy," the Life Binder said thoughtfully, tapping the blade of his knife against his lower lip.

"Oh, there's more," Elanna said, moving out of her corner of the seat and getting closer to the green-haired man. "You see, life is ultimately meant to be enjoyed. That is why we were created with the capacity to enjoy it! Our senses, for instance. They give us a constant barrage of pleasurable stimuli. Our brain releases endorphins to mask pain and to heighten pleasure. Even the natural things around us provide pleasurable stimuli for our sense of sight. So why make pain? Pleasure is so much more civilized and enjoyable for all."

"Fascinating," he said as he lowered the knife from his lip and rested the blade beside her leg on the stone lip. Quite near her right arm.

"Isn't it just!" Elanna said with a smile as she totally relaxed around the stranger. He wasn't so bad when he wasn't brandishing a blade like Michael Myers with flippers.

"Yes, it is!" he said as he considered her words. "I'm still going to cut you though." He suddenly lifted the blade and slashed a long thin line down her arm.

"Oww!" Elanna said quite calmly as she looked down at her arm, as if she couldn't believe he did that. Or even worse, that she couldn't talk him out of it.

"It is an interesting theory," he continued as he reached for Storm's arm. "I'll discuss it further with you later. So simple, it's almost brilliant!" he mused as he made a similar slice on Storm's left arm.

"May we continue now?" Storm asked as he sighed at the fates that gave him such a complicated, chatty woman.

"By all means," the Life Binder replied.

"You cut me," Elanna said, looking at the few drops of blood that welled up.

"Yes, I know," he replied.

"And you didn't use antiseptic," she said, and both men again looked at her as if she were crazy.

"You know, stuff to keep it from getting infected? Things to kill germs?"

The Life Binder blinked at her once—men seemed to do that a lot around her lately—and scooped up a handful of saltwater and liberally doused her arm with it.

"Ouch!" she hissed as she glared at him.

"There, now may we continue?"

"Please!" Storm sighed, as he shook his head in wonder. *If all matings happened like this, it was a wonder that any man did it at all*!

"Very good," the Life Binder said as he picked up Elanna's arm and placed the cut up against the slash he made on Storm's.

"With the mingling of your blood and life essence, I declare you one! One being with one purpose, one goal, one rhythm."

He bent Storm's head down and quickly cut a long lock of his hair. Then turning to Elanna, he pulled her head down, and before she could squawk, sliced a thin lock from her nape.

"You cut my hair!" she hissed.

"Yes, I know," he said as he quickly intertwined the two locks into one. "And a more lovely type of hair I have never seen. Just don't move your arm. We are getting into the serious stuff."

She blinked at him then. "Okay," she said. "But hurry, I'm getting hungry."

He nodded his head and continued, as promised.

"As I intertwine this hair, so shall your lives be intermingled, synchronized, united. It's a pity yours is so short," he said to Elanna as he rubbed the braid against his palm, shaking his head at the loss of the interesting texture her hair lent to Storm's, as if it actually created something from both of them, yet entirely different.

"That's okay," Elanna said to him. "My life is short anyway. I guess it's symbolic."

"Uh," the Life Binder began.

"Elanna, you don't know how sorry I am," Storm finally spoke, all of his amused annoyance at the proceedings vanishing in the blink of an eye. "This is all my fault. If I hadn't left that pouch…"

"It's not your fault, Storm," she insisted as she turned to him and lifted her left arm to run her hand against his face. "I did it to myself. If I had not meddled where I had no information, no right to be, this would have never happened."

"Er," the Life Binder began, but was cut off again.

"But it was my responsibility to take care of you. I am the one who saved you. I should have been more cautious."

"Um…"

"No, Storm! I knew better. I knew the consequences, and yet I took the risk. Me and only me. I alone am responsible, Storm. Don't you ever blame yourself!"

"Yes, well now…"

"But Elanna! You are special," Storm said, his eyes beginning to widen with emotions he thought he could never have for another female. And in futility as he knew the fate of his woman and was powerless to do anything. He could control the forces of nature, command the sea, but he could not pull the powders from one small female. "You are the one I have waited my whole adult life for. You are the one who makes me live again, feel again! I have waited a long time for you, searched for you, fought for you, and when you land in my lap, I lose you, because of something stupid that I did. That I did, Elanna. I have caused my own misery, and cursed us both!"

"Storm! You are not cursed! You are such a special man. You are loving, and decent and kind, and in no way to blame for what I have done. You're not responsible for the actions of others! You are only responsible for your own. You can't protect the world. You can't be everyone's conscience. You can only do what you can to the best of your ability. And that is something you do well. Take care of your responsibilities, that is. And I refuse to be another responsibility. I am a woman who takes her own blame. You are not responsible for me. You didn't make me do what I did. That was me. All me!"

"You were meant to be mine!" he cried, a few scales finally falling. "I held paradise in my arms, and I never realized what I had, until it was taken away from me. You are mine, Elanna. Do you hear me! I love you and you are mine. My responsibility if I wish it. Because it is an extension of my love."

"Oh Storm," Elanna cried out, her own tears breaking free. "You love me?"

"Elanna, I love you! It took me some time to recognize it for what it was, but I love you."

"Oh Storm!" Elanna, keeping their arms touching, reached out and lifted her head for his kiss.

She inhaled the sea smell of him and rested her mouth against his cheek. He tasted of the salty sea, sweet and bitter at the same time.

"My Elanna." His arm went around her, pulling her to the very edge of the stone, turning his head to capture her lips.

They groaned together at first contact, savoring the difference between them, feeling the heat of his body and the force of their emotions as they moved to deepen the kiss.

"My Creator," the Life Binder finally sighed, throwing up his hands in disgust. "You can move your arms now. There is no purpose to me even being here. Here!"

He thrust the hair chain at the two surprised people, who broke off from the kiss before it could get really good.

"Take this. You are mated. You never needed me here anyway. But for the council's sake, it's official. You are mated! *Go* in peace so that *I* may find some peace this day."

He sank beneath the waters mumbling, "Wasted my time here! To hell with tradition! Who needs tradition anyway! Young people! *Ha*! They need to be told *when* they are mated, not going off on tangents of their own! And I had the words perfect this time!"

"We are mated?" Elanna asked, raising her other hand to caress his face.

"All but for the act."

"The act," Elanna sighed, remembering the pleasure that she felt at his hands and wondering what the mysterious bulge was. But the time for wondering had passed! She was going to find out, and soon from the looks of things.

"Yes, the act," he breathed as he moved in to kiss her again.

Moaning in glee, Elanna lost herself in his kiss, carefully running her tongue along his teeth, delighted at the feel and taste of his mouth.

So happy was she that she almost missed the splash as a few people entered the chamber. Almost.

Pulling back from the kiss, she tried to turn her head to see who had entered the room.

"Storm?" she began, but he began to kiss her open mouth, each individual lip, her face, and her hair as he pulled her closer to him, causing her to wrap her legs around his body.

They both groaned at the contact. His heat was incredible, but there was that annoying splash again.

"Storm," she said, pulling back a bit, only to have her naked body pulled completely against his own, her breast now pressed deeply into his chest.

"Ignore them," he gasped as he delighted in the feel of her soft skin pressed tightly against his. Even their color contrast was a feast for his eyes. He looked at them, held so closely together, and moaned.

"Ignore them," she repeated as he gripped her hair in his hand and pulled her head back to nibble at her neck. She groaned as her eyes closed in the ecstasy of his touch.

"The witnesses. Ignore them."

"Witnesses," she breathed, losing herself in a sinking pool of desire.

Wait a minute! Witnesses?

"Witnesses?" she nearly screamed as she pulled back to stare at him.

"Witnesses to our mating."

She turned her head and saw the demented trio, along with Sting, were back! Sting even had the nerve to wave at her.

"Oh no!" Elanna said, pushing Storm away, then pulling him closer. She'd forgotten she was naked. "What are these people doing here?"

"They ensure that I don't hurt you and the act actually takes place," he said and he lifted passion-glazed eyes at her. "It is tradition."

"Fuck tradition!" Elanna screamed, feeling frustrated, loved and angry.

"Fuck?" Sting asked politely.

"*No way, Storm*! Not in this lifetime!"

"But Elanna," Storm began, running a hand shaking with frustration through his hair.

"*No!*" Elanna insisted.

No one was going to watch her consummate her love with her Fish Boy! And she meant it!

Chapter Sixteen

ಬ

"Elanna." Storm tried to reason with her. "They have to be here. We need witnesses!" It was hard for him to think with her legs wrapped around his waist!

He never knew legs could feel so good, so soft, so strong. And the heat was radiating off her skin. He had to resist the urge to wrap them tighter around his waist and just wiggle between them.

"I have waited a lifetime to get married, Storm. And I will not spend my wedding night as part of a peep show!"

"Peep show?" Storm asked, his attention drawn away from the novelty of having actual limbs other than arms surrounding his body. He closed his eyes and luxuriated in the feeling.

"Storm!"

"What does 'fuck' mean?" Sting interjected from behind, looking at them in wonder. Those legs looked like they could be fun. "And how does that feel, Storm?"

"Sting!" Storm groaned while running his hands along Elanna's thighs. "It is like nothing that I have ever felt before! You have to try legs!"

"They are not all that!" Rage snapped, looking jealously at Storm, who was now totally wrapped around that human female. "Do they work both ways? I mean, does the male of the species possess the ability to wrap legs, too?" *That might be more fun*, she thought.

"Will you all get out of here!" Elanna yelled. "I am not a sideshow! You will not get your jollies watching me and Storm get it on!"

"Get it on?" Sting asked, looking at Storm for an explanation.

But Storm was lost, awash in sensations he had never felt before! He felt himself harden, felt his stomach tighten with the feelings. He was barely capable of thought, let alone coherent speech.

"That looks weird!" Rage added, but it was clear her thoughts were still on human males and what they could do with their legs.

"Some people like to try different things," Sting sagely said to her, in his Merman-of-the-world mode. "We shouldn't make fun of them or treat them any differently. Although, the possibilities of legs escaped me before. Imagine, mating face-to-face, intertwined with your lover. It sounds different, but kind of nice."

"That's it!" Elanna fumed. "I will not sit here and be discussed like the main attraction in a circus! I've had enough of that all my life, and I won't tolerate it now! If you won't do something," she jabbed a finger into the drooling Storm's shoulder, "I am leaving!"

Then she showed them all a new use for legs. Dropping them down and ignoring his frustrated moan of protest, she brought her knees up between them. With one quick shove, she kneed him back far enough to get her feet between them. Then, planting her feet on his strong abdomen, she shoved him back with all of her strength!

"*Omph!*" Storm grunted as he suddenly found himself thrust from the gates of nirvana, back under the sea.

While he tried to puzzle out what had happened, Elanna neatly slipped from the stone outcrop and dropped neatly into the water.

"Female! Elanna!" Storm wailed, as he watched his human fair disappear into the deep waters.

"Lost something?" Sting couldn't help but interject, face devoid of emotion as he watched the confusion on Storm's face.

"Huh?" he asked, looking at the spot where Elanna had disappeared.

"Your woman, Storm. You lost your woman."

"I didn't lose her," he said quietly. "I think she swam away."

"I don't think she can swim in her condition," Sting pointed out.

"What?"

"She can't survive at this depth," Sting advised.

"You had better go and get her," Rage added, her sisters nodding their heads in agreement. "I want to see a human mating. I am taking mental notes."

"Oh Creator!" Storm suddenly gasped. "She can't swim in her condition!"

"That's what I said," Sting replied as he looked at the spot where she'd sunk below the surface of the water. "I think you should go and get her."

"And bring her back here!" Rage insisted. "I want to see what legs can do!"

"Elanna!" Storm growled in frustration, running a hand through his hair, before he dropped below the surface in hunt of his mate.

"I hope he brings her back," Rage sighed as she lay back on the surface of the water, floating in her element.

"I hope she isn't dead," Sting said, remembering what the human had done for him and Amadala.

* * * * *

I think I may have miscalculated, Elanna thought as she began to sink like a stone. Instinct had her holding her breath and keeping her eyes open.

She had never expected to sink so fast! For that matter, she never expected to get lost! But the only way she was going was straight down, and suddenly the water became very cold.

Where was Storm when she needed him? she thought. He should be here by now!

Crossing her arms, she let a small amount of air escape her nose, glaring at the bubbles that floated upwards, marking her position. It sure was taking him a long time!

But she had to get out of there, she reasoned. Those people were looking at her! They were waiting to see the sex act between her and Storm! She didn't even know what the sex act was for a man who was part fish. Well, mammal, she decided. He could breathe in the water and in the air. Or did that make him amphibious?

But she had no time to puzzle through his classification, for there was a flash of blue-green and then she was in his arms.

Knowing the drill, when he pressed his face close to hers, she leaned in and opened her mouth to his.

Almost immediately, she felt him pulling the air out of her lungs and replacing it with fresh oxygen.

She opened her eyes and glared at him. They seemed to say, *Why did you let me go through that?*

He wrapped his arms around her body, pulling her close to his body, instantly heating her skin and relieving the pressure that he only felt now was gone. His eyes answered, *What could I do, Elanna? It is always done like that!*

She narrowed her eyes and communicated, *Well, it won't be done like that for me!*

I know, his eyes answered. *But I was so lost in what you were making me feel.*

It is intense, but that is for us to share, Storm! I won't share you with anyone else!

I know, love. I know that now! I did not realize how our traditions might seem strange to you. That was insensitive of me. I will make it up to you.

How?

Like this.

With a kick of his fin, he propelled them out of the maze of caves and into the open sea. It was almost noon, and the sun was at its most powerful.

It created a glittering world of purple and green for her delighted eyes. As Storm propelled them towards the surface, the water heated, entering her pores, relaxing her in his embrace. The flow of the water around them washed away the last of her upset and anger, and Storm twisted and twirled in this undersea paradise.

Long ropes of purple kelp and light green seaweed waved as if being blown by air. Colorful coral in brilliant hues of fuchsia, yellow, blue and red dotted the sea floor below them, glistening like jewels in the pale light of day.

Jewel-toned schools of fish, living gems, darted past in synchronized movements, blending momentarily with their underwater tropical environments, then in a flash becoming visible, before they streaked away, bright bolts of life, creating a rainbow of movement.

Small white motes, sea dust, floated down around them like dove feathers or angels' wings. They drifted all around them, making the place seem like some magical dream. And through it all, he held her safe and secure, spiraling, flowing with the tides. Weaving in and out of enchantment, making time stand still, creating a moment, a memory that would stand for all eternity.

The silence was almost spiritual as they gently floated past, becoming one with their surroundings, with themselves.

This is so beautiful, Elanna said, her eyes turning to those of her mate's, the pale color no longer seeming strange to her. She raised her hands to cup his face.

Like you, be answered, his eyes dilating and glittering with his emotions. *Stunning in its natural beauty.*

She looked down, closed her eyes in her sudden shyness, but felt her heart begin to melt between them.

Don't look away, he said, his eyes drinking in the delicate aura that suddenly surrounded her.

You unnerve me.

You unman me.

She looked up, her eyes wide in shock.

In a good way, he added.

You make me complete, she decided, realizing she loved the rhythms of his body syncopating with hers. It felt as if they shared one heartbeat, one breath.

You make me, he said, closing his eyes and pulling her body close to his, forcing her to feel the hard bulge that grew between them.

Make me yours, she said, her eyelids dropping to half-mast at the feel of the maleness of him.

You already are, he answered.

Then with a swift flip of his fin, they were once again propelled towards the caves, leaving the bright majesty of the sea-born day, a seascape of exquisite delight, and soul stirring splendor, for the glittering future that lay just before them.

And in a deep quiet voice, he added, "Now we become one."

Chapter Seventeen

ಐ

Elanna groaned as they broke the surface of the water, sending crystal droplets of saltwater flying around them.

Tearing her lips away from his, Elanna took in great drafts of air, filling her lungs, breathing on her own as she held tightly to her man.

He had brought her to another cavern, but this one was closer to the surface and filled with warm, gently lapping water.

"Where are we?" she gasped, as it seemed the blues and purples, the warm colors tangling with the cool colors of the sea, followed them into this room.

Looking up, she saw that there was a dome ceiling with a large oblong hole in the center. From this hole, sunshine — bright, brilliant sunshine — flowed, filling the air with its heat and maintaining a comfortable water temperature.

"My special place," he answered as he nuzzled the side of her neck, his eyes still dilated and bleary. "No one, not even Amadala, knows of this place. It is my sanctuary."

"And you brought me here," she murmured, lifting her head so that he could lap the streams of saltwater from her flesh.

"You are my sanctuary," he answered, gently taking the lobe of her ear between his teeth and nipping.

Elanna moaned and buried both hands in his hair, forcing his gaze to meet hers.

"Your sanctuary is in here," she whispered, before she sank, chin deep, into the water and placed a kiss upon his heart.

"Elanna," he breathed, but she quickly moved on to more intriguing things, like his erect nipple just beneath her chin.

Grinning up at him, she took the tender bud between her lips and flicked at it with her tongue.

"Oh!" Storm groaned as he tightened his hold on her. What she was doing was…wondrous! Never had a female touched him there, yet he found it exciting.

"'Oh' is right," she purred as she released his throbbing nipple and placed tiny love bites across his chest. "You taste like salt," she murmured as she began to lick at the bites, to take away the sting.

"And you are too sweet to be real, hotter than any other woman, and you have legs," he moaned as her hands began to explore his chest, slipping around his sides to caress his back.

"Really," she softly said as she pulled herself back up to feast at his lips.

"Let me show you," he said softly, before his eyes started to glow a bit and the water began to bubble.

Not a rolling boil, but gentle massage bubbles rolled around them, awakening the nerves in their skin.

"Storm," Elanna gasped as he suddenly reached down and grabbed her legs, pulling them around his waist, exposing her woman's center to this erotic water play.

"Legs are great," he responded as he finished wrapping hers around his waist. "But what's between them is better."

Fastening her arms around his shoulders, Elanna threw back her head and whimpered as the teasing bubbles hit her sensitive clitoris, stimulating her tenderly as his hands began to roam across her body.

Okay! This was foreplay! This is what her other relationships had been lacking! She shivered and buried her nose in his neck, inhaling his special scent as she rubbed her breasts against the wall of his chest muscle.

"I want to feel you, Storm," Elanna groaned as his hands cupped her bottom and pulled her tightly to that mysterious bulge that she was so curious about. "Let me."

Storm eased his grip just enough for her to slip her hand between their bodies. With murmurs of approval, she ran her hands along his chest, stopping to appreciate the slabs of muscles that made up his abdomen, before venturing lower to the rougher skin that melded into his fin.

This was where things were starting to get odd. If Storm were a human male, she would have encountered his pubic bush before reaching his manhood swollen with need. On Storm, she felt his skin change textures before she again felt that pounding bulge. Running her fingers over it got a distinct reaction.

"Elanna!" Storm gasped as he lost control for a moment and sank below the water. He coughed as he sucked in a surprised lungful. His body, unused to such stimulation, was slow to adjust to the environmental change. He quaked with a sudden sharp spear of desire.

"Oh, Storm," Elanna purred, holding on as if she were riding a bucking...seahorse. "You have a hot button."

Renewing her attack, she clamped her teeth down onto his neck, just where it met his shoulder, and rubbed that bulge again for good measure.

"You are going to make me disappoint you," he breathed as he recovered and buried his fingers in her wonderful hair, pulling her face upwards to meet the crushing kiss he forced upon her.

Ever careful of his sharp teeth, Storm nipped at her lips, before plunging his tongue deeply within, as he wished to do with his straining manhood. Her flavor exploded within his mouth, bringing with it a sense of excitement as well as urgency. His human tasted of fire and lightning, and he desired more.

"I need to feel you," Elanna said again as she broke off the kiss. "I need to know what you feel like."

Storm groaned as her fingers danced along the slit, threatening to make him explode from the protective opening. His body trembled as his mind began to whirl. He lost control of his power and bubbles began to explode on the surface of the water—hot bubbles, surrounding them in a fizzing heat.

Elanna shuddered and writhed within his grasp as his fingers began to drift and explore her womanhood.

"Creator!" he gasped as his fingers played with her light dusting of hair and her feminine opening from behind. She was wet and not because of the bubbling water. Her body seemed to create this hot slippery substance that coated his fingers and sent his mind reeling with images of himself sinking into that heat. He felt a hard button, that when pressed, caused her to squeal and tense in his arms.

"Storm! Yes!" She moaned at his touch, and Storm, becoming more aroused by her actions, repeated this caress. This had to be the center of her pleasures, he decided, so much different than the Merwomen he had known.

Storm's caresses were driving her mad. The teasing of the water was driving her mad. This whole erotic game of cat and mouse was driving her mad! Elanna had had enough!

Feeling his opening with her fingertips, she gently but firmly pushed inside and was rewarded with the most velvet softness she had ever felt, surrounding a firm rod of steel.

"Elanna," Storm gasped as he clamped his lips to hers, stealing her breath, and sinking them below the surface of the waters.

The time for exploration had come to an end. Now it was time to claim the prize. With a groan, Storm let his slit open to her questing fingers and he exploded into her palm.

Elanna gasped at the size of what she was holding! Sting had said something about her fitting, but she wasn't sure what he'd meant. Now she had an idea!

But he felt too perfect for her to release! She had to squeeze him, enjoying his heat, stroking him, and gasped as he grew thicker in her palm.

He was shaped like any other man that she had handled, only his skin was softer and his head seemed broader. He grew to stunning largeness under her caresses and she wished she could see exactly what he looked like.

But her thoughts began to turn to mush as one of his hands slipped in between their bodies. His fingers rubbed and caressed before easing inside her opening.

"Storm!" Her essences exploded at the sensations of being filled, even a little, by him.

She trembled in his embrace as she tangled one hand into his flowing hair. She held on as he began to thrust his fingers deeply into her, preparing her for his taking.

She opened her eyes to see the colors surrounding them—the purples, pinks and greens swirling around them like magic. The dancing bubbles seemed to follow them as his fingers teased and tormented her. She wished that his mouth was not occupied breathing for them, so he could suck on her nipples, adding another dimension to this pleasure, but the bubbles popping along their distended tips as they rubbed against her chest made up for it.

His muscles bunched and tightened as she lifted her legs higher around his waist, an open invitation to initiate her in the ways of underwater love.

Oh, Elanna, female, my true mate, he thought to her from within his mind. *If only you could experience what I am feeling right now.*

He felt her legs slide higher and felt the crushing need to merge with her.

Helpless in the face of this compulsion, this overwhelming need, Storm lifted Elanna higher and placed the head of his shaft at her opening.

"I love you," he purred, before he gripped her waist between his hands and lowered her onto him.

Elanna tried to pull away, to scream but incredible waves of pleasure raced over her body. She felt him stretch her opening, felt his heat pump through with a small bit of discomfort that was quickly washed away in the flurry of sensations that swamped her.

Her stomach tightened noticeably as her legs and arms gave way to trembling. Her man was inside her, pushing deeper, taking possession of her soul.

Then he set up a steady rhythm, undulating his hips backwards and forwards in a constant steady motion. He was so large and still growing within her body, so that every stroke hit all of her pleasure points, sending lightning spiraling up through her body. The constant steady rhythm built tension up in her body she had never felt before! Her nails dug into his back, making him grunt and jerk as he began to spiral out of control.

Thrust and withdrawal, like the ebbing motions of the sea, built and increased in strength. He felt a tingling in his manhood, felt himself sing to the fullest inside her wet, tight heat! And most wonderful of all, he could open his eyes and see her face, know that he was pleasuring her, experiencing her sexual awakening through her eyes.

Soon it became too much for him to bear. The motions became erratic and spontaneous. No longer did he wonder about her needs. The needs of his own flesh were making themselves known.

With a flip of his fin that drove him deeper inside, he moved them back to the surface of the water, breaking through and tearing his lips away just as she let out a bellow of unprecedented joy. He felt her inner muscles contracting strongly about him.

"Oh my Creator!" he bellowed, as he felt answering waves tear through his body.

Never had Elanna felt those gripping waves of release before, ever!

Her body was not her own! Electric waves shot through the backs of her thighs, making her toes point and her stomach clench as she gritted her teeth and stopped fighting it.

Relief ripped through her body, turning her muscles to mush as she weakly maintained her grip on Storm, felt his tremors and shakes as he faced his own crisis. His eyes rolled to the back and his eyelids fluttered as his sharp teeth clamped onto his bottom lip.

Suddenly his eyes opened wide as the water around them exploded in empathy, sending torrents of rough white water flying towards the ceiling. The air reverberated with the roar of the towering funnels surrounding them, masking the roar that escaped Storm's throat as he felt his seed explode from his body, to splash inside her warm, giving body.

He buried his face in her neck, overcome as nature exploded around them, as his world narrowed to only her, him and the sea.

Almost as quickly as it had begun the rage inside the cavern ended, leaving Storm weak and drained.

He groaned as Elanna shifted a bit. His sensitive penis still nestled within her, his trembling arms holding her fast to him.

How I love you, he projected, still too weak for actual talk.

How I love you right back, she replied as she wiggled a bit, enjoying the feel of him resting inside her, his heat surrounding her, his strength comforting her.

"What did you say?" Storm suddenly asked, jerking his head up.

"I said I love you back, silly." Elanna laughed, a new husky, sensual laugh.

"But I didn't move my lips!" he said, cupping her face gently between his hands.

"You said…"

I love you, he added as he pressed his lips to her mouth, proving that he wasn't using his voice to communicate with her.

"What is happening?" she asked, eyes wide with wonder as she realized what had taken place.

"I don't know," he answered as tears began to fill his eyes. Would the fates be so cruel as to give her these talents when he only had her life's flame for a short time? "But I am going to find out."

Chapter Eighteen

"And why are you not witnessing Storm mate with that human?" Amadala asked as Sting popped up in her private cavern.

She had taken to her rooms, licking her wounds, and hiding her face from the world since the council incident.

"Because she left," he said with a smile.

"She didn't mate with him? What did the Binder say?"

She raised one pink eyebrow in surprise as she looked over at the dark-haired man.

"Oh, they were joined—the Life Binder saw to that, but we didn't get to see the mating."

"What? Long skinny legs not up to your standards?" she sneered, still hurting from what Storm had done to her.

"Oh, they are very lovely, Amadala, but I assume her customs are not like ours. As it is not a custom to put down those who have saved our lives."

"I didn't say anything about you, Sting," Amadala sighed. "For once."

"I am not referring to myself, nor would I ever seek glory for my own ego. I am referring to the human female, Elanna."

"Elanna?" Amadala nearly shrieked. "That scaleless creature of a land walker? What did she have to do with anything?"

Amadala narrowed her eyes in anger as she thought of the woman who had ruined her plans. But she softened her look as she gazed at Sting. He wasn't so bad, she supposed, once she had gotten used to him. And he had saved her life.

"No, Amadala," he said solemnly. "The only way I could have stopped Storm was to kill him, an almost impossible feat with that power of his."

"But you stopped him," she stuttered, eyes wide with shock. "I saw you!"

"I did nothing," he insisted as he moved closer to her, getting close enough to run his hand across her face, close enough to stare at her with his one uncovered eye. "It was the human who stayed his hand."

Amadala dropped her head, suddenly filled with shame.

"How?"

"She broke through his madness, Amadala. What were you thinking, bringing the council into this affair? You knew what would happen and yet you deliberately tried to manipulate that man. You know how he feels about them!"

What could she say? Everything Sting said was correct, so she said nothing, just looked into the waters of the sea, her home, the very thing that had been used against her.

"I thought you were this great ruler, Amadala," Sting continued as he raised one hand to lift her chin, forcing her gaze to his. "I thought I had never known a more fair and just queen. And you are an excellent ruler, except where Storm and your own selfish desires come in."

"I don't—"

"You do!" he hissed, becoming angry. "What kind of woman are you? Because you were told to do something, you react just like a spoiled little child! You almost tear a man's life apart so that you can wriggle out of an obligation. That is not the mark of a good ruler, to use your subjects like pawns. You know who Storm is, and yet he let you dictate to him for years, giving in to your every whim, until he decided he wanted some happiness of his own. Then you move in and almost shatter his life and his mind. That is not the act of a ruler, Amadala! That is the act of a dictator and a coward."

"Sting!" Amadala cried out, fear lightening her eyes. "I would never—"

"But you did!" he growled. He released her as if he had touched something repugnant. "But you did."

Her mouth opened several times, but nothing was said. No words could describe the hurt she now felt.

"I am thinking about withdrawing my suit, Amadala. You are not the woman I thought you were."

"No!" she fairly screamed as she reached out to take his arm. "No, Sting, no!"

When had he become so important to her? When had he made his way into her heart? When had she become so dependent on his presence, his words and his impassive face that hid his humor? When did she grow to love him?

"I cannot mate with a woman that I cannot respect, Amadala, and your actions are hateful, selfish and childish."

"But I only wanted…"

"Wanted what you decreed was right in your eyes, ignoring the needs of your people. Storm needs to take the throne back."

"But his mind is broken!" Amadala argued, as she began to grow cold and her body to shake.

"Even broken, he is a better ruler than you, and a better person."

She drew back as if he'd struck her, and in a way he had. She had always served the needs of her people, but in this one case, she had let her pride stand before her common sense. She had never hurt anyone, until Elanna and Storm, she thought sadly. Maybe Sting was right.

"Don't say that," she whispered as her fin began to tingle in a bad way.

"I'll say it because it is true! I will have to think about taking you to mate, Amadala. I will return with my decision."

Without a sound, he sank below the surface of the water, leaving the lone woman there.

It was a falsehood that Mermaids could not cry. No one could actually hear those mournful wails or see scalding tears trail down their faces, but they can and do cry.

Amadala floated, breath tearing in her lungs, nose stinging, as she watched the spot where Sting had disappeared.

"Sting," she whispered, her voice breaking on his name.

And in that moment, she proved that Mermaids could cry. The bright pink scales, once her pride and joy, softly dropped from her fin, scalding pink tears that told of a love newly discovered and lost in the same breath.

Amadala, Ruler of the High Seas, Master of the Oceans, Defender of the Merpeople, proved that Mermaids could cry if the pain was deep enough, sharp enough, cutting enough.

And the softly falling scales proved it.

* * * * *

"I'm tired," Elanna mumbled as Storm tore around the cavern he had dragged her to.

She was beginning to get a feel for this place, thinking it was laid out like a giant underwater castle, complete with stalactite chandeliers and her very own trio of court jesters.

Rage and her sisters had waylaid them coming from the sunroom, as she affectionately called it, and wanted to know details on human relations—the physical kind.

After escaping with as much dignity as he could muster, Storm dragged her to this room where he plopped her on a stone seat—she was getting used to the feel of good rock against her bottom—and began to pour through powders.

The room was almost like a pharmacy or a poorly stocked lab, she decided as she wearily examined the bags hanging around, separated by the color of the skin that held them and the size of the pouch.

Soon, I'll take you to the island so you can rest, Storm said, his lips not moving but his voice loud in her mind.

"Can you lay off the mind-speak?" she asked testily as she pulled her feet and legs out of the water to curl up and get as comfortable as she could. She examined her toes carefully as she shook the water from them. Was she growing webs between them? Well, she might, considering the amount of time she'd spent in the water. "You are giving me a headache."

"Sure, love," he said distractedly as he searched through the pouches, tasting this one, sniffing that one.

Closing her eyes, Elanna decided to try and get some rest before she hunted for dinner, and her fish had better be cooked!

Without realizing it, she drifted off to a deep sleep, her body temperature dropping as her heart rate and breathing slowed.

She was so tired.

She tried to sigh deeply, but that heavy feeling in her chest was back, and it disturbed her somewhat.

That feeling jerked her out of a sound sleep and into panic.

"Storm!" she wheezed, trying to get enough air to force the words out, but finding it impossible. "Storm?"

Having no success calling the man who was still surrounded by his powders and his desperate musings, she tried a different approach.

Storm! she called out in her mind.

Elanna? With a mighty splash, he was almost instantly at her side, turning her onto her back, pressing his hands to her chest.

I'm dying, she managed as even the mental thread began to grow weak.

"No, Elanna!" Storm begged as he closed his eyes and let his power search through her body. The epimorph had taken over! It was running through her blood, through her lungs and her brain. It was completely filling her body, and he had no way to force it out. "Please don't leave me!"

His eyes grew wide, and even though no liquid spilled forth, she knew that he was crying.

Storm, it's been fun, she wheezed, the mental line just as shaky as her voice would have been.

"Fun," he chuckled, knowing that there was nothing he could do, feeling her life seep from her body.

Fun, Fish Boy! She laughed weakly. *And you gave me my first and only orgasm. Thanks*!

She tried to smile, but found the muscles in her face were just too weak.

She no longer felt the cold, the hardness of the stone she complained about, and suddenly, she wished that she could feel them, feel the discomforts that made life, and have the time to complain about them anew. But stillness had come over her, a slow creeping darkness that leached the feeling right out of her. She could barely feel her lungs struggling to rise and fall or her heart fighting for one more beat.

"Storm!" she cried suddenly, tears filling her eyes and rolling down her cheeks, tears she could not feel. "I don't want to die!"

"Elanna," he sobbed, his voice cracking as he pulled her stiff body into his arms, feeling the coldness of death as it slowly overcame the flesh he loved, the body that was once filled with a shining, vibrant life force. "I don't want you to leave me! I want to beg and plead, but you are going! I can feel it!"

His breath raced as he remembered the first time he saw her, falling from the sky to land across his body, her sarcastic comments to him, the way she tried to take his head off with her words. Then he remembered her eyes, looking trustingly up at him, relying on him, needing him. He felt his heart rip, and a pain too intense for words began to wash through him in waves.

"Elanna, don't leave me!" he begged anyway, as he clutched her tighter, as if the very powers in his body could do the impossible and revive her. "Elanna! Creator, Elanna! Don't you fucking die!"

Such language, Elanna sent, a small smile tugging at her lips.

She struggled to raise her hand, to touch his face ravished and inhuman with his grief.

Storm saw what she was attempting, and immediately reached down to grip her palm, resting it against the fever-hot skin of his face.

"Don't you leave me alone!" he sobbed without a tear. "Don't you dare! You are mine! These eyes," he cried as he rested his forehead against her delicate and so beautiful face. "They are mine! And this face, it's mine! And your mind, Elanna, it's mine! Give them back, damn you! Give them back! Please! Fight it, Elanna! Fight, my love! Fight for me! I can't go on without you! Damn you, woman!" he screamed as the water began to turn a dark murky black and the air went still. "Don't you teach me to love, make me love you and then leave me!"

He dropped his head to her chest, gripping her palm, placing kisses—tender kisses, begging kisses—on her cold, still flesh. His body shuddered with the force of his pain, his grip tightened on her body.

"You are loved," Elanna breathed as she tried to remember what he felt like, how hard his muscles felt, how the wet silk of his hair flowed, his wonderful sea smell. "You are loved, Storm!" she said a bit stronger as the room began to grow dark.

"Love for me," she whispered.

Now the room was a tiny pinprick of gray light. The silence roared in her head. She tried to feel her chest move, but it had stopped.

Tears still ran down her face as that tiny light focused on the turquoise hair of her one true love.

"Storm," she asked calmly, "my love. Where have all the colors gone?"

"*Nooo!*" Storm wailed to the heavens, screamed as he held her tighter, but there was no life left in Elanna Richfield.

She had gone home to play with the angels.

Chapter Nineteen

※

"We should go and talk to him," Rage said as she huddled with Sting near the entrance to the cavern where Storm held a sad vigil over Elanna's body. "It can't be healthy for him to be in there with her dead body."

"You go and talk to him," Sting said sadly, trying to understand in some small way the grief the Merman had to be facing. "I think it's better we leave him to grieve."

"But it's been a whole day, Sting!" Rage countered. "He needs nourishment, he needs to be in fresh water, he needs to let us go in and dispose of her body."

"He needs to be left alone," a low voice said from behind.

Rage and Sting turned to see Amadala making her way slowly towards them.

"His heart is breaking and he needs time to deal with the changes in his life."

"Changes?" Rage asked. "What changes? He only met her a few days ago! He has made no changes for her."

Rage wasn't being obtuse, she just didn't understand this thing called love that caused people to react in so many unpredictable ways.

"He opened his heart," Amadala said quietly. "That is a hard thing to do. It's even scarier when your heart is rejected."

As she said these words, she stared straight at Sting, her eyes wide and hurt, her once sparkling tail fin devoid of color and luminance. Most of her scales had been shed.

"Amadala," he began. "Now is not the time. We are worried about Storm."

"I'll talk to him," she said as she stiffly turned from the one man she had unexpectedly grown to love.

"I think you are the last person he wants to see," Sting said as he reached for her arm.

But with a small wave of water, Amadala pushed away from his restraining hand and moved farther away from him.

"I said I would talk to him."

"Amadala," Sting said as Rage, sensing a conflict, took the time to bolt. "I don't think this is what Storm needs."

"Storm needs to grow up!" Amadala finally lashed out, turning to face the black-haired Merman, watching as his one eyebrow rose almost to his hairline.

"And you are a fine one to give advice," he stated coldly.

"He needs to grow up and stop feeling sorry for himself!"

"Storm needs understanding!"

"Damn Storm!" Amadala screamed, her patience snapping. "Damn him and his schemes, and his lost love, and his human! He needs to let her go, Sting!"

"He needs to grieve!"

"He needs to realize this was not his fault, just as Neima's death was not his fault! He feels guilty," Amadala insisted. "And what is he supposed to give up this time? His life's blood? He already abdicated the throne to me because of his guilt about Neima."

"He is in pain," Sting continued to argue. He could not begin to imagine Storm's loss, but he likened it to the loss of his lofty ideals and ideas about Amadala. That wound was still fresh and throbbing and he had to fight not to compare the two situations.

"Life is pain!" Amadala sneered. She took several deep breaths, feeling the agony of her shattered heart as she faced the one who had caused her such distress. "And you have to accept your faults and move on. That is the important part, Sting, moving on!"

"And how is he supposed to move on from this, Amadala? Two women he has loved, two women he has lost. How is he supposed to move on when his every breath reminds him of his loss?"

Amadala was silent for a moment, contemplating Sting's words. She had an answer, but she didn't think that he would like it. For a moment, she debated telling him of her opinions, but then her aggressive nature took hold and she let the words fly.

"He has to stop being selfish."

"Selfish?"

"Selfish, Sting! The human is dead. His mate is dead. Elanna is dead! She is feeling no pain, no suffering, she knows nothing. He is feeling sorry for himself over a human who could not care if she wanted to. Life is for the living. Do you think she cares whether or not he stares at her corpse and wills himself to death? She lost that ability when she ceased to exist. Storm is being selfish and pitiful because he can't face reality. Elanna is gone! It is time to move on with his life."

"That was heartless," Sting said quietly. "But in a way, it makes sense."

"Of course it does. He is still feeling bad about something he could not have prevented. He has to grieve, Sting. But he doesn't have to kill himself because the one he loved is gone. He is feeling sorry for himself, guilt-ridden, and there is not a thing Elanna can do to ease his suffering. Elanna is dead, Sting, but he lives."

Sting blinked his eyes as he stared at the woman before him. Was this the shallow, vain woman that he had grown to know? Where had these deep insights into Merman nature come from?

"So what are you going to do?" he asked finally.

"I am going to go and talk to him. He can grieve all he must, but he must *live* for himself, Sting. That human would never have wanted Storm to die for her, and he *is* willing himself to death."

Turning away from Sting, she sank beneath the surface of the water, her pale pink hair floating for a moment before it too disappeared, leaving Sting alone with his thoughts and the fading sight of her long pink hair.

"Be careful," he said quietly, but his words were never heard.

* * * * *

Storm sat beside the body of his beloved and felt the coldness that surrounded her.

He had laid her flat on the stone bed, her arms crossed over her naked chest, hiding the breasts that he had loved. Her eyes were closed, those once lively orbs stilled. Her brown skin looked gray and hard. Her hair, her wondrous tightly curled hair was dull and lifeless. Lifeless, just like her body, just like him.

He couldn't force himself to leave the room.

He knew he should allow the others to come and remove her body for disposal, but he could not let her go.

He sat there, stroking her hard cold skin, and tried to picture life as it had been, life without her.

He couldn't do it.

"Elanna," he breathed, his eyes wide and luminous. "Why did you leave me?"

"It's not like she had a choice," a female voice said from behind. Storm easily recognized the voice of his queen.

"No," he breathed, not even having enough energy to order her to leave. "She never had that option."

"Then why are you contemplating a question when you already know the answer?"

Still not turning away from the face of his love, he answered quietly, "Because it gives me something to think about."

"Why not think about letting us take care of the body?"

"Her name," he gritted out between clenched teeth as the water around him began to bubble, "is Elanna."

"She is gone," Amadala said quietly. "This is just the husk that held the human Elanna."

"Then I shall have the husk a while longer," he answered, still not looking at her.

"And then what?" Amadala asked. "Will you turn your back to your people, run away to live with the sharks? What would your precious Elanna think of that?"

Storm said nothing, just stroked the lips he'd once kissed.

"So you are going to die for her?"

"Not honorable," he mumbled.

"And locking yourself in with a dead body is?" she countered.

"Go away, Amadala," Storm sighed. "I don't need you here."

"Well, you need someone!" she spat. "And everyone else is too busy throwing you a celebration of pity! Poor Storm," she mocked. "Poor, poor Storm! He lost his love and lost his mind. Snap out of it, Triton. You have duties to perform."

"I suppose you want me to fetch and carry for you," he sneered. "Bring you seaweed from the Baltic, fresh fish from the Aegean?"

"No! I want you to do something really important. I want you to prepare her body for disposal."

"I can't!" he screamed in a broken voice. "I can't bear to let her go."

"*I* and *me* are all I'm hearing from you, Storm. You have to let her go. She is gone! Her life is gone! You are the only one holding her here! You need to end this."

"How can you say that?" he roared, as he finally turned from his beloved's body to face his tormentor.

Amadala swam a few lengths backwards as she faced a sight she never thought to see again. Storm was going insane.

His eyes were wide and wild, their pale color almost red. His face was drawn and gaunt, all of the flesh seemingly melted away, consumed by his own never-ending grief. His breathing was raspy, his hair a tangled mass from running his fingers through it. Even more horrifying, his scales were dry and flaking, all of their glimmer gone.

He looked to be on the edge of death himself, holding on by his anger and guilt.

"I can say this because you are killing yourself!" Amadala said. "You are dying, Storm! And I cannot allow that to happen."

"What are you going to do?" he asked, suddenly quiet, his stillness worse that his insane ramblings. "How will you save me, Amadala? Elanna sought to save me, and look where it got her. Will you be the next to die?"

The water began to roll and boil and Amadala again felt an uncommon shaft of fear as the water played around her. Because of her recent bout with Storm's anger, she was developing an absurd fear of the sea, the very thing which gave her life.

"Storm, you must end this!" she insisted, feeling the coppery taste of fear filling her mouth. "You must begin to live!"

"And what have I to live for?" he asked, leaving the body of his mate for the first time. With a snakelike movement, he eased through the rough waters towards Amadala, who paused, frozen in fear, eyes trained on the Merman who moved closer and closer with every breath.

"You live for her," Amadala insisted, trying to remember how to breathe and move. She kept taking small glances at the rolling water, and then returning her frightened gaze to Storm's face. "You have to because of her!"

"And what do you know of love?" Storm sneered. "Other than the love of your own reflection?"

"I know love that is lost hurts," she stuttered. "But you are the lucky one. My love died before I could experience it!"

Storm blinked once, then regarded the Mermaid who trembled in her skin, yet tried to stand up to him. Her bravery was the mark of a true leader.

"You've lost...love?" The waters began to calm.

"I lost love before I recognized it for what it was. I was selfish and stubborn. Don't make my mistakes, Storm."

"Sting?" he asked, as normalcy tried to fight its way through his feral eyes.

"He thinks that I am selfish and that I use people."

"So he knows you are a bitch!" Storm said, a trace of his old self in his voice. "He must have known from the moment he met you. I did!"

Seeing that talking was calming him down, Amadala continued to speak of the past.

"When I met you, you were ready to kill me."

"Still am!"

Bad choice of words, she thought as the water picked up its eerie boiling again.

"But then I went with you to find Neima."

"You fought off sharks," he said.

"And I prevented you from killing off the council," she reminded him.

"Yes," he replied. "And I walked away from them! I gave you what you wanted, Amadala, power. I gave you the ultimate power, my throne."

"You sacrificed your throne on the altar of your guilt," she said. "And yes, I was there to receive it. But the council's decisions were not your mistakes, Storm. Just as Elanna's death is not your fault."

"She would be alive if not for me!" he shouted.

"She would have been dead if you had not protected her."

"She is dead anyway," he said in a voice filled with regret, and abruptly the water calmed.

"Dead," Amadala said as she moved closer to Storm. She was still terrified of him, but he was her friend, even though she hadn't been acting the part lately. "Yet you are alive, Storm. You survived!"

"I am tired, Amadala." He sighed as she came close enough to touch him.

Then he seemed to collapse into himself, the guilt and anger that had sustained him melting away for the moment, and his body began to break down.

"Rest, Storm," she said softly, as she wrapped her arms around him and pulled him to her chest. "You will rest and then we will grieve together. You for your human and me for my lost chance."

"I will probably kill you later," he whispered as he closed his eyes and rested his head on her shoulder.

"Thanks for the warning," she chuckled. "And I thought that we were friends."

"Maybe once," he sighed, as he began to sleep and to dream. "But then you turned into a bitch. And don't touch her body. I am not…ready yet."

"But…"

"Tomorrow. I will be brave tomorrow," he said as he stopped fighting the waves of mental and physical exhaustion that swamped him.

"Tomorrow then," Amadala repeated, as she held Storm tight.

Chapter Twenty

ೞ

Storm remembered seeing what was left of Neima's body, blood-red billows spreading across the surface of the suddenly cold water, then he remembered little else.

But he remembered the council.

The members waited in their stone coffin as he, dressed in his wedding finery, slowly approached, the smell of blood and death surrounding him.

"What—what has happened?" the eldest member of the five-man council asked, fear masking any concern that he may have had.

"Where is Neima?" a second drawled. "Should we be prepared for weeping and accusations, Storm? We did what we thought was best, what we still think is best. Your powers should not be diluted."

"Quiet!" Amadala said, her own adornments torn and disheveled. "You know not what you speak of!"

"Look at that," still another council member pointed out, oblivious to Storm's blank face and insane eyes. "That is the bravery you want bred into your children, Storm! Is Amadala not the perfect mate? The perfect match for the throne, I say!"

"Please!" Amadala insisted, her eyes wide, frightened, her pink scales starting to shimmer as they began to drop. "Please listen to me!"

"Already she takes control of him," another elder observed. "This is what the boy needed."

"You killed her," Storm said calmly, as the temperature in the room began to plummet.

"What?" several confused voices asked at once.

"You fools!" Amadala hissed, glancing wearily at the council and to the barely contained man. She could feel his power begin to build violently. "Neima is dead, destroyed in your foolhardy quest!"

"Impossible!" the first elder stuttered, unwilling to accept responsibility in this scenario. "There is no way…"

"Sharks!" Storm growled as the water began to swirl around him. "Sharks don't leave much for burial."

There was a loud gasp as the members of the council were suddenly slapped in the face with their guilt, with what their actions had wrought.

"Sharks?" one said, as if the creatures existed only in nightmares.

"You murdered my conscience," Storm said quietly as he watched the members digest his words, then fear began to fill their faces.

They knew it was his inbred conscience that held him in check when his powers demanded a release in destruction, kept him from harming others and forced him to pay heed to the elders' voices.

Now with that barrier gone, there was nothing standing between them and the full power of a true Child of Triton.

"No, Storm!" Amadala screamed as she turned towards the council. "Please!"

She had looked into his pale amethyst eyes and had seen the gaze of death.

The walls trembled as strange underwater lightning began to strike at the stone cavern, tearing stone into bits of rubble as it tumbled downward.

White water bubbled and loud cracks of breaking stone filled the air.

Diving for cover, the council took refuge underneath the massive table that represented their power, a useless symbol now in the face of a Triton's abilities.

"They deserve to die!" he said calmly as he turned glowing eyes to Amadala.

"No one deserves death!" she pleaded. There were several family friends under that table, men she had grown up with and respected. She could not see them dead. "They do not deserve to die!"

"Did Neima?" he asked as his vacant eyes turned to the scene of the council scrambling for cover and cowering like the lowly scavengers they were.

"No, Storm! She did not! As they do not!"

"They are responsible!"

"They are not sharks!"

"They are worse. They are humans tainting everything they touch!" There were loud gasps at this insult, because humans were known as the despoilers of the sea. "No, they are not humans, they are less than human! They are bottom dwellers, planning and plotting against the underbelly of true power! You want power? You want to control my life? You want to rule and make my decisions? Then choose your death!"

Still staring at the five men who had caused him no end of shame growing up, who had manipulated him as they saw fit, who wanted to control the power coming to the throne, he smiled.

A loud clap of thunder made everyone's hair stand on end, before a blue glow began to fill the cavern.

"What are you doing?" Amadala screamed, gripping his arm with her sharp nails and pulling desperately.

"I am giving them power," he answered. "The power of unbreakable stone that will fall on their heads, crushing them, thereby giving them a true demonstration of power. Ingenious, no?" he asked as the glow began to intensify.

"You can't!" she argued as the wildly spinning water ripped her hair around her face. "You are not a killer!"

"What I am is not a ruler!" Storm said in a singsong voice. "No ruler would take joy in their demise. Besides, I don't want to rule any people who would follow filth like this!"

"But you can't kill them!" she argued.

"Am I not the ruler?" he asked peevishly, the first real emotions crossing his face since he'd seen his lady die such a horrid death.

"But you don't want this! A ruler can't do this!"

All the while they were speaking, the blue glow was growing brighter, hotter, the water rolling faster and harder. Still, Storm remained untouched, the water swirling around him keeping him in a calm eye as the seas around them began to wage war.

"What would a ruler do?" he growled, anger in his voice and now showing clearly in the flattened features of his face. "What would you do?"

"I would banish them!" she screamed, her eyes going to the men she had known all of her life. *Anything to save them, her teachers*, she thought.

"Good!" Storm said suddenly, throwing her emotions off with this sudden change of mood. "Then you are ruler! Hear that, you old misguided pack of barracuda! I am no longer the leader! From this day, this gracious pink-haired one..." He didn't even remember her name.

"Amadala!" she said, realizing what he was doing with some awe.

"This Amadala," he corrected "is now the ruler. She chooses to banish you as a just leader would. But since I am no longer the leader, I can choose to do with you what I will!"

"Please!" Amadala said, recovering from her shock as a fierce determination to keep this office filled her even as death loomed around them. "Please, let me handle this! You passed power onto me, let me exercise it!"

"But they killed her!" he bellowed, as the cavern began to shake. "They killed her because of me!"

"No!" she insisted.

"Yes! Because of me!"

His hands tore through his hair as frustration, anger and confusion crashed down upon him, all at once.

"If I had not loved her, if I had not chosen her, if I had left her alone, she would be alive!"

"Storm," Amadala said cautiously. "This was not your doing!"

"But it was done in my name, for the purpose of controlling me. *Me*! That means I am to blame."

Even as his cool exterior cracked, very real emotions poured out of Storm, emotions he had never felt before in his life.

What was this pain in his heart, this ache in his stomach, this fear that filled his mind?

In his confusion, he lost his hold on the elements, the blue glow leaving the room as the cavern stopped trembling.

Still cowering, the council watched in awe as the only true Child of Triton to be born with such powers broke down and sobbed like a child.

And even more disheartening was the fact that Amadala, the chosen power-hungry bride, was staring at them, a look of disgust on her face.

* * * * *

"I have nothing left to strive for," he said as the memories began to fade, then jumped as a pair of strong arms surrounded him.

"Live for you," Amadala said as she wrapped her arms around his massive shoulders, shoulders that were now bent in despondency.

"I don't think I can do that," he breathed brokenly. "She was my world, and without her I am nothing."

"When you are ready," Amadala said uncertainly. Was she doing the correct thing, saying the right words? "When you are ready, you will find a reason to live."

"I am ready," Storm said as he pulled away from Amadala. "Let us prepare her body."

Chapter Twenty-One

୬

He hadn't expected many people to show up and he was not disappointed.

Elanna had very few opportunities to meet Merpeople, and it showed as a treasured few filed past the stone altar that held her remains.

Stoically, Storm stood by her body, acknowledging the condolences of the few people Elanna startled, made curious and befriended.

Storm looked down at her body, draped in iridescent mother-of-pearl shells from her neck to her pretty little toes. He remembered Elanna had been distressed by anyone seeing her naked, so he provided what cover he could. Cloth was hard to come by here underwater, and he wanted something special to acknowledge her importance to him.

Her hair was that exotic pouf of curls he so adored, sprinkled with crushed shells and pearls as it framed her head in a soft brown halo. At her ears hung the largest and rarest black pearls, their sheen almost seeming like rainbows where the light of several torches touched them. Around her neck hung several strands of matched black and pink pearls, harvested by Sting and Rage earlier that day.

Her body lay on the softly glistening mother-of-pearl shells, which continued up and around one shoulder, leaving the other bare. They draped over both breasts, hiding the rich darkness of her skin so odd to his race, and narrowed to a thin stripe across her stomach, only to widen below her navel and cover her from her crotch to toe.

She was a sparkling, glowing, undersea angel, an angel who died and took his heart with her, leaving him alone to mourn his loss.

Storm felt numb as he watched the few who showed up file past to pay their respects.

He tried his best to put on a façade of confidence and strength, but his face looked blank, devoid of all emotions. This whole ceremony was killing him inside by slow degrees.

Finally, the last Merperson swam past, looking down at the empty shell that had once contained his life's love. He knew it was time for him to say good-bye.

"Storm," Amadala spoke as she slowly made her way to his side. "For what it means, I am truly sorry."

"That's the trouble," Storm said, his voice as emotionless as his face. "Everyone is always sorry, yet nothing can be done to change things."

Storm turned and looked down once more at Elanna, the one who had opened his heart after that long season of loneliness, and felt his scales begin to tingle.

He reached out with one trembling finger to trace, for the last time, those lips he loved so well, those eyes that saw his world with wonder and excitement, the hair that still continued to fascinate him. And the first scales began to fall.

"Elanna," he breathed as his words backed up in his throat. "I will indeed miss you, human."

He closed his eyes and sighed deeply, feeling the weight of his sadness on his chest. But he knew he had to face this, so he opened his eyes again and looked down upon her body.

With the rest of the mourners watching, Storm began to make his final farewells to Elanna Richfield.

"You were my life and yet you were here for such a short time."

He smiled a bit at a memory, but then his face fell into its emotionless mask again.

"I think I started loving you when you vomited on me."

There were a few restrained chuckles from the observers, but most remained silent.

"But then," he continued, "then, you threatened to scale me and I began to fall. I have no idea where you came from, Elanna, and I do not care! I would have lied to keep you by my side. I would have killed to keep you here with me. I discovered that I truly needed you."

He looked down again, almost lost in his confused jumble of emotions, and then he looked up, his eyes angry and hot.

"But damn it, you left me! Why didn't you fight? Why didn't you try harder? I know in my mind you had no choice, but I am very mad at you."

His eyes dropped down to her face once again and he reached out to grasp her hand, so stiff, so cold.

"But I forgive you," he sighed. "I forgive you and I will do my best to make you proud. I will not blame myself, or any others, Elanna. I swear. I will do my best to live, but don't expect too much too soon."

He leaned down to kiss her hand, again marveling at how small and delicate it was. He sighed as he lowered his face to rub that tiny hand across his face, finally resting it against his forehead.

"I love you," he whispered. "I love you more than my life, and now I let you go."

Rising in a cloud of softly falling blue scales, Storm took one last look at Elanna and let her go.

As he moved back, several Mermen, the drummers, stepped forward, and began to pound out a slow, steady beat.

Then the people who knew Elanna, the ones who had aided her or had any contact with her, began to file forward.

First came Sting, carrying a large conch shell, the insides a soft swirling pink and white.

"For courage," he said as he lowered his one black eye in a moment of sadness, then placed the shell upon her chest. "And I was so fascinated by your legs, too." He glanced quickly at Storm as a small blush tinged his cheeks. "But I suppose there are other humans out on land. Good-bye, female." Then he turned and swam away.

Next came Rage and her two sisters. Each carried a colorful variety of underwater grasses in vibrant reds and oranges.

"For beauty," Rage said as she and her sisters arranged their offerings around Elanna, outlining her body in the colors she so loved. "We didn't get to play dress up with you, human, but we sure had fun listening to you and Storm argue."

With that, she turned, with a flip of her tail and swam away, her sisters following close behind.

Next approaching the altar was the Life Binder. He held in his hand several colorful rocks, geodes that were cracked open to show the yellow crystals inside.

"For wisdom," he said solemnly. "All of you young think you know everything, but you need to learn to meditate and reflect on what you actually do know. And despite your claims, human, you did not know it all. But you recognized what you had, and that was a grand start."

With a nod in Storm's direction, the Life Binder swam away to the rear of the small crowd who had already made their offerings.

Last, Amadala left Storm's side to face Elanna, her adversary, and the winner of their little tug-of-war over Storm.

"For strength," she declared as she pulled an intricate knife from a jeweled belt at her waist and laid it across Elanna's chest.

"You had fight in you, human," she said as she stared at the corpse of one she had so hated. "I can respect that. And I now understand why you fought so hard. I wish I could follow your example, but I know what I have lost."

So saying, she turned and waited for Storm to make his final offering to his beloved mate.

Taking a deep breath, Storm faced his mate for the final time.

"For love," he said quietly as he produced a pouch and slowly untied its thong. Upending it across her body, he sprinkled a thin layer of purple powder across her body. Almost immediately, a rainbow of colors swirled around her, brightening up the room, heating with its joyful hues.

"You should always have rainbows," he whispered as he bent to place one last kiss upon the lips that would never smile again.

"I love you, Elanna," he sighed as the drummers came to a halt.

The silence in the small chamber was deafening as the mourners filed out, waiting for the final part of her ceremony.

Once everyone had exited the tomb, Storm would cause a rockslide to cover the entrance, sealing in his love and her journey gifts, and her rainbow for all eternity.

As he backed away from that kiss, from the press of his mouth against her cold, still lips, he tried to gather the strength to do what he must.

The torches were extinguished, leaving the room in darkness but for the sparkling rainbow that covered her, which would continue to cover her until the powders lost their effectiveness.

"Good-bye," he whispered as he backed from the room.

As he turned to gather up his energy, there was a small cough from the altar.

My imagination, he decided as he raised his arms high in the air.

Then he heard the cough again.

Swimming in the tomb, he stared at her still body in confusion. Then he heard something that almost made him pass out.

"Sand," she gasped as her body began to tremble. "My butt! It itches!"

Then Storm, the bane of the council and the most powerful Child of Triton ever born, passed out cold.

Chapter Twenty-Two

It was so peaceful here!

Storm floated on a soft bed of water, the warmth of the liquid penetrating his pores and relaxing muscles that had been tense for days.

The morning sun shone down upon his face, not too hot or drying, but just enough to heat his body comfortably.

Gently the waves splashed against his face...*slap*... A little harder than expected, but it was still nice!

He needed this break, this time away. *Slap*!

Hmm, the waves were growing rougher.

But still, this time of peace was...

"Wake the hell up!" a voice screamed as another stinging slap was delivered to his face. "What did you do to me?" With a jolt, Storm opened his eyes and stared in amazement at what he saw!

There, in all of her outraged beauty, was his mate, his love, his Elanna!

"How?" he stuttered, but was cut off as she gripped a handful of his hair and pulled his face up to meet hers. "Ouch!"

"What... Did... You... Do?" Elanna said, spacing each word carefully as her brown eyes bored into his.

"You were dead!" he gasped as he tried to clear his thoughts and figure out what was going on. "I was about to entomb you."

"You were going to bury me alive!" Elanna hissed. "You were going to leave me in that chamber covered in shells and sitting on sand! Sand itches!"

Storm blinked as he slowly reached up to cup her beloved face. Ignoring the pain in his scalp, he stared deeply into her eyes and smiled.

"Elanna, you came back to me," he breathed.

Elanna stared back, blinked twice, and then let go of her unsuccessful attempt at holding back tears.

"I thought I would never see you again," Elanna gasped, as her tight hold on Storm became one of tender embrace.

Lowering her head, eyes wet and lips trembling, she placed her mouth against his and let all of the feelings in her heart flow through that perfect kiss.

Moaning, Storm buried his hands in the hair he so adored and pulled her closer, deepening the kiss, accepting her emotions and returning them in equal measure.

Finally breaking off the kiss, he ran his hands frantically over her body, touching her, making sure that she was real and not a mirage.

"You are back," he laughed. "You are here with me!"

With a joyous shout, he pulled her onto his body, giving her the full embrace his heart demanded that he give.

Laughing, both of them laughing, they rolled on the stone altar that held them. Turning and laughing and placing teasing kisses on each other, they rejoiced at once again being reunited. Until they fell off.

With a splash, Storm and Elanna plunged off their hard bed and landed on the equally hard water.

Elanna's laughter turned to a shout of fear and rage as she screamed, "Laura!"

* * * * *

"I remember!"

"Shh," Storm soothed as he pulled her from the water and back onto their perch. "It is a dream."

"No!" Elanna insisted as her hands latched around his neck and she buried her nose in his now wet hair, inhaling his scent. "It is real! I remember it, Storm! I remember it all!"

Her body quaked as the memories began to flood through her body.

The gun, the look on Laura's face, the dusky circle of that terrorist's face growing smaller as he watched her plummet to her death.

The gut-wrenching fear as she saw her death reaching out to grasp her.

"Oh, God!" she gasped as she swallowed deeply, trying not to vomit as her emotions and memories turned and churned into one huge tangle.

"I have you!" Storm soothed, sitting up and pulling her into his arms. "I have you, Elanna, and I am not going to let you go."

"They wanted to kill me," she breathed as huge tears filled her eyes. "They wanted to see me dead, Storm! And for what? For some stupid, twisted ideal?"

"You are not dead, Elanna," Storm murmured as he rocked her from side to side. "You are not dead."

"But I should be!"

"No! You are where you are supposed to be," he whispered as he began to run his hands over her cool skin. "You are safe, in my arms."

"Safe?" she whispered, her mind still struggling with the concept that suddenly seemed foreign to her.

"Safe," he breathed. His hand cupped her chin, and he lifted her face as he lowered his. "Safe with me. I'll keep you safe."

His lips brushed lightly over hers, careful, always careful of his sharp teeth, and nibbled at her bottom lip.

Elanna's startled gasp opened her mouth, allowing his tongue to plunge deeply inside, tasting her unique flavor and sending a rush of warmth through her body.

The whimper that floated out of her throat surprised them both. But she tightened her arms around his neck, pulling him closer, welcoming his deep, penetrating kiss, longing for him to take it further.

"Let me show you safe," he breathed as he broke off long enough to trail light kisses along her face, making her shiver as heat cascaded down her shoulders and back.

"Safe," she whispered as she threw her head back, exposing her neck to his expert caresses.

"Yes," he moaned as the trembling in her body began to shift from fear to something else entirely.

Dropping his hands to her hips, he shifted her until she was straddling his waist, her soft warm thighs surrounding his hips as she took enough of her weight on her legs to lift up and let her breasts hover above his face.

Gleefully accepting her offer, Storm lifted his head and nipped and licked at her right breast, teasing the swollen flesh around her nipple, but never taking that tempting fruit into his mouth.

"Please," she whimpered. "Storm, show me!"

Then his lips surrounded her nipple, his tongue laving the hardening tip.

Her groan rose up from deep within her soul and her eyes closed as she lost herself in the sensations flowing through her body.

Storm tightened his hands on her hips, holding her in place as her lower body began to slowly gyrate, mimicking the motions of his tongue as he carefully nipped at her flesh, then lapped the small pleasure-pain away.

"Do you feel me?" he asked, as he pulled away from her breast long enough to take in the slack look on her face and feel the small tremors shaking her body.

"More," she breathed. "Please, Storm?"

He answered by pulling one of her hands from around his neck and dragging it down the front of his body.

Her fingers danced over the cool skin of his chest, pausing to scrape her thumbnail firmly over his nipple. She smiled a bit as he hissed at the hot shot of sensation racing through his body.

"Yes," he moaned. "Do that again!"

And when she did, he lowered her body to rest on his lap as she bent to run her tongue along the small welt she had raised.

"Elanna," he moaned, tangling his hands in her hair, holding her closer to the source of his pleasure even as he tossed his head back, thoroughly enjoying her ministrations.

Her hips began to grind against his bulge, tempting his slit to part and the milky head to peek out. Feeling his slick hardness against her, not quite at her opening but near, Elanna decided to redouble her efforts.

Forget foreplay! This was the man she wanted, he was right there, and damn if she didn't feel safe in his arms.

Growling, she dragged her tongue up from his chest to attack his neck, nipping and biting at the firm flesh beneath her lips.

He tasted so good, so salty and masculine, and so much like the sea.

"Mmm," she purred, running her tongue up to his jaw, nipping at the shell of his ear.

"Creator!" he breathed as Elanna writhed about in his grasp. The only thing he could do was…react.

Gritting his teeth in an aroused snarl, he gently raked his hands and nails down her back, feeling the small bumps rise again over her skin, hearing her whine and whimper as he reached the firm flesh of her ass.

How hot human skin is, he thought as he kneaded another one of those parts that so fascinated him about his mate.

It was chunky, firm, soft and springy all at the same time. He could feel her muscles shift, as she pressed harder against his opening, spilling her hot juices across his emerging erection, coaxing it out of hiding without any manual help at all.

Damn, he loved her!

Balling his fist in that amazing whirlpool hair, he pulled her head back, exposing her neck for his play.

"My turn," he breathed, sinking his teeth into her skin hard enough to draw an impassioned moan, but not hard enough to break the skin.

"Again!" Elanna demanded as he teased the surface of her skin with his teasing nips and loving licks.

Soon, she was again rising up, offering her breasts into his care, a chore that he eagerly commenced as his fingers left the plump flesh of her ass to slide down over her thighs and tease the hair that hid her mysterious human secrets.

The folds of flesh were slick and hot to the touch, swelling under his exploring caresses even as he marveled at how different yet the same humans and Merfolk were.

"God, yes! Touch me!" Elanna moaned as her head dropped to rest on top of his, overcome by the twin sensations of having her nipples suckled and her clit stroked just right. Her Storm knew enough not to provide too much pressure, but just enough to raise her sexual tension up another notch.

Her groans of approval were definitely the sweetest of siren songs to his ears.

"I have to be in you now," Storm finally breathed, still intrigued by this new way of making love, of her slick molten core he so remembered, of…legs!

"Yes!" she breathed back, sliding her hands lower on his chest, letting one exploring finger slide through his protective slit and stroking his hard cock out into her palm.

He clenched his eyes and hissed as the feel of her fingers wrapped around his hardness.

But when she began to gently stroke him, his eyes grew wide and his teeth sank into his lower lip, tearing into the delicate flesh.

Then she was positioning him, dragging him through the curly hair, teasing her moisture-slick folds of flesh with his extremely sensitive cock head. And then he was pressed against her molten opening, the contrast between their bodies astounding him even as they slammed his desire up another notch.

"Elanna!" he breathed as she began to slowly lower herself onto his hardness, to feel the massive head of his erection part her body and began to seat him deep within her.

Damn, she thought. *How can something hidden in a pouch be so big?*

But she felt her body begin to stretch to accommodate his girth, felt him swell even further as he slid into her wet heat, felt a shock of extreme pleasure as his cock slid past a point deep within her inner walls.

"Storm!" she wailed as his thickness spread her lower lips to the max, and the cool steel of his cock rubbed at her clit.

"Again!" he hissed, lifting his hands to her waist and raising her up a few inches. "I am not all the way in!"

"Mmm," she moaned. "It is so deep this way, Storm, so full."

Her words made him shudder even as he lowered her onto his quivering cock, mentally reciting his powders in his pouch in order of potency — anything to keep the seed he felt building within the base of his cock from exploding and ending this amazing feeling!

He had to make it last, have it longer! It was too good to let it end so quickly.

But his options were almost snatched out of his hands as Elanna rose to her knees, discovered her leverage and began to pound down onto the delightful stiffness that was slamming into her every erogenous zone, sending her mind reeling and white-hot stars bursting behind her eyes.

"Yes! Oh, God, more!" she groaned, picking up the pace.

Holding on to her waist for dear life with one hand, Storm dropped the other to their stone perch and began to slam himself deeply inside her, fully penetrating with each thrust.

"Oh, yeah!" Elanna screamed, her passion-drenched voice echoing around them, sending her desire flying out of control as they tried to find a steady rhythm of thrust and counterthrust.

And still it was not enough!

Suddenly out of desperation, Storm clamped his arm around her waist and slid them off the perch, sending them splashing into the water, though his hips never lost their rhythm.

Spinning around, he slid both hands up her back, protecting her even as he pulled her closer, forcing her against the stone, giving him something solid to brace them.

Then his hips began a gyrating, slamming rhythm that tore endless screams of ecstasy from her throat.

"Yes! Harder! Harder!"

And he did his best to comply, the electric feeling of imminent release spiraling up his spine and making his head swim with colors.

"Elanna!" he growled, burying his face in her neck as his thrusts slammed deep. "Oh, Creator, Elanna!"

"Storm!"

And then she was coming, exploding, her muscles spasming around him as her legs clamped about his waist, holding him tight. "Storm!"

Storm felt her muscles tighten about him, felt the liquid rush of heat that signaled her release, but he still wanted more.

"Elanna," he breathed, his hips quivering against her. "More! I have to have more!"

"Take it!" she said harshly, sounding tired, passion-drenched, and determined.

She had to bring her man to release, she thought as she clenched her walls around him and shivered at the feelings of desire still flooding her system.

It appeared she really could offer him more, and take more for herself at the same time.

"Take me!" she breathed, nuzzling against him until she nosed aside his wet hair and sank her teeth into his shoulder.

"*Ahhhh!*"

The wordless sound exploded from his mouth as he slid home another powerful thrust, the deep colors of the sea at sunset swirling behind his eyes.

"Mmm," Elanna responded, raking her hands down his back and gripping his scale-covered ass. "Again!"

Then she was gasping as he gave in to his desires and started to fulfill both of their needs.

There was only the ebb and flow of the water around them, the hot press of their bodies, the molten heat clasped around his swelling cock.

He could die and never regret one moment of their possession, for as much as he was taking of her, she was taking of him.

Faster and faster they moved, Elanna feeling the hunger inside her rising again to engulf her being, turning her into a panting, begging thing that craved only release that the man riding between her thighs could give her.

Feeling her desires rise again, Storm tightened his grip on her shoulders and prayed that he could hold on long enough to bring her off again.

But even as the thoughts crossed his mind, he felt the spasms start at his back, felt his cock swell incredibly large within her and knew that his climax was at hand.

"Elanna!" he roared as he felt his cock spasm, shooting life-giving seed deep into her womb, felt the climactic shudders take his whole body, felt his muscles tighten until he thought they would break, and then blessed release!

"*Ungh*," he grunted as his hips instinctively jerked against her, sending more spouts of his hot cream flowing deeply inside her.

As for Elanna, the feel of him swelling so impossibly large hit her clit in just the right way, sending her spiraling for the second time just moments behind him.

"Sta...Sta...Storm!" she gasped as her second orgasm tore through her body, sending her nearly flying headlong into oblivion even as her body went totally limp within his protective arms.

"Elanna," he moaned, feeling her spasm around his sensitive cock as he rode her climax, hoping his cock was still hard enough to prolong her release.

With one final shudder, Elanna slumped in his arms, a weighty, sated creature, trusting him completely.

"Elanna," he breathed her name out as he tightened his grip on her and rolled over onto his back, leaving her legs straddling his body as he positioned her comfortably on his chest.

They both groaned as he slipped from her warm, slick sheath, but quickly adjusted to this new position, the water cradling their exhausted bodies.

"Now," he breathed. "Will you tell me about it?"

* * * * *

Storm and Elanna floated softly on the surface of the water inside Storm's secret cavern, Elanna resting against her lover's chest as he easily supported the both of them.

After her loud outburst, it had taken Storm almost an hour to calm her down.

Then they'd had to run the gantlet of questions Sting and the others tossed at them. Storm, still shocked and amazed to see his love alive and full of vigor again, decided enough was enough.

All questions would be pondered over and answers given when they returned.

Sting was curious, almost to the point of being rude, but he finally quieted and left, heading for the council to question them about their long history with humans.

Amadala was stunned into silence before she too jumped into the free-for-all that had become their lives.

She wanted to know what game Elanna was playing, scaring them like that! Then she wanted to know how she had accomplished such a feat. She wanted to know what the epimorph did to her body, what changes were there and why she could speak to them at all when she should have been dead.

Rage was a bit more subtle, when she asked if Elanna knew what was going to happen. Then she turned to Storm and said, "You had better hold on to this one. She beat death to be at your side." Her sisters, ever silent, nodded and the trio departed.

The Life Binder just nodded and said that some ties were forever.

They escaped to the small, sun-filled cavern, trying for a little peace as they assimilated what had happened to them in such a short time.

Then Elanna told Storm of her memory.

"You remember what?" he asked. "What death feels like?" He was deadly serious and quiet as he gently held her in his arms, her leg resting on his fin.

"I remember my past," she responded as she squeezed her arms to force his arms tighter around her, comforted by his large bulk beneath her.

"And?" he prompted as he placed a kiss upon her forehead, marveling at the feel of her flesh, soft, warm, and blessedly alive, in his arms.

"And I need to go back," she said quietly.

"Elanna!" Storm all but shouted. "No!"

"I have to!" she insisted. "What I know is of great import to the world."

"What you are is of great import to me!" Storm argued as he began treading water, turning her to face him as both of their bodies became vertical in the warm blue water of the sea.

"Try to understand," she began, and her eyes teared up as she stared at him. "What I know could save lives, Storm! It could save a lot of my people!"

"I am your people," he said as he gripped her arms tightly. "We are your people!"

"I am human, Storm! I can't turn my back on them for my happiness."

"But you can turn your back on me?" he asked as his body tensed up, all the relaxation and happiness he'd felt replaced by a deep sense of foreboding.

"I am not turning my back," Elanna argued, though she was unable to meet his eyes, and her very words caused her pain.

"Then what do you call it?"

"Being responsible!" she argued. "I call it doing what I have trained my whole life for, meeting my goals, realizing my dreams!"

"And what of me?" he asked. "I thought I had become our dream!"

"You are!" Elanna said, jerking her gaze, shimmering with unshed tears, to his. "You are the most perfect thing that I could ever imagine."

"Then why do you abandon your dream?"

"For the good of my people!" she said again.

"We are—"

"You are my heart, my life, Storm! But what good is my life if I sacrifice thousands of people for my happiness?"

Storm could formulate no answer for that one. He, as once a ruler, had to use this line of reasoning to comfort himself as he made a decision that affected his life for the good of his people. There was no good answer for the question. What was the life of one when compared to the lives of so many?

"I can't let you go, Elanna!" Storm finally said, releasing her arms and floating back from her a few feet. "How can I?"

"We have now," Elanna said, looking pleadingly up at him.

"What good is now, when I live for the future?" He asked, "You are the one who taught me that, living for the future."

He felt a cold dark pit building in the center of his chest as he observed his mate, so recently rediscovered, and now about to become lost to him yet again.

"I have to help my people," she repeated as she clenched her fists and her tears began to fall freely down her cheeks.

"You are correct," he said quietly as he watched the silvery trail fall down her face and drop, causing faint ripples in the surface of the waters. "You are not one of my people. Mermaids cannot cry."

Discovering the need to be alone, he slowly sank below the surface of the water, leaving a stunned and devastated Elanna behind, treading water and crying silent tears.

Chapter Twenty-Three

෨

"So, you can, like, breathe underwater now?"

Elanna turned to see Amadala, of all people, staring at her.

She had treaded water in the same spot for what seemed like hours, and thought of the decisions she had made in her life.

What was the right thing to do?

She had always tried to do the right things in life, even if it cost her.

She had studied because she knew she had the intellect to do what she wanted to do, and to make her parents happy.

She had studied medicine, because her professors had told her that she could contribute to society, to make the world a better place for her fellow man.

She took on the frustrating cancer research, because, if God had blessed her with the vision to muddle through problems, then she should tackle the biggest problems man had to offer.

Now, she knew she was the only one who could complete her research, to follow up on the cure she had discovered, to adapt it to other ailments from AIDS to the common cold!

It was the right thing to do.

But was it worth giving up her very happiness?

Was that not too, a gift from God?

So she stayed there, treading water, sickened by the pain she had caused her mate, the man who had suffered so much and would suffer again when she was gone.

But, she didn't want to go!

Was there a way that she could fulfill her obligations and still keep the treasure that she had in Storm?

"What?"

She looked in Amadala's face but couldn't remember what the woman had said.

"Are you one of us now? Can you breathe underwater? Can you communicate with sound waves? Will you drown if I hold your head under?"

"I don't know," Elanna sighed, her eyes downcast and her body trembling as her tears continued to flow. "Why?"

"Because I would dearly love to drown you, human, for what you have done!"

Amadala's pink eyes flashed fire at her as she curled her lips in disgust.

"What did I do?"

Elanna was shocked by this display, and a bit frightened. She backed away from the angry Mermaid, determined not to give her the chance to make good on her wishes.

"What did you do? Humans! You are all so blind and egotistical, not to mention selfish!"

Amadala flung her pink hair behind her shoulders and placed her hands on her hips, her anger apparent.

"You, human, had it all! You had a man who treasured you above all others! He loves you and you tear his heart out!"

"I wouldn't—"

"You did! You destroyed him! He had just reclaimed you from the jaws of death, and now you plot to send him into insanity once more!"

"I couldn't—"

"You could and you did!"

"But I have a responsibility to my people!"

"Since when did you care about races, Elanna? Since when did you look at Storm and decide that he was not worth saving?"

"Storm is worth more than anything!" Elanna argued hotly, her eyes imploring the other woman to understand. "He is the best thing to ever happen to me!"

"Then why are you throwing your happiness away?"

The anguish in her tone told Elanna that something was wrong. The desperation in her eyes only increased that belief.

"Amadala…"

"I have lost the one man who would have truly loved me, human. And the tragedy is, I never realized what I had until it was gone! You know that feeling, do you not?"

Elanna looked down, awash in the memories of the moments after her joining, when she thought that she would never see her Storm, her quirky, irritating Fish Boy again. Never had she felt pain so great as when she knew that she was dying. Never had anything devastated her so completely.

"Yes," Elanna said quietly. She remembered that pain, she felt it now!

"So tell me, what is more important, human? The fact that you live your life catering to the responsibilities of others, dead inside, or that you live your life?"

"But I can't abandon my people!"

"The same people who threw you away?"

"Not all of them are bad! Most of them are kind and honest, and just."

"So, my people are worth throwing away."

"I didn't say that! I would never wish to leave this place! It breaks my heart just thinking about it!"

"Then what will you do, human? You cannot live in both places. You had better choose the side on which you stand for."

"Why do I have to choose? Why can I not have them both?"

"Because we are too different, Elanna. You have two legs and we have gorgeous, multicolored fins with scales that shine and glow!"

"Well, you are missing a few sparkles, Glenda," Elanna snarled, looking down at Amadala's once beautiful tail fin which now was dull and lifeless, the sparkle missing. "And I thought all good witches were supposed to sparkle."

"Witch?"

"Never mind!" Elanna sighed remembering the futility of calling her witch names when she had never even seen *The Wizard of Oz*. "There has to be a way."

"So why don't you give the humans what they want, and then come back."

Elanna froze. Her legs stopped treading water, and she dropped like a stone.

It was so simple! The plan was foolproof! It was so basic and straightforward it would work!

Sputtering, she propelled herself to the surface, smiling and laughing at the same time.

"Amadala, you are a genius!" she laughed as with one mighty kick, she reached the woman who had given her such torment but now gave her a grand idea! Gripping her by the shoulders, she dropped a kiss on her startled lips before releasing her and dropping below the surface of the water.

"*Ish*!" Amadala wailed. "Human spit! I am contaminated!" Then she paused in her furious mouth-scrubbing and tilted her head to the side.

"Human," she called out, curious and confused. "What did I do?"

* * * * *

Without thinking, Elanna sank below the waters, her mind on finding Storm and telling him this brilliant and so simple plan.

But then she realized something…rather important.

She was breathing! She was breathing water! She was breathing water and she was not dead!

Elanna paused, mid-stroke, and just sank. This was impossible! This was unreal! She was breathing water!

A broad smile spread across her lips as she realized that she could see clearly, too. No saltwater burned her eyes. Everything appeared to be lit up as bright as daylight. No hidden shadows scared her, nothing could sneak up on her. She could see!

Storm! she called out, laughing as she realized that she was sending the words as high-pitched squeals, almost like the dolphin language. And even more surprising, was that she now heard thousands of voices, so many they became background noise breaking the silence of the sea.

The waters were alive!

There were millions of voices out there, calling out to each other, greeting each other, sending welcome and telling of danger, ringing out warnings. There were millions of them and she could hear them all!

Like a child with a new toy, she threw back her head and laughed her joy to the world.

She spread her fingers and felt the thin, almost invisible membranes spread, giving her the buoyancy to swim with greater speed. She felt her lungs, taking in water painlessly, and sending it back through her body, leaving precious oxygen behind. She felt her whole body tingle as it adjusted to the cooler temperatures of the deep sea, the waters now caressing her, welcoming her home.

She was not the same person who plummeted from the plane so many days ago. And yet, she was the same inside.

She had a man! She loved her man! She had a plan to help her keep that man.

She was going to succeed in fulfilling her obligations, or the whole world could go to hell in a handbasket!

But first she had to find Storm and explain.

She had to explain that she was leaving, but she was coming back. And nothing, come hell or high water, would keep her from her man.

* * * * *

"Human!" Amadala wailed, as she dropped below the surface of the water, to give chase to the excitable woman. Humans were so high-strung. "Human! Elanna, wait! What are you planning?"

She spied what she thought was the flash of the human's—yuck—legs, and dove towards it, pouring on all the speed she could muster.

But then, as fates would have it, she rammed headfirst into something large and hard with powerfully muscled arms.

"Oomph!" she grunted, as she jerked back and attempted to get the tangle of hair from her mouth and eyes.

"Amadala?" Sting asked, as he gripped the woman by her arms and held her until she regained her equilibrium.

"Sting?" she squeaked, as she ripped the hair from her eyes and stared, wide-eyed, at the man whom she tossed away.

"Amadala, I need to talk to you."

"No, you don't!" she denied, as she felt the unmistakable tingle of scales threatening to fall. "We don't have time."

"What is the problem now?" he asked, looking grim. This place grew problems like rocks grew mold!

"It's the human! She is going to do something, and I don't know what it is."

"Leave that human alone!" Sting roared, losing his patience. "Haven't you done enough to them, Amadala?"

"I was only—"

"Trying to help?" he barked. "Haven't you helped enough? Leave them alone!"

"But Sting—"

"Amadala, no! This ends right now. I cannot have a mate who is this troublesome! The council agrees. I will become co-ruler and we will share the decision-making, Amadala. Nothing more!"

"The council!"

"They agreed, Amadala. You are a good ruler, but you take on too much of others' personal lives. You need to be controlled before you do harm!"

"Me? Harm?"

"You, Amadala! You caused so much trouble with your schemes that we almost lost the true Child of Triton and his mate."

"Oh, now the human is his rightful mate?"

"Amadala…"

"I know my name, Sting! And I care not for the council's ruling. They can go to the sharks! Elanna is about to do something rash, and I have to stop her!"

"Amadala…"

"I said no! Do what you will, Sting! I shall return after I invade their lives once more. She needs help, and I intend to give it to her! It's a pain thing. We both understand it well."

With that, she jerked away from Sting, leaving him with a sour taste in his mouth.

Had he overreacted? What was wrong with the human? He had to find Storm. This did not bode well.

Chapter Twenty-Four

৯০

Where was Storm?

Elanna searched all over for her mate, desperate to find him and tell him of her plans.

She checked the cave where he had first taken her, the flames still burning bright from careful tending.

She checked the place where he stored his powders, shuddering as she entered and remembered the last time she was there.

The space was neat and orderly, but no Storm.

She even checked the bathing room where she had first met the triplets and Amadala had almost perished at Storm's hands. But no luck there.

Where could that man be?"

She ran her hands through her hair in her frustration, for once not even complaining about the ravages of saltwater on natural hair.

She still marveled at what her body was able to do, tolerate and accomplish, but the miracle—and it was a miracle—paled without her mate beside her.

Depressed, her eyes stared at the sea around her, teeming with life and bubbling with energy, and it all looked gray.

A tear filled her eye, but was quickly washed away in the salty water. The sea was no place for tears. It was made up of them.

Then she heard it, a mournful wail that touched her heart and brought her loneliness to the forefront.

It was a low, exacting sound, hauntingly beautiful and so eerie it sent shivers down her spine.

Entranced, she paused, floating in her sea of tears, and concentrated on the sound.

The distorted cry pulsed through her body, making her eyes close and her head tilt back, embracing the lonely cry, letting it become one with her.

The ancient voice filled her waters, filled the seas, its slow pulses filled with some fathomless emotion that called to her.

Her body began to sway with the sound, her mind connecting not with the meaning of the chords, but with the emotion they conveyed.

It twisted her heart, made her eyes burn with unshed tears. It stilled the beating of her heart.

"Whale song," she heard in her mind, her brain transferring the clicking sounds into an understandable language.

Slowly, as if she were forcing her movement through a vat of mud, she opened her eyes and turned towards the foreign sound. Nothing should disturb the tranquility of these wails and cries, she thought, as she faced the intruder to her misery.

Amadala floated there, her bottom lip trembling as she faced the human who had taught her so much about herself.

"Whale song," she repeated. "They cry for us, you know. They cry for all that we are, that we were, for all that we had the potential to be. They see us as we really are, and they mourn."

"It does sound like a keening dirge," Elanna allowed after examining the woman for a moment.

Pain was etched on every surface of her countenance. It seeped from her arms, crossed defensively over her chest, to the dull sheen in her eyes. Amadala was pain.

"They are the wise ones," she whispered faintly.

"What are they saying?"

"No one knows. They sing the old language, forgotten by us in our quest for growth and development. We have forgotten the old ways, and our sacrifice will not go unpunished."

"Sacrifice?"

"Yes, sacrifice. We gave up all that we were to follow the new ways, the ways of progress, and in doing that, lost the core source of our beliefs."

"And that would be?" Elanna turned to study the Mermaid closer. Amadala had not been the best of friends to her, but she was honest.

"Love, human. Respect for ourselves. Honesty, integrity, faith, selflessness. These are the things we gave up to be what we are now."

"But…"

"I am not saying that we have become a brutal bunch of savages, Elanna. But we have managed to overcomplicate what should be something quite simple. We overburdened our lives, human. With power and greed, we have created our own trap. And when they ask us why we strive, why we fight for progress, we say so we can relax and have time for ourselves and the ones we love in the future. When in actuality, if we had stuck to the old ways, taken care of ourselves without our vices, would we not have that time to relax and love?"

"Prophetic words, Amadala," Elanna breathed. "But what do they have to do with you or me?"

"Nothing and everything, human. I don't know what I'm saying. I babble."

"Amadala…"

"What are your plans, human?"

"My plans?"

"What will you do? Will you let the vices of the old world, wrapped in hypocrisy and selfish acts, taint the new world you now have?"

Did Amadala consider her going back and sharing her knowledge with humankind her bid for glory?

"I have to go back."

"Then the whales cry for you!"

Amadala began to turn in a flood of pink hair, but was startled when a warm hand gripped her arm. "I am going, Amadala, but only to drop off my information, and then I am coming back."

Amadala slowly looked from the hand gripping her arm to the intent face staring up at her.

"You would give up your research, your findings, your glory?"

"What is glory without the one I love?"

There was a pregnant pause, filled with the sounds of the whales and their mournful cries. Both women shared a silent moment of understanding, and then Amadala turned fully towards Elanna.

"Well said, human."

"And the sooner I start, the sooner I get back."

"But—"

"No buts, Amadala. I refuse to let them cry for me! I will do what I have to do and return as quickly as possible."

"But Storm—"

"Tell him where I have gone, and tell him I will return! How can I exist without the other half of my soul?"

"Human! Elanna! Wait! Let me—"

"No time!" Elanna called as she turned towards the east, and land she instinctively knew. "I have to go so that I may return! Tell my love I will be coming back to him!"

"The humans will not accept this, Elanna!" Amadala cried out desperately. "They will hurt you, study you, destroy you!"

"They are my people, Amadala! Just give Storm my message! I shall return!"

"Elanna!"

Amadala screamed out in panic as she watched the dark figure of the human who had changed so many lives disappear towards the land and the humans she knew would harm her.

Sting! she screamed through her mind, turning quickly.

There was no time to bring her back! Elanna would not listen to her. She needed to find Sting and Storm. They would bring her back! Her place was here, beneath the waters of the sea with Storm.

She needed to get help!

Turning in a flash of bubbling water and pink scales, Amadala raced to find the man who has so scored her. She needed his help now, for her intuition told her that nothing but trouble lay ahead.

And as she quickly swam away in search of the one she had caused so much pain, the one she had sacrificed for vanity and stubbornness, the whales sang songs of mourning and loneliness. They sang for her and never before had she felt so alone.

Chapter Twenty-Five

ಐ

"I just don't understand women!" Sting moaned, finishing up his diatribe about the fairer sex. "I mean, I expect them to act one way and then they turn around and do something completely…" he struggled for a moment, searching for the correct word, "odd!"

"You are requesting my aid in understanding women?"

Storm and Sting sat on the rocks near the island where he had taken his human to recover.

The day was hot, but both men used their fins to splash water on each other, offsetting the painful burn that could develop if they were overexposed to heat and sun.

Both men wore long faces, their depressed looks matching as they stared off into the sea, trying to do something men had been contemplating doing for eons, discovering what women want.

"You have a human. Humans have to be different."

"Female is female," Storm sighed. "No wonder human males are casting them off into the sea. They would drive them insane if they didn't do otherwise."

"You don't mean that," Sting argued. "Humans aren't casting them away for sanity's sake. They are doing it to drive us into extinction."

"How do you figure that?"

"Well, first the women move in and drive us mad, then they infect the other women!"

"What?"

"Think about it. The other women start acting unpredictably and they drive us to kill ourselves. With the men gone, there is no reproduction and then our entire race is gone."

"You are calling my Elanna an infection? A disease?"

"Well, look at yourself!" Sting swore hotly. "You are sitting here, face longer than a seal's, and moping."

"A seal?" Storm's blue eyes began to glitter as he stared at the one-eyed, black-haired man.

"A seal! And…and…look at you! Sitting here complaining because some woman is acting crazy!" Sting spoke in desperation, frightened, because he saw himself in Storm's depressed face.

"And look at you, Sting, sitting there like a wounded carp, pining because Amadala turned out to be a bigger bitch that you realized!"

"Bitch?"

"*B-I-T-C-H!*" he spelled out. "Big bitch! *Whale-sized bitch*!"

"She is *not*!"

"*Yes*, she *is*!"

"*Is not*!"

"*Is too*!"

"She may be a bit…odd, but she is no…not a big…well, she is just a little bitchy, but *so what*? No one is perfect!"

Both Mermen glared at each other, the light of battle heating their eyes.

Both refused to give ground, both refused to look away. Neither knew what they were arguing about, but neither would back down.

Storm!

Both men jumped and turned to the waters as a ringing cry and an explosion of water and pink heralded the approach of Amadala.

"Where have you been?" she screeched as she practically flew on water to his side. "Elanna needs you!"

"Elanna is going home to the humans, to be the savior of the legged species, and has no time for me!" he replied bitterly.

"No! She is going—"

"I thought I told you to leave them alone?" Sting snarled, finding a target for his anger, but stopping before he went too far. "My apologies, lady."

"Whatever," Amadala said, ignoring him completely, focusing on Storm. "Elanna is going, but she is coming back!"

"She will have to stay and see to her patients, Amadala." Storm sighed as he calmed himself and shook his head sadly at her. "I am a healer, and I know this to be true."

"No, Storm!" she whispered desperately. "She could not give you up! She is going to tell her people what she knows and then she is returning!"

"When did she decide this?" Storm asked, hope growing in his eyes and he stared at his friend of many years.

"She always knew, Storm! How could she leave her heart and soul behind?"

Storm gave the impression of leaping in the air, even though he moved not a muscle.

"Infection," he sneered at Sting, who stood there gazing at Amadala as if he was waiting for the punch line.

"But there is a problem!" she added.

"*There*!" Sting snorted to Storm. "There is *always* a problem."

"Sting, control yourself," Amadala stated with the decorum shown by true queens.

"My lady." Instantly, he fell into protocol, remembering who Amadala was and what power she held.

"What problem?" Storm asked, already his heart racing in fear. What had happened to his human before they had a chance to make up?

"I feel that there is danger surrounding her!"

Storm reached out, his hands gripping her upper arms as he stared deeply into her pink eyes.

"I know that you are of the Power, Amadala. I will not discount any advice that you have to give."

Amadala was born from blood that had been immersed in power. Her family, her line, everything about her spoke of power. Just because it didn't manifest itself in her body didn't mean it was not there.

"I may not be a true Child of Triton, Storm," she began, "but heed my words carefully. Danger surrounds Elanna! Danger she does not expect. You have to go to her!"

"Where?"

"To the east! The volcano the humans call Hawaii. And Storm, please be careful. I have lost so much, and I refuse to lose more."

Storm glanced over at Sting for a moment, before nodding.

"Some things were not meant to be, Amadala," he said as he pulled her into his embrace. "Your discovery is still out there. And so is his."

Releasing her, he smiled tenderly at her, before turning to face Sting.

"Maybe not a *big* bitch, but a small annoyance," Storm said as he leapt clear of the rocks and disappeared into the sea.

"Perhaps you are right," Sting mused as he stared at Amadala.

"Did he call me…?"

"Nothing that I haven't called you before," he replied as he returned to business again. "Now tell me, what is the nature of this danger, Amadala?"

"Immediately, to your male reproductive organs," she hissed, eyes glaring, but trying to find a comfortable place to be with him. "But I feel danger around Elanna, Sting. I am worried."

"Let us wait, then," he replied, letting go of regrets and trying to develop some sort of relationship with Amadala. He realized they could never be lovers. There was too much…incompatibility between the two of them. But maybe they could be friends. "We shall intervene if we are needed."

"Then we shall wait," she decided. "But I can't be around you right now. I'll find you if I sense something further."

"I…I understand," Sting said quietly, watching her disappear beneath the blue water.

Full of regrets, but knowing that it was not meant to be, Sting focused his one eye on the horizon as he waited.

He knew something big was about to happen. He just didn't know what.

Chapter Twenty-Six

ஐ

Confidently, Elanna stroked through the waters, reveling in what her body could do.

She didn't seem to feel the miles pass as she doggedly made her way towards land. In fact, all she felt was a burning need to finish her task and hurry back to her love.

Her resolve was set. She had never wanted to unburden herself more.

The whale song, the lonely mournful cry of times past and things lost would not be sung for her. She would do what she had to do, then return quickly.

Her diplomas, her name in the scientific community, all the letters printed on her office door were meaningless if her heart did not lay in that direction. And her heart lay with Storm.

As she raced along, she paid no heed to anything but her need to end this business. She gave her surroundings no second thought until she felt a weird creeping in her spine.

She paused, turning about as she scanned the surrounding area for the source of her unease.

The memory of Storm's story, of his past love and her demise, flashed across her mind. Were there man-eaters, hungry sharks that were out for her blood?

She shivered as images of every shark attack she had ever seen, coupled with a few frames of the movie *Jaws*, flashed through her mind.

She could even hear the eerie theme music, the low bass chords, as she fearfully continued to swim, trying to make as little motion or sound as possible.

Sharks were drawn to movement, right? Movement and blood?

She looked down at her body, all at once conscious of its nude state, something she had begun to ignore while she was with Storm. Now, she had never felt more vulnerable in her life, even though in her mind she knew a suit and a pair of pumps would offer no protection from a shark's toothy bite.

Swallowing deeply, eyes wide, she continued, again turning her head every few seconds. The feeling of being alone, isolated and hunted filled her being.

It was too much!

Facing forward, she began to swim swiftly, damning her earlier notions about movement in her very real fright. She swam faster than she had ever been able to, faster than she thought was possible, then the first body brushed against her.

"*Shark*!" she wailed as she turned to bat at the thick-skinned body that lay against her.

It was a good thing that the epimorph had done its transformation, because as wide as she opened her mouth, she surely would have drowned if she had been totally human.

But as it was, all her scream did was bring an echo of laughter.

Shark, she said, a chipper voice laughed.

Shark!

Shark! Human cried shark!

Then there was a lilting laugher, the sound she believed only mischievous fairies could make.

Calming herself mid-scream, she turned again and saw what was teasing her.

It was a pod! A small family of dolphins swam around her, their gray bodies twisting like joyful puppies as they circled her.

She counted three happy dolphins, their bottlenoses dipping and raising in the water as if scenting her.

Human, not the kindred, one dolphin said clearly.

Elanna was startled that she could understand it.

Smells like human and kindred, another voice added.

Human! a third confirmed. *No flippers. Human in the sea! Humans belong on land!*

"Hello?" Elanna tried, breaking into this conversation.

Human speaks! dolphin one clicked. *Human is kindred!*

Human is human! number three argued, her distinct clicking sound identifying her.

Is both! the second voice argued. *Both human and kindred.*

Impossible! the first and third crowed together.

"Excuse me?" Elanna tried again, this time putting a bit more force behind the sound that emerged from her mouth.

Take to shore! the first said finally, ignoring her.

Take to shore, the third agreed and turned to look at the second.

Take to shore, he sighed. *But I would like to play first.*

Play later, the first and obviously the leader of this pod said. *Take to white-coated humans first.*

"That's it!" Elanna cried, all of her tension melting away. "Take me to the white-coated humans."

There was a beat of silence, as all of the dolphins turned to look at her.

Pushy human, the second declared, though his humor could be heard in his…voice.

Playful human! the first insisted, as he brushed against her side, making Elanna smile. *More fun than the white-coated humans with their noise boxes*, he decided as Elanna laughed at the contact.

She had always wanted to swim with the dolphins.

Let's play! the second dolphin, the one she mentally named Chipper, declared before he dove beneath her body and hooked her on his back.

"Let's play!" Elanna laughed, not wanting to give up this opportunity.

Then her breath *whoosh*ed from her chest as Chipper took off, an explosion of movement that propelled her to the surface of the water.

Everything rushed by. The shapes of the other two dolphins blurred as they raced past. The water, churned white and foamy by their movement, seemed to be so many soft pearls that filled her field of vision, surrounding her like the tickling bubbles of champagne, streamed over her body like a million teasing hands.

Elanna threw back her head and laughed as she held tightly to Chipper's dorsal fin, held on to his thick warm skin and went on the ride of her life.

Surfacing long enough to take a breath, Chipper and Elanna dove again into the warm waters, spinning and dancing as they passed the others, leaving them in their wake.

We greet the sun! Chipper called out, and not knowing what this meant, Elanna tightened her grip on Chipper.

With a sudden burst of speed, Chipper dove deeply into the water, then suddenly reversed his course.

"We are going to jump!" Elanna gasped, fear and excitement in her voice as they sped past the others, gaining speed, playing in water, leaving every thought and notion behind.

Then she felt it—the barrier of the water parting from her, the sudden shock of warm air as the sea expelled them from its womb. She felt a jerk as if gravity refused to give up its hold on her, then they were flying!

Up and up, higher and higher they rose! The sun, the bright yellow sun greeted them, kissed her flesh for a moment, warmed the world around them, spun her vision into a delightfully twisted kaleidoscope of shape and color, before they were descending, saying good-bye, slamming with a welcome scream back into the body of the sea.

The shock of the water, cool after being kissed by the sun, made her gasp, but then she was laughing. Tossing her head back, she roared with laughter, delighting in the freedom that she had felt.

Human is fun! Chipper chattered as he pulled out of his dive and began to surface.

Elanna laughed, cried, and shrieked her joy for the undersea world to hear. Never had she been so…so…euphoric. Except, maybe, while exploding with Storm in his arms, sharing the rapture of release.

But this was a close second.

Elanna, a huge smile on her face, popped to the surface of the water, hugging Chipper to her body, and wishing for another jump.

Before she could request a repeat performance, a voice jerked her back to her surroundings.

Chipper had played with her as he declared, but he had also listened to the elder members of his pod.

Elanna rested on his back, hugging his body tightly to hers, at the base of a huge platform.

And there, several white-coated scientists stood, mouths open in amazement as they watched the woman speak to the dolphin.

"Uh, hi?" she offered, as a deep feeling of unease filled her.

The white-coated humans, Chipper squeaked, and absently Elanna answered in small clicks and squeals of her own.

"Yes, they are," she said quietly as she watched them race for nets, phones, cameras, all with excited looks on their faces. "And I am wondering if I've made the biggest mistake of my life."

Chapter Twenty-Seven

ಞ

Elanna sat in the corner of the large glass chamber, and shook helplessly as the horror of what happened to her came over her once more.

She had tried to run, tried to flee with the dolphins, recognizing the look in several of the doctors' eyes. She was the new experiment to examine under a microscope.

But a well-aimed dart from a rifle ended any hope of that!

She remembered Chipper's horrified squeal as she was tranqed, then nothing more.

She awoke to find that she had only been out for half an hour, that she was strapped to a table, that a white-suited scientist was peering at her through a biohazard suit and painfully taking her blood from her arm.

"Stop it," she mumbled, weakly struggling against the thick black cuffs that restrained her arms and legs. "Leave me alone."

But the young-looking man only started, and ran out of the room calling for his supervisor.

Elanna groaned as her head began to pound and her throat went dry. She needed water and a bathroom in the worst way. She looked up to see a huge water-head hanging over her, cameras placed all around and a wall filled with what she knew to be two-way mirrors. She was being stared at like a creature in a zoo.

She was still attempting to voice her necessities from a parched throat when a man entered, sans the big white suit, but the glee on his face was just as frightening. Instead, he wore a wet suit and had a headpiece attached to one ear. He almost rubbed his hands together in delight as he observed her.

"Hello, my dear," he said as he eyed her naked body. "Can you understand me?"

"Water!" she gasped as she struggled to keep her eyes focused on this man. It seemed important that she remember his face.

"Water? On land too long," he muttered to himself. "Shelby, we need water."

Immediately, the hanging water-head opened, sending gallons of seawater crashing over her.

She gasped as the water filled her mouth and nose, choking her, pounding her muscles into a pain-filled mush.

Her eyes opened wide in shock as the pressure on her chest built, bending her ribs and denying oxygen to her lungs.

"Too hard, damn it, Shelby!" The doctor, protected in his wet suit, yelled into his earpiece over the roar of the water. "I don't want to lose this find!"

The pressure and the force of the water eased just as suddenly as it began and Elanna's body shook, drawing massive gusts of air into her empty lungs, filling her painfully full of the air that it craved.

Her loud, gasping breaths filled the sudden silence in the room and her eyes closed, unable to deal with the reality of what she now faced.

A low whimper escaped her open mouth and tears filled her eyes.

"Are you recording that?" the doctor yelled. "It may be another attempt at communication!"

"Let me go," Elanna gasped, hearing his words.

"What?" The doctor moved in closer, straining to hear what she was saying. "Damn it, Shelby, you had better be recording this! This is my Nobel! I have captured the first real live Mermaid!"

"Let me go," Elanna gasped again, finding that her breathing was easing off. She opened her eyes and stared into the deep blue ones that examined her, noting the shock on his features.

"You speak English?" he asked, as his eyes scanned her body again, making a note of each of her struggling breaths.

"*Let me go*!" Elanna screamed, finally drawing in enough breath to demand her release.

"Remarkable!" the doctor gasped, backing up a step. "Did you record that, Shelby? She is conscious of her surroundings."

"How could I not be, you dingleberry!" Elanna screeched, giving in to her rising frustration and anger. "You have me strapped to a table like I'm some alley cat ready for dissection and you nearly drown me with seawater! Let me go!"

"Idiom!" the doctor gasped. "She has a grasp of idiom and syntax! This is remarkable! She holds a great understanding of the English language."

"English, Latin and Spanish, dillweed!" she screamed, ignoring the pain in her throat as she tried to get her message across to these two scientific boneheads. "My name is Dr. Elanna Richfield and I demand that you release me! *Now*!"

The doctor jumped as if scalded, and peered closely at his find.

"Elanna Richfield is dead," he muttered. "You do have some passing resemblance to her, but you cannot be her. She was dumped—"

"Into the ocean!" she growled, her eyes narrowing on her tormentor.

"Yes," he breathed. "The ocean."

"And now, I want you to remove these restraints and get me out of this room," she growled.

Silence.

There was absolute silence broken only by the drip of water leaking from the large head above her, making her jerk as each drop splashed against her bare stomach.

"Elanna is dead," the doctor said again. "Maybe you found her body and took it over, maybe she told you what happened before she died, but no human can survive a drop from a puddle jumper going at that speed into the sea."

"I did."

She made her statement with authority, but the doctor shook his head again.

"No human has webbed toes and fingers, or gills on their lower back," he said as he dared her to argue with his findings.

"This one does," she said just as confidently. "And this one needs a bathroom, a set of decent clothes and a phone."

"Clever little creature," he breathed as he stared into her eyes. "But not clever enough. I will release you to see to your needs, but you will remain in my care. You are too important to lose. And you cannot be Elanna Richfield."

"Dr. Richfield," she corrected automatically, not noting that his eyebrow went up in surprise. "And why can't I be?"

"Because Elanna Richfield was a brilliant scientist and more machine than woman, but she could not speak to dolphins!"

He left soon after that and Elanna got her first look at Shelby.

He crept into the room, embarrassed and apologetic as he began to uncuff her ankles.

"I am real sorry, ma'am," he said, his deep brown almond-shaped eyes pleading with her for understanding. "But the doctor gives the orders around here."

He moved with a grace she had only seen in martial artists, and in Storm and his people.

Storm!

Her eyes grew moist at the thought of her beloved. She had made him a promise, and she would not, from the look of things, be able to keep it.

"No! Don't cry," he said as he ran his hands through his long, silky black hair. "It won't be that bad! I am here to take care of you."

Shelby had to be Asian, Elanna instantly classified as she absently regarded her new jailer—Asian and something else. But his voice was kind.

"I want to go home," she breathed as her hands were released.

"Nothing funny," he warned as he reached down to help her sit up on the steel table. "And you can't go home. Maybe they will release you later, but this is home now."

"This is not my home," she cried as her breath began to catch in her throat. "This is not the home I remembered and these are not my people."

"Who are your people?" Shelby asked, pain squeezing his heart as he held the shaking Mermaid up.

He didn't trust her enough to get too close. Who knew what damage she could cause, but he did feel sorry for her. She was just in the wrong place at the wrong time.

"My people live under the sea," she laughed, another play on one of her favorite Disney cartoons. "And I want to go back."

"Ma'am," he began, his own heart breaking as he watched her small shoulders tremble with her tears.

"Polynesian," she panted, struggling to kill the waterworks before she dehydrated more than she already was.

"What?"

"You're Polynesian. It shows in your build and in your features. I was wondering," she breathed.

"You are correct," he whispered and felt the deep affinity with the sea his people held strain over what he had to do.

"Well, Shelby," she sighed as she forced her red-rimmed eyes up to meet his brown orbs, filled with pity and…shame? "My people welcomed a human who had been cast off. Not all of them were nice or kind, but they are extraordinary. I left my…soul behind and I need to get it back. I will not try anything with you—I have no hatred of a lackey who is forced to follow an idiot. But I will return to my home, under the sea."

Shelby's eyes hardened as she voiced his very thoughts about himself and the whole affair, but he said nothing.

He brought her water, which she drank from a thin paper cup, and left her to evacuate her bladder and bowels in the proper receptacles. It too, no doubt, would be taken and studied.

Then he left her alone, sitting in a corner, trembling in the face of what her world had become.

And all he could do was shake his head at his own sorry self, and envy the freedom she had lost.

Chapter Twenty-Eight

ഇ

"Something is not right!" Amadala decided as she flowed fluidly from her chambers, her long pink hair trailing behind her. "We need to get to them!"

She began to search frantically for Sting, sending out a call on his personal frequency as a last resort.

"My lady! What troubles you?"

Sting popped out in front of her, startling her as his one black eye gazed at her face.

He had been expecting this call, but since his powers didn't run to premonitions, he had waited and taken his time, preparing silently for war he felt might happen.

"We have to get to them!" she urged, reaching out and grabbing his forearm, not even noticing the retracted spikes whose tips sliced into her fingers.

"Lady! Have a care!"

He pulled his arm back, not wanting to hurt her, taking her hand into his and examining her palm.

"They need us!" There was some urgency in her voice, assurance that belied any disbelief that he may have harbored.

"Where?"

His one eye sparked as he released her and to absently reach up and adjust his eye patch.

"Near the humans, Sting! Elanna and Storm are in terrible danger!"

Without a word, Sting began to mentally transform himself.

He locked down all emotions, becoming the hardened death machine that had so impressed the council. He began to calculate his plans, silently reviewing humans' weak points.

"What are we going to do?" Amadala interrupted his preparations. "I am worried, Sting! Storm is the most powerful of us…"

"And the most unbalanced," he said as he turned a cold eye to her. "Elanna is the only thing preventing him from turning his fury loose on the humans. If they have harmed her…"

"Storm would never do that!' Amadala argued, but Sting just lowered his eye past her full bare breasts, past her waist to her tail—now almost completely devoid of scales—without words reminding her how Storm had nearly killed her.

"I'm going with you!"

"No, you are not!"

"Then I will follow!"

"No, you will not!"

"Who is ruler here?" she gritted out, pink eyes flashing with her anger and concern.

"We both are!"

"But are you crafty enough to overthrow a claim of co-rulership and set up a nice, painful execution while you are away?"

Silence.

Then, "You may come, but try not to get into trouble, and stay out of my way!"

"Oh, I wouldn't dream of it!"

* * * * *

Storm raced towards the island, sure he would overtake Elanna and bring her home where she belonged! He didn't care if she had discovered the secrets to eternal life. He was going to bring her home. It was what she wanted, what they both wanted.

Inside he smiled, all the while picturing locking her in his cavern for a few weeks!

But how had she made it this far, this fast? he wondered as he picked up no trace of her.

Sending out a call, he waited for a response from her, any response at all! He knew that she could understand his language, but why did she not answer? The sound waves carried for miles. It just made no sense.

He was really starting to get worried, when he heard the chatter of light happy voices, a complete opposite to what they were saying.

Bad white-coats! one young-sounding dolphin spat. *Bad, bad, bad! We never should have taken the kindred human there*!

To her own kind! an older, worried voice answered, unsure.

In the sea! the young voice argued. *She belongs to the sea*!

We tell kindred, another old voice responded. *They need to know*!

"What? What do we need to know?"

Storm recognized the voices of the dolphins, though this pod was small and unrecognized by him.

Kindred, all three cried, then surrounded him, all the while sending out furious shrieks and clicks.

"One at a time!" he demanded, feeling a sinking deep within his stomach.

Air! the older two said as they swiftly rose to the surface, only to return within seconds.

She wanted to tell the white-coats something! the young one chirped. *But she was not human! She greeted the sun! She breathed Mother Sea and she spoke properly, not in grunts and moans*!

"What happened to her?"

Storm was frozen in panic! It had to be Elanna they were speaking of! Something had happened to Elanna!

While the young one went up for air, the older two carried on the conversation.

She indeed greeted the sun, the eldest said. *And we took her to the white-coats. But they shot her with something and dragged her off. Who was she?*

"She is joined to me!" Storm breathed, and felt his mind begin to splinter as his rage began to take over. "She is still alive!"

The humans shoot death, the eldest dolphin said sadly, his voice still sounding upbeat and cheerful. *We have lost several in the past! Once shot, they do not return. I am sorry, brother kindred.*

She will return to me! Storm vowed, just as the youngest returned.

I will take you to her! he chirped, excited and anxious at once. *She greeted the sun well. She swam well.*

The white-coats, the eldest one reminded the youngest. *They have taken the human kindred.*

They will not harm me! Chipper said with a sarcastic snort. *As long as I scream at the box and spit on them they will be happy and pay no attention to me.*

"Then let us depart!" Storm said, quickly moving to follow the young dolphin.

But turning to face the elders one last time, he made a request.

"Will you take a message to my kingdom?" he asked. "The Kingdom of Calis by the twin islands. Seek out Sting and Amadala of the Pink. You will know him by his eye patch and black hair. He is a Child of Triton and will understand my urgency. Tell them to come quick. They may need to save the humans."

Your joined? the second oldest dolphin, the female, asked.

"No," he snarled, his eyes beginning to glow a pale blue. "The humans that took her!"

Shark Hunter! Child of Triton! Storm! the elder breathed, then he and his mate were off, seeking out the people he mentioned.

There was going to be a war, they decided. And they prayed that Storm would leave a few humans alive.

Chapter Twenty-Nine

ಐ

Amadala and Sting quickly made their way towards the island named Hawaii. They moved with a swiftness and stealth only possible for their kind. They were on a mission and nothing could stand in their way.

"Did you contact the warriors?" Amadala asked as they sped along, dodging underwater mountains and large schools of colorful fish.

"If we do not return within a certain amount of time, the warriors will gather and surround this island. Then, if my signal is not heard, they will attack."

"But dare we risk exposure?" Amadala shivered as she thought of hunting expeditions launched to eliminate all of her people.

"Elanna is special to both of our peoples, Amadala. But Storm is irreplaceable. If they capture him, they will seek to discover the source of his powers, and that will kill him. Then they will hunt us anyway, out of curiosity or fear. You make the laws, Amadala. I will enforce them. That is the way we will share rule!"

Amadala said nothing as she followed the black shadow of her co-ruler and associate. Maybe one day she would consider him a friend, but that would take time and healing.

"If you are sure, Sting," she sent out, "I will follow your decisions. But the Creator have mercy on all of us if we are too late or you are wrong."

"I am rarely wrong, Amadala," he returned as he kept his face and concentration straight ahead. "And if I am, I remedy the situation as quickly as possible."

* * * * *

Storm swam beside his dolphin guide, all senses alert, watching for any sign of danger.

Near here, the little one clicked as they came to the area where the platform was set up.

"This is not the island," Storm pointed out, but the dolphin gave him a strange look.

Metal island, rock island, all islands.

"I see," Storm mused as they floated near the surface of the water.

The sun was beginning to descend in the sky, and the young dolphin knew that the white-coats would be back with their boxes for their evening "chat" sessions.

"Where?" Storm asked as he observed the empty platform.

They come soon, the young one chirped. *You hide!*

Grunting his agreement, Storm sank below the surface of the water and waited.

After a few moments—no more than half an hour—the doors opened and two men appeared on the metal deck.

"Doctor, we have to report this," the younger, long-haired man decreed. "This is unethical. If this is the real Dr. Richfield, we are guilty of kidnapping."

"We will do no such thing, Shelby."

"But…"

"*Listen* to me, young man! *We* are scientists! If that creature really *is* Dr. Richfield, she would understand what we are doing. Drs. Manda and Port agree. We have to keep this discovery a secret until we know more. Can you imagine what can happen, Shelby, if word got out? There would be Mermaid hunters all over, destroying their way of life before we got the chance to study them! That I cannot allow."

"What about her, Dr. Woods?" Shelby bitterly growled, looking down as his guilt and his professionalism vied for dominance in his tortured mind. "She has a mate and wants to go home. What will happen to her? She is going to pine herself to death."

"There are always casualties, Shelby. You know this."

"But she is a human being!" he hotly argued, eyes coming up to stare at the doctor's face.

"Whatever she is, she is not human, not anymore."

"So you *do* believe that she is Dr. Richfield!" His eyebrows rose up to disappear almost into his hairline.

"I didn't say that!"

"But *you* implied it!"

"Just do your job, Shelby! And no one will get hurt!"

Shelby started to protest, but the look in Dr. Woods' eyes more that scared him. He began to realize how vulnerable he was here on this platform, how easy it would be to dispose of him and say that the sharks had gotten to him or that he had had some other accident. Wisdom shadowed his actions and he stood down.

"Yes, sir," he said quietly, any respect that he had for the world-famous marine biologist evaporated in that moment. "I'll go and see to our guest."

He turned on his heel and stalked away, brushing past the other doctors who came up onto the platform, carrying the black tone box.

"What's eating him?" Dr. Port asked, pushing back her long blonde hair as she watched the intern's retreating back.

"Excited about our discovery," Dr. Woods answered. "Worried about her care."

"Well, so am I," Dr. Manda added, pulling down his glasses as he examined his colleague, Dr. Woods.

The man was obsessed, had been for years, about speaking to the dolphins. Now that they had this Mermaid, this living creature of legend, he became almost unbalanced about learning her secrets.

"I didn't get a good look at her," he said, "but she seemed healthy enough. I assume she needs a diet of fish and the like. It seems to be the main staple in the seas, anyway."

"I think she looks sad," Dr. Port suddenly put in. "I mean really sad. We should worry."

"How do you know that she has feelings?" Dr. Woods sneered. "Not every creature does! Most live by instinct alone!"

"And we know," she stated calmly, "that dolphins, whales and other mammals often sicken and die when separated from their partners! Those are feelings, *emotions*, John. We need to take that into consideration."

"And do we know that she is a mammal?" he sneered, but the conversation was cut short.

A young dolphin, possibly the same one who had carried in their Mermaid, surfaced and began to chatter.

Hello, shark-face! Chipper squeaked and laughed, and the humans seemed delighted.

One ran to turn on the box and another eagerly stripped out of his coat, exposing his tight black fake skin.

Chipper winced as the box was turned on, its piercing sounds making no sense, but gamely moved closer.

Where is the human kindred? he chattered cheerfully. *I have brought her mate and he promises death.*

The humans smiled at each other and turned the knobs on the box, sending out more of the loud noise into the air.

"They were speaking of my bonded one!" Storm growled softly, as he listened so he could learn all he could before he made his move.

"I think the dolphin is looking for her," Dr. Port said as she adjusted the knobs. "Maybe they have a connection."

"Different species," Dr. Manda said as he lowered himself into the water, yet held on to the platform. "But maybe he acted as a guide. We will have to find out what relationship they hold."

"I will examine her later after she recovers," Dr. Woods said, a snide smile on his lips. "In fact, I will go now and see to preparations."

He turned and left the two fools with their pet fish and went to see to bigger things. Like what made this woman tick. Even if it *was* Dr. Richfield, he would not have cared. He deserved some answers and was determined to get them.

* * * * *

"Why did you come here?" Shelby asked as he walked into the room with the woman, who still huddled on the floor in the corner.

"I wanted to help," she answered, deciding that he could say that much. Shelby wasn't that bad, she decided, as he drew her tattered mental facilities together. "To help my people."

"There are more like you?"

"Humans," she sighed as she lowered her legs, but kept them crossed to cover her nakedness. "Can I have some clothes?"

"No."

She stiffened as he settled on the metal table still in the center of the room, staring curiously at her.

"Doctor's orders."

"The doctor can go to hell," she snarled. "I refuse to be naked around a bunch of strangers!"

Shelby thought for a moment, then shrugged out of his lab jacket.

"Thank you," Elanna said as she snatched the offered coat and quickly, with as much dignity as she could muster, slid it on.

"I don't think this is right," Shelby said, finally, ashamed to his bones to be party to this.

"And still you help them." She shook her head. "What? Is he going to take away your research privileges?"

"No," Shelby sighed. "But both of us may be dead before this is over."

"What?"

"I think the doc is a few donuts shy of a baker's dozen," he said as he got to his feet and began to pace in the small room.

"What?"

"Crazy!"

"Well, tell me something I don't know!" Elanna said as she climbed to her feet, and almost fell as legs, unaccustomed to walking after so much time below the water, fought to hold her weight.

"Here, let me help!" Instantly, Shelby was at her side, helping her to stand.

"Thanks," she breathed as her legs wobbled like overcooked noodles.

"I am thinking that we have to get out of here! If I try to help you, I have a feeling that I just may become chum for the next shark cage experiment!"

"Then we both have to get out of here," Elanna said, leaning heavily on the man. "We have to make a break for it and fast!"

"I…I… My people would be ashamed," he said finally. "I have had mixed feelings about this for some time, well, since he shot you with that dart. Dr. Woods is going insane and he is going to take a lot of people down with him in his madness."

"Oh, come on," Elanna said as she motioned that she wanted to try and take a step. "We have to get out of here! Think of a way!"

"I could slip you out at night, when no one is up, but I argued with him today. He is going to be watching my every move. And I wouldn't be surprised if he came up with some cockamamie story about you killing me with poison darts while trying to escape to protect himself."

"That is a good one!" a voice from behind said, startling them both. "I have to remember that!"

"Dr. Woods!" Shelby gasped as he turned to face his mentor.

"Shelby!" he *tsk*ed as he stepped deeper into the room. "I am so disappointed, but not surprised. You Polynesian natives could never separate yourselves from the legend. Too bad."

As he stepped forward again, he lifted a syringe from his pocket.

"This is plain old everyday tap water," he said when he saw he had both of their attentions. "I can stick this in Shelby here and watch as all of his red blood cells explode or I can add a few air bubbles and see what his heart does. Then I can blame it on you, my fine little Mermaid. That would give me all the time I need to experiment with you and see what makes you tick. How does that sound?"

Without waiting for an answer, he lunged at Shelby, making Elanna scream in anger and fear, her voice echoing through the metal platform and flowing out, magnified, towards the sea.

* * * * *

"Elanna!" Storm bellowed as he broke the surface of the water, scaring the doctors and the dolphin that had begun to chatter at the sound of Elanna's scream.

"What the fu—!" Dr. Manda gasped as a blue-haired, blue-skinned man exploded from the water.

"Jesus!" Dr. Port screamed as she reached for the dart gun, always at her side.

"Where is she?" Storm gritted out as his wet hair began to flow wildly around his body and the seas began to boil. "Where is Elanna?"

Dr. Port quickly aimed at the crazed blue man. She pulled the trigger, letting the dart fly, but it never made contact.

She screamed as the dart blew back towards her, as the sea came up to circle the man, as his pale eyes, the eyes of death, locked on to hers.

"Where is my mate?" he snarled softly as the waves began to rock the platform.

"I… She…" Dr. Crystal Port stammered as she scrambled backwards on her hands and stared in horror at the creature that exploded angrily from the water.

"If she has been harmed, you will all die! She is mine!"

So intent on his demands and his anger, Storm never even noticed Dr. Manda pull his dart gun from a pouch at his side and quickly fire off one round.

Crystal watched, heart banging in her chest, her eyes wide and breathing all but nonexistent, as the man jerked, then turned to face James.

Her skin had begun to crawl as she had tried to fire off the shot, but somehow, the wind seemed to aid the creature.

And who was Elanna? Was she the Mermaid they had pulled from the sea earlier?

Not for the first time, she began to have doubts about what they had done! But it was for the betterment of humanity.

Right?

Storm growled as he cursed himself for taking his attention off the male. He had stuck him with some stinger that burned as its poisons entered his skin.

He reached down, pulling his eyes away from the frightened woman, to face the man again as he pulled the dart from his side.

"If she is harmed, you will die!" he gritted out as the substance in his veins began to make his vision blur. Shaking his head, he growled as he reached for the man, now hanging on to the platform and trying to scramble to safety, the gun dropped and floating away in the rough water.

"She is fine!" Crystal screamed, trying to distract him and save James. "She is inside!"

"Why?" he growled turning to face her, leaving James to scramble onto the platform and race towards the inner doors for help.

"We had never seen... We wanted to study..."

"You stole her," he snarled as the water surrounding him began to slow and the winds to die down. "She wanted to help her people and you stole her!"

His hair settled around his body as his eyes began to droop.

"The dolphins told me. She wanted to help you and you are killing her!"

"We… We are…" But she could think of nothing to say as she watched the pain in this man's eyes.

"I want her back. She wants to go…home. She is screaming. What are you…doing…to…her?"

With his last words, Storm cursed himself a fool as he began to see black. Instead of helping Elanna, he had wound up captured himself! Love did strange things to a man, like taking away his common sense, but he at least would see Elanna. Then together, they would make it out of his mess.

Crystal sighed as the man dropped forward into the water, unconscious.

Still shuddering, she moved forward slowly, trying to see what he was or how he had done that thing with the wind and the water.

But as she neared the edge of the platform, she gasped! The man had no legs! Just a very large fin that was colored a darker blue than his skin or hair!

This was a real live Merman! They were real! But if he was a Merman, who or what did they have below?

* * * * *

James raced into the lab, frantically searching for Shelby and John. Crystal needed help and they needed to get that creature away!

He was looking for the female, so they should just give her to him.

Racing into the specimen chamber, he saw John and Shelby facing off, the Mermaid leaning against Shelby.

"John!" he called, not noticing the syringe that was quickly hidden in his pocket. "Come quick! There is a strange blue man outside! He has Crystal!"

Blue man? Elanna thought. "Storm!"

"She speaks English?" James' mouth dropped open as he looked at the woman. "Elanna Richfield?"

"Crystal!" Dr. Woods called as he turned and darted from the room, leaving a confused James and Shelby to follow.

When they reached the deck of the platform, Crystal had already hauled the man up.

"Jesus God!" John gasped as he saw the man, his tail and his complete blueness.

"He wants his mate," Crystal stuttered, still in shock by what had transpired and the discovery she had made.

"She called him Storm," James said, realizing what the woman who had so looked like the missing doctor had said.

"He called her Elanna," Crystal said just as Elanna herself stumbled onto the platform.

"Storm!" she screamed as four pairs of eyes watched her stumble across the deck to drop to her knees bedside him. "What did you do to him? Answer me!"

Her piercing brown eyes speared each one of them, placing blame, marking them for death.

"He is—" Crystal began, getting over the shock of seeing the Mermaid speak English and fawn over the fallen Merman. She reached out to them both.

"Don't touch him!" Elanna yelled, making Crystal take a step back, disturbed by the anguish on her face.

"This is all my fault," Elanna breathed as she lowered her face to burrow into his long blue hair. "I did this to you! This is all my fault."

She struggled to flip him over, laying his head in her lap as her eyes traced every feature on his beloved face.

She let out a tortured groan as she hugged him to her breast, wetting the lab jacket with seawater and tears.

"We are together, my love," she sobbed. "We are together and we will make it out of here! We are together and nothing will tear us apart." She crooned softly to him as she rocked his limp body back and forth.

Four pairs of eyes stared down, four pairs of eyes with four very different thoughts. And only one had thoughts of setting them free.

Chapter Thirty

✼

Chipper took off the moment Storm exploded from the water. He had to find his pod and let them know what had happened. There was no time to spare!

The elder two dolphins had already intercepted Amadala and Sting by the time Chipper showed up.

The others turned to face him, curiosity and horror on their faces.

They have him! They have the king! Chipper chattered, as he rose to the surface on a quick breath.

"Who?"

The white-coats! Chipper nearly sobbed, though his voice sounded happy and gay. *Human kindred was screaming and now they have them both!*

"Screaming?" Sting snarled as he turned to face Amadala. "Then it is to be war."

His cold black eye bore deeply into hers, and for once, Amadala was in total agreement.

* * * * *

Storm came to by degrees, his discomfort making itself known in his confused brain.

He was dry, too dry, and it was beginning to get painful. And he was flat on his back on something hard! Had he fallen asleep on a rock somewhere?

He tried to move, to shift his head but was met with resistance.

Groaning, he struggled to open his eyes a small crack, but that move was met by blinding pain as bright light seared his sensitive eyes and shot white-hot pain to his brain.

"Don't move, love," he heard Elanna whisper to him, and again struggled to turn his head towards the sound of her voice, ignoring the straps that cut across his forehead. "And don't struggle so. You'll only make it worse."

Storm sought to open his eyes again, just a hair, and managed to catch a watery glimpse of his mate, strapped to a table beside him.

"What goes…? Who…?"

"The white-coats."

With her words, memories began to pour into his mind.

He remembered confronting the humans, the two on the metal island, and the two that joined them.

"They will all die," he whispered, his voice rough with the effects of the drugs. "Every last one of them."

Elanna said nothing, but she stared intently at her lover's face, feeling the pain that he must be feeling as well.

"How long, Elanna?"

"Hours, days, weeks. Does it matter so much, Storm? They have us and they are not letting us go."

"How long, Elanna?" he repeated, opening his eyes more as he grew accustomed to the light.

"A day or two, Storm. They locked us down here and haven't showed their faces at all."

Storm grunted, then began to twist his wrists, trying to loosen the straps that held him.

"There is one that may help," Elanna continued as she turned her head to stare up at the metal ceiling. "But I am afraid our captors will do something to him. He said his people had an affinity with your people, once. He tried to help me."

"The only good human is a dead human," Storm growled as he gave up his struggle and flopped back to the metal table, tired but not defeated.

"And what am I?" she asked, amusement tugging a smile at her lips.

"Exceptional," he replied as he closed his eyes and tried to draw in what energies he had left.

"What are you doing?" Elanna asked, looking on in concern. "You're going to deplete yourself."

Snorting, Storm focused in on his inner power and the room began to vibrate.

A light blue aura began to surround him as he drew more and more power from the very air.

Suddenly, there was a spark. Lightning flowed from his body, through the metal of the table, and the smell of ozone filled the air. As Elanna stared on in amazement, the leather bands that held him began to smoke, then snapped as he gave a sharp jerk.

First one arm, then the other.

An eerie smile began to grow on his lips as the glow faded from his body.

He reached up above his head, felt the strap holding his forehead in place, and began to shred it with his sharp nails.

Soon, that band too gave way and Storm was pulling himself in a sitting position.

"Hello, love," he purred, discovering that as long as he was sitting up, the hanging lantern above his head did not sear his eyes with its light.

"Hello," Elana giggled, fear, relief, and nervousness running through her mind. "And don't even think to try that with me. Metal is a good conductor of electricity and you would fry me before I could open my mouth to scream."

"The only screams that come from your lips will be the ones of orgasm, Elanna," he replied, as he reached down and tugged the straps holding his lower appendage.

Tears again bubbled from Elanna's eyes as she watched her mate. He was so beautiful, so exotic, and he was trapped here because of her.

"Don't cry, Elanna," Storm soothed as the straps gave way and he undulated to maneuver his body into a more comfortable position. "You need to save your moisture. It appears they plan on roasting us slowly under these lanterns."

"This is all my fault!" Elanna gasped. Her sobs filled the air, ringing throughout the metal room, sending painful vibrations straight to his heart.

"No, Elanna. You had to do what you thought was right. That is why I love you so much — you think for yourself."

"If I had listened to you…"

"You would have had regrets for the rest of your life. Don't live like I was, Elanna. Let go of the past. We have to find a way out of here so that we will have a future."

Still Elanna sobbed, rough, tearing sounds made all the more harsh because she could not move her head or cover her face. That added to her shame. She didn't look good when she cried, and she was helpless to even have the comfort of shielding her face from view.

"Elanna," Storm began, but the lights flickered and loud footsteps sounded.

Storm rolled to face the door, to see what new misery this visitor would bring. He would protect his mate with everything that was inside him.

He began to glow an eerie red as something scraped against the metal door.

*****

"We have to let them go!" Crystal snarled as she stomped across the small office. "Who knows what they can do, John? Who knows what they will do to all of us?"

"We keep them both." John was calm as he stared at the collection of worried people in his office. "They are contained, Dr. Port. What harm can they do?"

"The blue one was controlling the weather, John. You weren't there, but I was! I will never forget the sight of my own dart flying back at me! We have to let those people go!"

"They are not people, Crystal. They are fish! Talking fish!"

"We don't know that!" she countered leaning over his desk, her eyes boring into his.

"We will when I finish my experiments."

"Experiments are all well and good," James Manda replied, as he watched the two of them spar. "But you both are overlooking one thing. She mentioned people, specifically, their people."

"So?" John sighed as he shifted his gaze to the young black doctor.

"So, if one of them could find her, then don't you think the others will be able to as well? You were not there, John. I saw what the creature could do. What if he can do more than make big waves and wind tunnels? How can you handle a tornado, John? A contained tornado directed at us? I got lucky with that shot because he was concentrating on Crystal. If he had been more aware..." His words trailed off as he sadly shook his head.

"I don't see a threat." John sighed again as he thought of how to rid himself of the doctors.

"Then you are blind!" Crystal railed. "I say we turn them back out into the sea and be done with it! You have some blood samples, John. You have photos of her, videos of her. You have her piss, for cripes' sakes! Let them both go so that we can survive to find them again!"

"I would expect that from a woman." John's gaze cut to James. "Too much emotion."

"Where is Shelby?" James suddenly asked, ignoring the doctor's quips. "I haven't seen him since we strapped that creature in."

"Shit!" John gasped as he rose to his feet and raced for the door.

James shrugged at Crystal, and soon both of them were racing after the doctor.

Chapter Thirty-One

ஐ

"Elanna?" a voice whispered as the door began to open a crack. "Are you okay?"

"Shelby!" Elanna hissed back, sure that their conversations were being recorded. "You are going to get yourself killed!"

"Sooner than you know, human!" Storm growled, as he thrust out his arm and a blast of cool air rushed around the room. Shelby was sucked helplessly inside as the door slammed shut.

"Storm!" Elanna screamed out, trying to check his motions as the lab assistant flew several feet into the air. "Don't hurt him!"

"He is human!"

"He is my friend!" she sent back, glaring at her mate.

"What she said!" Shelby called out as he began to drop. From four feet up suspended by nothing, four feet seemed a long way down.

"You will release her," Storm demanded as he gave Shelby a shake.

"That is why I'm here!" he shouted back, fear overcoming any manners that he might have had. "And for goodness' sake, don't drop me!"

Let him go! Elanna mentally commanded her mate. *Please*!

"As you wish," he answered as he glared at the human, but gently lowered him to the ground. "But you will release her, human."

"That's what I came in here for!" Shelby breathed, his eyes locked on to Storm.

"Then do as I command," Storm repeated after a moment of silence with Shelby staring at him in open-mouthed wonder.

But Shelby stood there, rooted to the spot, his eyes glazing over.

"I think he's in shock," Elanna said, catching a glimpse of the statue-like young man.

"He's going to be in pain if you are not soon released," Storm growled, as the wind began to circle around the room.

"Right," Shelby gasped as he seemed to jerk back to himself. "Release Elanna."

Almost tripping over his own two feet, Shelby raced to the strapped woman, fingers fumbling as he released the leather cuffs. "Sorry. But…but he's real!"

"And dangerous," Storm added in a low menacing voice as he watched Elanna stiffly roll to her side before she attempted to sit up.

"Let me help," Shelby sighed, seeing her condition.

"Touch her at your own peril," Storm growled, not liking the two-legged creature holding his woman.

"Like you are going to walk over here and help," Shelby muttered under his breath.

"I heard that, human."

Shelby blanched.

"Um, he has very good hearing," Elanna said as she was hoisted into a sitting position, her weary muscles protesting each move.

"Fascinating," Shelby muttered, his eyes going back to the blue man.

"I need water," Storm said as he took in the condition of his fin. It was dry and painful to move, his scales losing a lot of their glimmer.

He ran his hands through his hair, finding it stiff and salt-caked. His skin burned from the heat and the bright lights still blazing in the room.

"Me, too," Elanna whispered, her throat dry. But she discovered something else as well. She felt a sharp tearing pain between her fingers and her toes. Her webbing had dried out. The pain was sharp and intense.

"Oh, I have something," Shelby replied, pulling a bottle out of his lab coat even as he shrugged out of it. "Bottled water."

That said, he began to pour the cool liquid over Elanna's hands before dropping the jacket around her shoulders, hiding her nudity.

That seen to, he cautiously approached Storm.

"I'm just going to dump this on your…lower fin. I can't believe I just said that!"

Shelby rolled his eyes skyward and shook his head as he took another step towards the Merman from the depths of the sea, this creature his people told of in legend.

"Do you have a way off of this metal island?" Storm asked, raising one eyebrow as Shelby approached and began to put what was left of the bottle over his body, making him close his eyes for a moment as the water sank into his thirsty scales.

"Metal island? You mean this platform?"

"No. I mean the metal bench that I am resting so comfortably on," Storm snapped.

"Sarcasm," Shelby breathed, his eyes opening wide in shock. "He really does speak English!"

"And several other languages you humans speak as well," Storm sighed. "You've only been broadcasting them across the oceans for centuries, polluting our waters and our hearing."

Shelby blinked as he took in the scope of this pronouncement.

"Several languages?"

"Are all human males this dense?" Storm asked Elanna, who struggled to hold in a laugh.

"I am not dense!" Shelby defended himself. "It's just that I never thought you existed, let alone could understand what we were saying."

"Human, since your kind developed on land, we have been observing you, and not liking what we were seeing. Human arrogance! Is there anything greater? You act as if you are the only sentient beings who have a right to exist and possess intelligence! Then you have the nerve to act superior and surprised when you discover something other than you has a greater understanding. Pathetic!"

"Not true!" Shelby spoke hotly as he poured the last of the water over Storm and glared at the blue Merman. "When we discover something new, we learn from it!"

"By dissecting it," Elanna hissed, remembering Dr. Woods' plans for them.

"Not true! Not really! Dr. Richfield…"

"I only know that I was strapped to a table and humans took my mate from me," Storm cut off his protest. "I know that my people are not something new, we have been here for eons, and yet we have never taken one of you humans captive. And yet, here I am…drying out in this ridiculous metal floating hulk!"

Shelby said nothing, then turned towards Elanna.

"I'm going to get you out of here. Both of you."

"Because," Storm insisted, glaring at the human, the only one there for him to release some of his ire upon.

"Because this is wrong, okay?" he growled, turning back to Storm. "This isn't right."

"It's a pity you feel that way," a voice echoed through the chambers.

"Dr. Woods!" Shelby called out, looking around the room, trying to spot the source of the voice.

"And did you think this room would not be bugged?" Elanna asked as she rolled her eyes at the innocence of Shelby's youth.

"Very good, Doctor," Woods chuckled. "You have done this before?"

"No. It's what I expect from a sadistic asshole like you!" she shouted back, her eyes narrowing in anger.

"Not very complimentary," Woods sighed. "But so fascinating to watch."

"Let us go!" Elanna screamed, only to be answered with a laugh.

"Good one, Doctor! I didn't know that you were a comedian as well."

With that, water began to flood the bottom of the room.

"What are you doing?" Shelby screamed, the smell of salt filling the room as water flowed through lower vents.

"Why, our specimens are getting too dry, Shelby. It was not very well done of you to not give them water."

"I had to sneak in here, you bastard!" Shelby screamed, a frightened look coming into his eyes.

"Yes…" John drawled, then snickered at the sound of his former assistant's panicked voice. "It's a shame too, that the creature drowned you as you sought to aid him. Too bad, really."

"What the hell are you talking about?"

"It was an accident, you see. No one knew you were in there, and they just held you down so that you couldn't scream for help."

"What are you doing?"

"My discoveries, dear boy!" John laughed, the sound echoing off the walls. "They can breathe underwater. And alas, poor Shelby, you cannot!"

"This is murder!" Shelby screamed as he felt the water begin to soak his pants up to his knees. "You can't do this!"

"I can do whatever I want!" John cackled. "And as an extra added bonus, your death will convince Drs. Manda and Port that those creatures must be destroyed before they do any more harm. I can find out what I need to know with the autopsies. So you see, your death will not be in vain, Shelby."

"*No*!" Shelby screamed as he felt the water close in around his waist.

"Good-bye," John laughed as the microphone squeaked and then clicked. Silence, but for the rushing of the water, filled the room.

"This is good," Elanna said, a smile crossing her face as Storm dropped into the water, then disappeared from view.

"Yeah, good for you, Fish Lady!" Shelby nearly screamed. "I can't breathe underwater!"

"You won't have to."

Shelby jumped as the Merman surfaced beside him and wrapped his arms around him tightly, and smiled, showing razor-sharp teeth.

"*No*!" Shelby screamed, the sound echoing around the room and carrying out into the sea.

* * * * *

"What was that?" Crystal breathed as a high-pitched scream echoed through the walls.

She and James had lost John as he raced through the complex. They were now seriously hunting for the deranged man.

"I don't know, but we had better find John and Shelby." James ran a tired hand over his face. "I don't know why I signed on for this project! John Woods is seriously cracked!"

"We should let those people go, James, and destroy what evidence we have of them."

He paused in his walking to turn and stare at Crystal as if she had lost her mind.

"Think about it! You saw the power that one blue man had, James! What if there are more of them? What if they are on their way here, right now? We could be up against a war that will devastate humankind, all because of one man's race for glory!"

"Humankind, Crystal? Come on!"

"Seriously, James! What if we can never venture into the sea again? What if they scare away the fish, destroy our equipment, and call up a windstorm to destroy ships? And you saw it talking to that dolphin, James! What if it can do more? Like talk to whales and sharks? We don't know what we are getting into!"

"Crystal, you don't know that will happen!"

"And you don't know that it won't!"

The two glared at each other for a moment, before they were interrupted by rushing feet.

"Thank God!" John cried out as he raced towards the two of them. "Something dreadful has happened!"

"What?"

Seascape

"Shelby! He went in to aid those monsters! He turned the water on to wet them down! But they did… something! They got free and they are drowning him!"

Instantly, James and Crystal took off for the submersible lab, never even looking behind.

If they did, they would have noticed that John Woods had a huge grin on his face.

Chapter Thirty-Two

ಚ

"What the hell!"

James gasped as he looked through the observation window down into the metal tank room.

Crystal came up behind him, her eyes wide in shock!

"Drain the room!" James yelled as he frantically pushed buttons on the console.

"It's too late, James," Crystal gasped as she stared at the floating bodies in the room.

"But we have to get him out of there. What are they doing to his body?"

Inside the room, there was a huddle of bodies—Elanna's, the blue man's, with Shelby's floating somewhere in the center.

His legs floated out between the tangle of fin and legs and the trio drifted somewhere in the middle of the room, not close enough to the window for them to get a good view of what was going on, but close enough for them to worry.

"I'm draining it," James growled as he located the proper switch, and with a gurgling sound, the room began to rapidly drain.

When the water was visibly going down, James turned and pulled a key from around his neck.

The weapons cabinet was in this room, and with a fierce scowl on his face, he reached in and pulled a large-caliber rifle from the sealed box.

"What are you doing?" Crystal asked, alarmed at the expression on James' face.

"I'm going to get his body. And I am not going in without protection!"

"Something is not right, James." Crystal said as she placed a hand on an arm knotted with tension.

"Yeah, Shelby is dead and those two are behind it."

"No! Think, James! Why would Shelby start the water and then go into the room? He had been watering the female with the shower. It just doesn't make sense!"

"What doesn't make sense is what any of us are doing here." James turned to stare at his colleague, his brown eyes intense. "But I know that after I get him out of there, this whole project is done."

Leaving her behind, James raced down the steps and stopped before a wide metal door, reading the water gauge inside.

When the water reached one-half foot, he spun the locking mechanism and pulled the door open with a jerk.

"All right in there! I've come for the body. Back off and no one gets hurt!"

Silence greeted his pronouncement.

Entering the room, barrel first, James stepped onto the wet floor, ignoring the rush of water wetting his pants and pressing against his forward motion.

The only sounds were dripping water, and then…

An enraged gasp of breath.

Jerking his rifle in that direction, James swiveled his body and paused as he aimed at the nearly naked woman in the wet lab coat.

"Where is he?" James asked, his voice low and dangerous. "What did you do to the body?"

"Behind you," a voice rasped, and James jerked, spinning towards the sound, his finger pressing reflexively on the trigger.

There was a loud boom that echoed across the room, then the sharp ping as the bullet ricocheted off the walls.

Instinctively, James ducked, his ears ringing, but his eyes were trained on something that he never thought to see!

As his hearing slowly began to clear, he was aware of a woman screaming and the sound of feet rushing across the room.

"What have you done?" Elanna screamed. She nearly leapt over the crouched doctor, ignoring the rifle in his hand as she raced towards the body that had fallen the moment it had been fired.

* * * * *

In his office, John Woods heard the boom of the rifle, and the resulting scream as a woman cried out.

"Finally," he sighed as he crossed his hands behind his head and mentally began to do math.

One day for the autopsy for the male, maybe two as I make up some excuse about not knowing how to treat his wounds. If he is not already dead, he will soon be.

Hmm, the woman. We can do the syringe thing and say that she died because her mate did. And then we get to see what changed Dr. Elanna Richfield into the mutation that she was.

Yes, and then maybe he could find that mutation agent and create a bigger stir than the doctor herself did when she broke that genetic code. The government would pay trillions for it! Truly amphibious soldiers, underwater spies...the possibilities were endless.

* * * * *

They scream! Chipper trilled as he raced towards Sting and Amadala. *Kindred*! *She screams*!

"We can't wait anymore!" Sting growled as he gave the signal.

The Children of Triton had amassed and at the given sign, the furious warriors began to move forward, encircling the small metal island. Others grouped together, ready to head towards the island called Hawaii.

Whether or not the second attack force would be deployed was up to whatever they found on the small metal island.

"We are ready," Amadala spoke quietly as she swam up beside Sting. "Our people will do nothing until we give the order."

"We?"

"You and I, Sting. We both made this decision and we both will face the consequences."

"Very well." Sting nodded as he moved forward. "Be prepared, Amadala. This thing with the humans ends now."

Chapter Thirty-Three

೮౧

"What the hell are you doing?"

Elanna stared at the stupefied man, but James Manda had a look of shock and fear on his face.

"Shelby?" he gasped, staring as the man eased to his feet, his hands held up as if to protect himself from further harm.

"You shot at me!" he muttered as Elanna helped him to his feet.

"You're alive!"

"You shot at me! You fucking shot at me!"

"Shelby!" Elanna admonished as she pulled the stunned man to his feet. "And of course he is alive, no thanks to you or that insane bastard you work for!"

"But...but..." James stammered as he rose to his feet, the rifle clattering to the water-covered metal floor. "You were dead!"

"Oh, he was not dead. We kept him alive." Elanna sighed as she kept her eyes on the nervous doctor.

"Elanna Richfield?" James gasped as his attention turned towards the woman.

"No, it's the Little Mermaid, sans flippers. Of course it's me, you idiot."

"But... But you're dead."

"This conversation seems to be going around in circles," a droll voice said from behind him and James turned, only to come face-to-face with something that could not possibly exist.

"You!"

"Me!" Storm sarcastically spat back as he rolled his eyes. Once again he sat on one of the metal tables, but this time, he was soaking wet and more comfortable.

"But I saw…"

"The kiss of life, Doctor!" Elanna sighed as she moved a bit closer to him, arms held out as if to show that she meant no harm. "And we had to fight him to make him accept it from a man."

"I don't go that way," Shelby groused, a blush highlighting his features.

"What way? Alive?" Elanna snarled, before she turned to face James.

"But he said you were dead, that they killed you," James stammered as he took a step forward, his rifle forgotten as he ran his hands over Shelby. "How could you survive so long underwater?"

"He breathed for me," Shelby admitted, pointing to Storm. "He saved my life."

But they were interrupted again, as Crystal ran into the room, armed with a rifle of her own.

"James! I heard a sho— Shelby?"

"He's alive," James related unnecessarily, a smile on his face.

"But how?"

"He breathed for him," James informed her as he pointed to Storm.

Crystal stared in shock.

"But… But they were holding him…"

"Breathing for me," Shelby explained again. "They saved my life and we had better get out of here fast. John has lost it, big time. He is going to kill us all."

"How right you are."

All four people jumped and spun around as John Woods walked into the room, the pistol in his hands pointed directly at Crystal.

"Drop it, dear girl. I don't want to have to kill you, but I will."

"This is the white-coat who took you?" Storm asked as Crystal's weapon clattered to the floor. There was no way she could bring it up fast enough to shoot him. She was a scientist, not a marksman.

"White-coat? How juvenile." John chuckled as he stepped deeper into the room, forcing the three humans back towards a quiet Storm. "But you all must understand why I must do this."

"Murder?" Shelby screamed as he stared at the doctor he once admired.

"Murder? Such a nasty word, Shelby. I prefer to call it...downsizing."

"And how are you going to explain this?" Elanna asked as she stared at the man with hatred running through her veins.

"John? What are you doing?" Crystal asked finally. "Are you trying to kill us?"

"All in the quest for fame and glory," Elanna sighed as she stared at the scientist.

"You lied to us! You said they killed Shelby!" Crystal added, putting two and two together and coming up with a number that didn't bode well for any of them.

"Well, I had hoped that you two would overreact, like you did. And I had hoped you would take care of preparing the cadaver for autopsy, but you didn't. Too squeamish, I suppose, but the one thing I can't understand is why you are still trapped in your mortal coil, Shelby? You should be floating belly-up right about now."

"The reason would be me." Storm chuckled as he tilted his head to the side. "And I suggest you end this right now, or you and your metal island are going to be less than nothing."

John exploded into laughter. He moved far enough into the room to kick both rifles under a metal table, and still he laughed.

"It speaks!" he chortled as he turned to face his second discovery for the first time. "It can actually speak English."

"And several other languages as well, human."

"Oh! You and Elanna there are a good match."

"I told you she was Elanna Richfield!" Shelby called out, glaring at the doctor.

"But how?" Crystal whispered, turning her head to stare at Elanna.

"Storm saved me." she replied, tilting her head in his direction.

"You make a habit of that," John groused as he stood back and took aim.

"And I am not yet done," Storm added, a smile on his face.

"What, you can dodge bullets now?" John chuckled as he drew a bead on Elanna.

"First, I think I'll take care of Dr. Richfield. She is too mouthy for my tastes anyway."

He pulled back the hammer, just as something hit the station and the whole thing began to shake.

"What the hell!" John gasped as he stumbled backwards, but maintained the hold on his gun.

Before he could recover, there was another loud boom and the scream of twisting metal as the platform began to vibrate.

"That is the sound of several angry Mermen," Storm informed them, calm as ever. "They are planning to tear this place apart piece by piece, until they get what they want."

"What do they want?" Crystal screamed, her eyes going wide in shock and fear.

"Why," Elanna answered as a grin twisted her lips, "us."

* * * * *

Sting gave the signal again, and a powerful wave of water struck the metal island, shifting and denting it on several of its smooth metal sides.

He and Amadala stood back, observing as a young Triton, Wave, raised his arms and sent thousands of gallons of water crashing on the platform.

"It should not be long now," Sting informed her. His eye glittered with anticipation.

"You are enjoying this," Amadala said finally, tilting her head to glance at her co-ruler.

"Yes, I am. Otherwise, I would not be so good at what I do."

"Storm and Elanna are in there."

"So are the ones who took them, the ones that need punishment."

"And when they come out?"

"They will return the true Child of Triton, or face the consequences."

"They are still in danger," Amadala said quietly. "But it is not as bad as before."

"Then we do good here," Sting decided and signaled for the island to be hit with another volley.

"I also feel…"

"What, woman?" Sting sighed as he turned to face her, wondering how such a beautiful woman could be so contrary.

"Change is coming, Sting. And I don't know if it is good or bad."

"Change is the one constant in life, Amadala," Sting replied as he signaled for yet another volley of water.

"I suppose," she whispered, turning to stare at the crumpling metal egg that housed the ones she cared about as well as the things that she feared. "But is it for the better or for the worse?"

* * * * *

"My God!" Crystal screamed as the walls dented in more and more. "John, you have to stop this! Let them go!"

"Never!" John shouted back, turning his gun towards Storm. "Make them stop!"

"Why should I?" Storm asked, lying back on the table as if bored.

"Because I will kill you if you don't!"

Snorting, Storm closed his eyes and rested his hands behind his head.

"You want to die?" John shouted, growing anxious as the platform screamed and rocked again, a few metal rivets exploding from the walls with sharp pings.

"Makes no difference to me, human. You will be dead anyway."

"I'll kill the woman!" John shouted, sweat beading on his forehead as he frantically searched the room, as if looking for a way out.

"I won't let you," Storm said, just as quiet and smug.

"I swear! I'll do it."

"Try."

Growling, John pointed his gun at Elanna and began to pull the trigger.

Before he could move it more than a millimeter, a gust of wind grew out of nowhere, jerking his gun up, causing it to fire into the ceiling with a loud boom. Everyone ducked as the bullet ricocheted off the walls several times to land spent in some unseen corner.

Everyone stared in wide-eyed horror at Storm.

"I can use electricity next," he decided. "I wonder if your brain will shut down first, or your heart? Which will explode, I wonder?"

"No!" John screamed. "I am too close! I won't let you stop me!"

Again he pointed at Elanna, and again the bullet pinged around the room, making a lot of noise but causing very little damage. As long as Storm controlled the wind, there was nothing much John could do.

But he always had a plan.

Lunging across the room, he reached for Elanna, daring to touch her, to press his weapon against her neck.

But he never got the chance.

The second he raced forward, a bolt of blue lightning exploded from across the room, hissing as it slammed into his chest, sending him flying back several feet.

As his body hit the water that still covered the floor, the humans in the room screamed, leaping back, terrified the powerful electric blast would strike them as well.

But they didn't need to worry. Storm directed the lightning bolt. It went where he commanded and nowhere else.

John Woods, would-be star of the scientific world, fell dead on the floor, a quick and meaningless death for a selfish, evil man.

"My God!" Crystal breathed, turning to stare at Storm, who still casually lounged on the metal table.

"He's dead," Shelby gasped as he stared at the smoking hulk that once had been one of the world-renowned experts on marine life.

"Storm!" Elanna streaked across the room to toss herself on his supine body.

"Elanna, love," he gasped as she collapsed on top of him, wrapping her arms around his neck, hugging him and dropping kisses all over his face.

But what would have happened next was halted immediately by something striking the metal hull, shaking the platform and making the lights flicker and spark. The platform was being destroyed.

"God, you have to stop them!" James demanded, turning to face Storm, panic clearly written on his face. "They are going to kill us all!"

"Not quite," Storm replied, his eyes glowing red as he stared at the collection of humans in the room.

"This platform can't stand the damage! It's breaking up! You have to stop them!"

"I could," Storm replied as he dried his face in Elanna's wonderful whirlpool hair. "But why should I?"

Chapter Thirty-Four

ಞ

"We're going to die!"

"Correction, *you* are going to die," Storm said to Crystal as yet another wave rocked the platform.

"But you can't do that! You have what you want! You have to stop them!"

Crystal was frantic while James and Shelby looked on in shock.

"I don't have to do anything, human. The only one I would even consider worth redeeming is the young one over there," Storm replied calmly, as he nodded his head in Shelby's direction.

"Storm," Elanna whispered as he pulled away from her mate. "You have to stop them."

"These people, these humans you tried so hard to protect?" he asked, sarcasm heavy in his voice. "The same humans who took you captive and spawned the one who wanted the rest dead?"

"Not all of them, Storm. Just the one…and he's dead now."

"Yet the rest, save for the young one, didn't even attempt to right his wrong."

At his words, James and Crystal flushed and looked down, something that Storm took as a sign of guilt.

"You don't know that," Elanna sighed as she gripped Storm harder, protecting herself from the rocking of the platform.

"And I refuse to offer an excuse," James said finally. "But I did argue that what we were doing was wrong."

"And that means so much," Storm snorted, sitting up and glaring at the group.

"It means a lot to stand up to an authority figure, Storm," Elanna said, her hand resting on his shoulder.

"So these are the humans you wanted to help, Elanna? These are the humans that you almost tossed our love aside for? These humans here? They are pathetic creatures, Elanna, not worthy of your attentions."

With a negligent wave, he discounted the people standing in the room as worthless and beneath his contempt.

"Wait a minute!" James argued, stepping forward.

"Wait for what?" Storm cut him off. "Wait for you to run into the room with another weapon…after the damage has been done?"

"Well, that's not fair!" Shelby cut in. "You have no idea what you are talking about!"

"I know what I have seen, human," Storm said as the lights flickered and the platform shook, another dent appearing in the wall. "I know that you took someone I love and you almost killed her with your treatment."

"So just go ahead and do it."

Crystal's quiet words were filled with anger as she moved forward and the two men moved back.

"Just go ahead and kill us and be done with it! At least John," she snarled, pointing to the body on the floor, "would have done it quickly and gotten it over with. You are worse than him and you claim such disdain for humans."

"Worse?" Storm growled, his eyebrow rising as he sneered at the human female.

She was quite different from his Elanna, though they appeared similar in form.

Her hair, though, was a mass of straight red strands, not unlike some Merpeople he knew. And her skin was pale, with just a few red spots on her face. She was slimmer than his Elanna, not as rounded in form, but there were definite similarities.

"Worse, you bastard!"

"Wait a minute!" Elanna cut in, her eyes turning a furious brown as she glared at the redheaded woman.

"No, Elanna." Storm interrupted, patting her arm with a tender hand. "I would hear what the human has to say."

Elanna had her own words about saving the lives of the people on the failing platform, but she too wanted to know what the woman, Crystal, had to say.

Crystal glanced from Storm's impassive face to Elanna's peeved one, and sighed.

"Look," she began, "I know we are not perfect. We make mistakes. We are only human. But what you are doing is wrong. The one responsible for this is dead. What more do you want?"

"Revenge," Storm stated quietly. "I assume you all have voices, arms, legs, hands? So why didn't you stop him? Even two is greater than the one. So your words mean nothing to me."

"Okay!" Crystal screamed. "We were curious. I-I was curious. I have never seen one of your kind before. I never even got the chance to see Elanna. John had her trapped and on the platform before we knew what was happening. But yes, I pulled you back onto the platform. I was curious, damn you. I wanted to see what you were. To study you. To learn about your kind. But I never advocated murder, and I definitely would not have hurt Elanna Richfield, if I knew she was onboard."

"But because I am unknown to you, I am not worthy of respect?" Storm asked, raising that eyebrow again.

"No."

"But you just said that you would have treated Elanna differently if you knew who she was. What about me? Or what if a curious child surfaced near you? Would you have someone so defenseless and helpless at your mercy? Would you treat her with respect? Or would you strap her to a metal rock?" He thumped the table he was sitting on. "Strap her down so that she couldn't move." He pulled at one of the leather straps on the table. "And would you subject her to murderous conditions?" He pointed to the lights as they flickered and died.

There was a deep inhalation from all in the room, except Storm and Elanna, whose eyes could easily see in the dark as they were created or had evolved for viewing things deep in the sea where no sunlight could reach.

An alarm sounded and within seconds, pale red emergency lights blinked on.

"Would you?" Storm asked in a silence that was so complete it seemed to be a tangible thing.

"I don't know!" Crystal answered at last. "I have never been in that position."

"And I have never been strapped to a table and roasted beneath a bright lantern while my mate cries out in agony."

Silence, yet again.

"Forget it," James cut in. "Just kill us and be done with it. You never had any intention of saving us, you monster. Crystal is right. You are just as bad as John, but John would have granted us a quick death."

"There you go again, comparing me to that human," Storm sighed as he shook his head. "See you any weapons? Do I have plans to cut you up and exhibit your body to my people? I never asked to be brought here, and now, because you have brought me here under such…accommodating circumstances, you have to deal with the aftereffects."

"Storm," Elanna said quietly. "Let them go."

"You would free these humans?" he asked, raising his eyebrow at her.

"I would."

"After what they have done to you?"

"I would."

"Why?"

"Because," she said. "It shows humanity."

"Humanity?" Storm asked, turning to face the humans again.

"Humanity, Storm. What they did was wrong, and they are not begging for forgiveness. But they did what they did out of curiosity. They are human, Storm. They can't communicate by thought, or listen to the language of the creatures around them, or are governed by traditional law like your people. Humans muddle along, trying to learn all they can with their methods. And they don't know that their methods hurt most of the time, until it is too late."

"Human, Storm." Shelby broke his silence. "Some of us are good and some of us are bad. But most of us try to do what is right. That's why I helped Elanna. Because it wasn't right what John was doing."

"So one of you possesses this so-called humanity," Storm stated, as if the small cross-section he faced was being judged for all of humankind. "What about the rest?"

"That is unfair!" Crystal yelled back. "We made a mistake, but we didn't know—would have never condoned murder. If we understood—"

"But you never tried to understand," Storm cut her off. "And now you want me to understand what you are feeling? How does it feel, human, to be helpless? How does it feel to know that your death is inevitable, to want nothing more than to go free? And to know you will never get what you wish?"

"It feels… Damn it. I want to live!" Crystal screamed, breaking down into sobs. "I want to live. I don't want to die. Is that what you want? You want to see me on the floor begging?"

She dropped to her knees, even though James tried to pull her up.

"I am begging. I am pleading with you, damn it. I want to live. I don't want to die. I don't want to…die!"

Her passionate outburst over, she hung her head and began to sob, not caring who watched, not caring about pride. Fear had taken over and she wanted it to stop.

"Are you satisfied?" James snarled as he knelt beside Crystal, taking her in his arms, trying to comfort her through his own fear and anger. "You have made us all victims! Is that enough for you?"

"Victims?" Storm asked, looking at the three, Shelby included. "You all feel like victims?"

"What the hell do you think?" Crystal screamed, stopping her forward lunge only because James held her back.

"Hmm," Storm mused out loud. "Interesting."

He closed his eyes and lay back on the table, mentally calling out.

* * * * *

Sting raised his arms, preparing for a final volley. After this strike, he would send in his warriors, and the humans would regret ever laying a finger on his people.

But just as his arm was about to drop, he felt the mental call.

Enjoying yourself? Storm said, a chuckle in his mind's voice.

Have you secured the return of your female? he sent back, motioning for the tiring young warrior to halt. *Have you secured your freedom?*

Come over here, Storm ordered. *I have some humans you should see. One is very emotional and would like to examine us for...knowledge.*

I am a Child of Triton! Sting mentally replied, indignation showing in every line of his body. *No one examines me as if I were the garbage of a bottom dweller!*

This one is nothing like Amadala or Elanna, Storm continued. *This female seems articulate and almost makes sense. Like my Elanna. But...different.*

Different? There was curiosity in his voice.

Different.

Still filled with anger but intrigued nevertheless, Sting motioned for his people to stand down.

"What is it?" Amadala asked, her eyes curious as that strange feeling began to overtake her once more. "What has happened?"

"He wants us to cease. He wants me to go over to the metal island. Do you sense a trap?"

"No," Amadala whispered after a moment. "I sense no subterfuge in Storm and I feel nothing from him or Elanna. Yet I feel..."

"I am going," Sting told her as he began to swim towards the island, easily traversing the choppy waters to where a door was slowly opening.

"Wait!" Amadala called out as she hurried after him. "I am going with you!"

On the defensive, Sting raised one hand to his eye patch, his scowl fierce as the opening of the door grew wider and he drew nearer.

Amadala swam behind, her hand on his shoulder, her eyes growing wide as that strange feeling deepened until it almost consumed her.

Then as the door swung open, a tall, dark-haired human peered out before stepping fully into the sun.

"I expected the sun to be hidden in clouds," he said, as if speaking to himself, looking around at the waves that only moments ago were tearing the platform apart.

"Where are they, human?" Sting snarled and Shelby jumped as if struck.

"My God," he breathed as he took in the dark-haired Merman, the pink one with the immense boobs just behind him, and the army of rainbow-hued heads treading in the not-so-far distance.

"Storm? Elanna?" Sting demanded again, his hand beginning to raise the eye patch as he glared at the human.

"Here!" Elanna called out as she rushed through the door, and without any hint of fear or hesitation, dove into the water, sinking out of sight before surfacing with a laugh.

"Storm?"

"From the bottom!" Elanna laughed as she swam to her friends, pulling Sting's arm away from his patch. "He is coming out through a lower trapdoor. We are safe!"

Her lab coat floated around her, looking like a limp white life preserver, but she ignored that as she threw her arms around Sting.

"Amadala!" she then giggled, even happy to see the surly Merwoman.

"My God! There are thousands of them!" Crystal breathed in awe as she followed Shelby out of the platform, her eyes straining to see the people in the distance.

"You were right," James said, his own eyes wide as he stared out at the army of Merpeople, all prepared for war. "They could have killed us all."

"And still may," Storm snorted, popping up behind Elanna, still glaring at the humans.

"Forgive them, Storm," Elanna whispered in his ear. "Forgive and forget."

"I may forgive," he replied as he turned to stare at each human for a second, as if etching their faces in his brain for all eternity. "But I shall never forget."

"Neither," Crystal surprised him by calling out, "will I."

"Examine that one," Storm called out to Sting as he wrapped his arms around Elanna and began to sink underwater. "She reminds me of someone I know."

Without a sound, Storm disappeared beneath the sea that spawned him.

Elanna paused, looked back over at the humans and smiled.

"Elanna Richfield is dead," she called out. "You will never hear from her again."

"And her secrets?" James yelled back. "And the knowledge she was going to give to humanity?"

Elanna paused for a second, then tossed James a wide grin. "Read my notes, James Manda. If you have any questions, and if you happen to be in the neighborhood…"

"I'll call on a doctor I know!" he replied with a grin.

"Wait!" Crystal called out. "What about all of this? What about these people? What can they teach us?"

"So now you are asking?" Storm sighed as he popped back up, his eyes glaring at the pushy human.

"I need to know!" Her eyes shot daggers at Storm.

"Me, too!" Shelby added. "My people have believed in you for centuries. But to find out it wasn't myth or legend… It can't end like this!"

"The platform is still there," Elanna reminded her, with a smile. Crystal was beginning to grow on her. The woman had courage in spades.

"But John…?"

"John Woods died of electrocution," James cut her off. "Playing with his dolphin box outside in a storm. You can stay here if you want, Crystal," he added. "But I've had enough of water. I'm going back to dry land."

"And these people?" she asked.

James looked around at the warriors, the calm Storm and the dark-haired Merman who carried about him an air of danger.

"Who would believe me?" he sighed. "Who would I tell anyway? I'm done. I'm going home."

"But I can't stay here alone!" Crystal said, turning to face James.

"I'm sorry, Crystal. I never wanted to sacrifice my life to science, and it's too dangerous here for me."

"I'll stay," Shelby said suddenly, his eyes on Amadala as she let out a gasp and sank lower in the water, hiding behind Sting.

"Shelby…" James began, his tone brooding.

"It's okay, Dr. Manda. I want to learn."

He managed to tear his eyes away from Amadala long enough to grin at James.

"Besides, the sea never scared me. Nothing in it would harm me."

"Keep thinking that, human," Sting snorted, staring at the collection of humans in confusion.

"So now we don't kill them and attack the big island called Hawaii?"

All parties gasped at his words, James taking a step back as he realized what they had almost unknowingly set loose.

Storm shrugged as he took Elanna in his arms.

"Do what you will, because you will anyway, but just not for our benefit. They understand what it means…to be trapped."

His words sent a shiver of fear down the humans' backs as his eyes once again searched their faces.

Silence met his announcement, and Storm took this time to dive below the water, dragging Elanna with him.

The humans stared at the remaining Merpeople, and the Merpeople stared back.

"Just what are we supposed to do now?" Sting all but growled, as he waved a hand and dismissed his people.

Silently, they disappeared into the now calm water, not a ripple left behind to show their passing.

"Um, introduce ourselves," Shelby decided, a smile pulling at his lips and he swept his damp hair back with a smile. "I'm Shelby. It's going to be fun getting to know you."

"Bah!" Sting growled as he cast one last glance at the humans who would be staying in these waters, then disappeared in a flash, leaving Amadala behind.

She stared up at Shelby and her heart began to pound. But she was a queen! And queens didn't give their time to humans.

"Bah!" she echoed Sting, before she too sank out of sight.

"This is going to be a beautiful friendship," Shelby sighed as the last of her pink hair sank out of sight.

"This is going to be a nightmare," Crystal added, but she stared in contemplation at the blue water. "And very interesting."

Sting, she thought she heard him called. "The Merman, Sting," she breathed softly as she turned and made her way back into the battered platform. *Sting*.

Chapter Thirty-Five

៛

Elanna swam through the water, a sense of freedom filling her with new purpose as the lab coat floated, forgotten, through the water.

The water had never felt so warm, the caress of it flowing over her skin, exciting her body, making her throw her arms out in a rush of pleasure.

She tossed her head back, her laughter filling the waters as she relished her life, and the man who made her feel so alive.

"Elanna."

Storm's voice made her turn, and the sight of him made her breath catch.

His body undulated through the waters, his long hair flowing behind him in the gentle currents as they swam.

His eyes glittered, his scales sparkled with the fractured sunlight, his powerful mother-of-pearl fin propelling him to her.

She paused, again overcome with the memories of loss, of the fear that gripped her when she saw him lying helpless on the deck.

Her heart seemed to skip a beat and pain filled her chest.

"Elanna?"

Then he reached out to her, his hands caressing her face, his eyes searching hers.

"I could have gotten you killed, them killed, started a war!"

"No," Storm sighed. "You did what you had to do. And I love you even more for it. You followed your heart."

"And my heart almost led me to disaster."

"Your heart gave them what they were looking for, Elanna. And you still plan on teaching them."

"I, ah…" A blush spread across her cheeks as she remembered the implied promises she had made.

"I understand. And I will help."

"You?" Elanna gasped, the shock of his words enough to jolt her out of her misery. "But you hate humans!"

"No, I don't," he replied as he leaned in close and ran his cheek along side hers, caressing her gently with his smooth skin. "I don't trust them, but I don't hate them. After all, they gave me you."

While she basked in the tenderness of his words, Storm pulled back, grasped her hand, and began pulling her through the waters.

"Where—?"

"Shh!"

All thoughts of the encounter, as she would refer to it, were pushed to the back of her mind as he propelled her through the currents at lightning speed.

Elanna let her body relax and go limp, as she gave in to her mate's demands. Silently, he pulled her along the waterways at hyper-speed, past the pod of three, past the caverns of their underwater home, past the returning armies of Merfolk in their rainbow colors and their excited chatter.

He tugged her along until they reached warm, familiar waters.

As they exploded from the enveloping embrace of the sea, Storm flung his hair back wildly, slinging the water from his body as he jerked his mate up to his side.

Elanna emerged from the water with a laugh on her lips, her eyes instantly adjusting to the waning sunlight that bathed the waters in crystalline colors of blues and pinks.

She felt her mate's arms wrap around her, pulling her tight against him as small waves broke against their bodies.

She sighed as she felt his warm fin tickle her feet as he kept them both afloat.

"It began here," he whispered, leaning close and lapping the water from her face. "I found you here."

Turning around, Elanna stifled a laugh as she saw her island nearby and the scorched sand where she had made her fire pit.

Before she finished picking out landmarks, Storm propelled her closer and closer to the sandy beach, until she felt the rough sand against her bottom.

"What are you doing?" she asked as he eased her back onto shore and loomed over her, half of their bodies submerged in the water, the rest reclining on the sand, which still held the day's heat.

"What I should have done when first we met," he whispered as he lowered his face for a gentle kiss.

"Mmm." Elanna moaned as his tongue invaded her mouth, and his flavor exploded on her tongue.

Her hands tangled in the wet silk of his hair, pulling him closer. She felt his rough hands span her waist.

She was eased higher onto the shore as she parted her legs and let the bulk of him settle between her thighs.

Elanna wrapped her legs around his waist, delighting in the feel of him, where she desired him most to be.

"Elanna," Storm sighed. "I thought I'd lost you. I thought I would never hold you in my arms again."

He pulled back from her, letting her glimpse the anguish and the passion that suffused his face.

Leaning up on his elbows, he visually traced her body, the full breasts with their dusky tips, the tight stomach that seemed to quiver as he touched her with his fingertips, the mat of curly hair that shielded her feminine secrets, so different from any woman he had known. And then there were her legs.

Oh, to lie between a pair of legs, to feel the heat from the center of her body, to feel those same legs wrap around him in passion…

"I have to have you!" he gasped as he lowered his head to her nipples, nibbling and biting at the turgid peaks.

"Whatever you want, Storm!" Elanna gasped, her arms going above her head in mute surrender as her back arched up into the ministrations of his nipping teeth, his laving tongue, his suckling lips.

She closed her eyes and moaned as he began to move lower, leaving a damp trail from one nipple to the other, before slowly licking his way down to her navel.

"Hey! Tickles," Elanna chortled, her legs sliding up his strong sides as she rolled her head in the sand, one hand coming down to touch his head.

"Tickles?" he asked, all innocence as he laved concentric circles around her navel. His tongue finally settled in the sexy indentation, making her go from giggles to groans as a sudden desire tightened in her stomach.

At her impassioned reaction, Storm lowered his head a bit more, his nose nestling in her damp curls.

"Storm?" she whispered, uncertain as his hands gripped her thighs, lifted her from the water, spreading them farther apart.

"You smell so good," he replied softly, burying his nose in deep, touching the top of her slit and inhaling. "You make me hungry."

His words were matter of fact, but his eyes glistened as he looked up at her face.

"I have to taste," he begged, his breath flowing through the thin curls as his tongue darted out to lash at her, caressing her clit as it slowly emerged from its hooded cowl.

"Storm!" she gasped as he lowered his head more and began a series of teasing laps over her rapidly swelling lips and clit.

"You taste of the sea," he purred, his fingers parting her moist lips and grazing over her pink opening. "I want more."

Elanna's hands dropped down to grip his hair as she felt his tongue dart inside her cunt, pressing against nerves she never knew she had.

Oh, the taste of her, the smell of her, the soft texture of her skin! Storm thought as he became lost in the textures and flavors of his woman. Never had he felt such a powerful reaction to a woman! And he had no idea what made him perform this wanton act of carnality on her!

But when he felt her, smelled her, he knew he had to have this part of her as well, to drown in the taste of her.

He felt his cock throb inside its sheath, felt himself become slippery with his natural lubricant, felt his slit opening as her thighs tightened around his head.

And her reaction…she was crying out his name, arching up, tightening her body around him, and he found he liked it. No, he desired it more than anything else.

"Storm!" Elanna screamed as she felt a tingling in her thighs travel to her cunt, felt her muscles bunch beneath her skin. "Storm, I can't! I can't! Please!"

And then he was taking his finger, wetting it in his mouth and plunging that one digit deeply into her, searching for that spot that had made her howl in rapture once before.

"Storm!" Elanna screamed, spreading her thighs wider, granting him access to her most tender, delicate parts.

And being the warrior that he was, Storm gladly accepted the surrender and moved in.

His tongue found her clit, pink and swollen, and laved it with his tongue, stroked it softly, then harder as her screams increased in volume. His one finger became two, and the two became coated in her essence which ran down his hand as her sheath widened to accommodate his possession.

His head began to swirl with the heat he found in her, with her reaction to his touch, and he found himself addicted, wanting more.

Elanna trembled, she shuddered, she groaned. Her body wasn't capable of much more as wave after wave of increasing pleasure washed over her body.

The things he was doing to her…the things he was making her feel! Never had her body reacted in such a hungry matter!

It was frightening, it was raw, and it was real.

She needed more of it, as she felt her desire for release increase until it blotted out all thought in her mind.

She wanted Storm! She had to have him riding hard between her thighs.

His fingers felt good. They touched on a spot inside her that made sparks fly in her mind, but they were not enough!

She wanted to be spread, to be filled to overflowing, to be stretched to capacity by the thick cock he possessed. And she wanted it now!

Tugging and pulling at him, she wrenched him up and away from her, while she practically threw him onto his back.

"In me now!" she panted as she desperately straddled his body. "Now, Storm!"

Blinking up at her, Storm grasped her hips between his hands and steadied her over his bulging crotch.

"Ready me," he groaned as he ground his encased cock against the moisture pouring from her body, caressing her clit with his motions, making her throw her head back with a sharp hungry cry.

Frantically, her hands reached down between them, stroking and caressing his bulge, searching for the slit that held his magnificence from her. She wanted cock and she wanted it now!

Her fingers moved across his opening and he sucked in a deep breath, moaning as the feel of her penetrating his sheath momentarily stole his energy. Then it came roaring back, doubled in intensity as this need filled him to the breaking point.

"Yes!" Elanna hissed as she gently widened the slit and his cock sprang out, thick, hot and wet.

"Guide me," Storm growled as he lifted her over his straining cock head that eagerly sought the warm depths of her body. "Put me in, Elanna. Put me where you need me most."

Shuddering, Elanna found the control to grasp him at his base and hold him steady as she began to lower herself down on his thick cock.

"Oh God! Feels so good," Elanna groaned as she sank deeper and deeper on Storm, his cock filling her body to overflowing, scratching an itch that seemed to form deep inside her.

Storm shuddered as he felt her wet heat sinking onto him, his body penetrating deeper than it had before.

His hands urged her to lean forward, and as she did, his lips latched onto her nipple, sucking hard at the tender fruit.

Elanna whimpered as this new position pushed the thick head of his cock against her hot spot and sent shudders wrenching through her body.

"Make love to me," Storm urged as he released one nipple and took the other into his mouth. "Satisfy us both! Give us what we need!"

No other words were needed as Elanna slowly rose and fell on his supine body, her knees tightening against his waist as he began to pick up speed.

Storm's hands caressed her side, running over her breast, caressing over her ass and thighs, increasing the skin-to-skin contact and making her inner muscles tremble.

Finally, Elanna reared back, riding high and proud over his body as she began to sink down rapidly, pulling out to the point where his head nudged her opening, then slamming down again.

Storm tossed his head from side to side, holding on as his woman moved to pleasure them both.

Finally, his hands reached up and grasped her waist, holding her steady as he arched his hips up, slamming into her on the downstroke.

"Yes!" Elanna screamed at this additional stimulation. "Yes, Storm, yes!"

She rose up and slammed down. Storm met each thrust, and a quick rhythm was established as both of them closed their eyes in ecstasy.

Suddenly, Elanna froze, her muscles tightened, her body unable to move as the pressure building up within her snapped!

She screamed as her muscles began to dance around his cock, milking it as her climax tore through her body!

Elanna whimpered as her whole body shook, as waves of release pummeled her, melting her control, turning her muscles into mush as she collapsed on top of him.

Storm threw his head back, groaning as he felt her body spasm over his! He felt a tingling deep within his spine as she shuddered and collapsed on top of him.

"Elanna," he whispered as one hand left her waist to tangle in her whirlpool hair. "Elanna, I need more. May I continue?"

Still unable to speak, Elanna buried her head in his neck and nodded. Though sensitive, she wanted to feel his body explode inside her, to give him the joy he had so selflessly delivered to her.

Storm ran his hand over her back, kneading muscles, as his hips began to sharply prod upwards!

The world began to spin as he felt himself sliding through the moisture her release left behind.

He felt small spasms as her inner walls trembled in aftershock. They seemed to tickle the swelling head of his cock just right.

"Oh, Creator! Oh, Elanna!" he gasped as his hips began to thrust up uncontrollably. "Yes!"

Storm swore his head exploded as he felt his lower body tighten and his hips thrust one final time, sending spurt after spurt of his creamy hot seed deep into her body.

His arms tightened around her and he lost the fight not to scream out his climax. His quivering muscles reduced him to seaweed.

"Elanna!" he muttered over and over, burying his face in her hair as the spasms eased and his body dropped back to the warm damp sand. "Elanna."

"I love you, Storm," Elanna breathed, delighting in the feeling of completion she achieved as she felt him go crazy within her.

Rolling to his side, Storm felt his cock soften and ease back inside his sheath, but the sense of relaxation he now felt made any other movement impossible.

"How I need you," he said softly as he slowly ran his fingers through her hair. "How could I live without you?"

"You won't ever have to find out," Elanna sighed, snuggling into his arms and letting her cares and woes float away with the tide.

Storm held her tighter, breathing in her scent, as he took in the seascape before him.

His woman in his arms, the sun setting over the waters, the colors of the day fading into the deep purple of night.

He closed his eyes and basked in his sense of utter completion.

He would deal with the humans, because he had to. He would deal with Amadala and Sting because it was required of him. But he would live…and love, because of the wonderful woman in his arms.

How blessed he was, the day she fell from the sky. She changed his life, his perceptions, his world.

And for that, he thanked the Creator.

Why an electronic book?

We live in the Information Age—an exciting time in the history of human civilization, in which technology rules supreme and continues to progress in leaps and bounds every minute of every day. For a multitude of reasons, more and more avid literary fans are opting to purchase e-books instead of paper books. The question from those not yet initiated into the world of electronic reading is simply: *Why?*

1. *Price.* An electronic title at Ellora's Cave Publishing and Cerridwen Press runs anywhere from 40% to 75% less than the cover price of the exact same title in paperback format. Why? Basic mathematics and cost. It is less expensive to publish an e-book (no paper and printing, no warehousing and shipping) than it is to publish a paperback, so the savings are passed along to the consumer.

2. *Space.* Running out of room in your house for your books? That is one worry you will never have with electronic books. For a low one-time c ost, you can purchase a handheld device specifically designed for e-reading. Many e-readers have large, convenient screens for viewing. Better yet, hundreds of titles can be stored within your new library—on a single microchip. There are a variety of e-readers from different manufacturers. You can also read e-books on your PC or laptop computer. (Please note that Ellora's Cave does not endorse any specific brands. You can check our websites at www.ellorascave.com or

www.cerridwenpress.com for information we make available to new consumers.)

3. *Mobility*. Because your new e-library consists of only a microchip within a small, easily transportable e-reader, your entire cache of books can be taken with you wherever you go.

4. ***Personal Viewing Preferences.*** Are the words you are currently reading too small? Too large? Too… ANNOYING? Paperback books cannot be modified according to personal preferences, but e-books can.

5. ***Instant Gratification.*** Is it the middle of the night and all the bookstores near you are closed? Are you tired of waiting days, sometimes weeks, for bookstores to ship the novels you bought? Ellora's Cave Publishing sells instantaneous downloads twenty-four hours a day, seven days a week, every day of the year. Our webstore is never closed. Our e-book delivery system is 100% automated, meaning your order is filled as soon as you pay for it.

Those are a few of the top reasons why electronic books are replacing paperbacks for many avid readers.

As always, Ellora's Cave and Cerridwen Press welcome your questions and comments. We invite you to email us at Comments@ellorascave.com or write to us directly at Ellora's Cave Publishing Inc., 1056 Home Avenue, Akron, OH 44310-3502.

The
☥ Ellora's Cave ☥
Library

Stay up to date with Ellora's Cave Titles in Print with our Quarterly Catalog.

To recieve a catalog,
send an email with your name
and mailing address to:

CATALOG@ELLORASCAVE.COM

or send a letter or postcard
with your mailing address to:

Catalog Request
c/o Ellora's Cave Publishing, Inc.
1056 Home Avenue
Akron, Ohio 44310-3502

Ellora's Cavemen
Legendary Tails

Try an e-book for your immediate
reading pleasure or order these titles in print from

www.EllorasCave.com

Ellora's Cave
The Best in Today's Romantica™

Got Sex?

Share it with the world or just make a BOLD statement in the bedroom with an Ellora's Cave Got Sex? T-shirt.

$14.99

The world's largest e-publisher of Erotic Romance.

ELLORA'S CAVE PUBLISHING, INC.
☥ WWW.ELLORASCAVE.COM ☥

COMING TO A BOOKSTORE NEAR YOU!

ELLORA'S CAVE

Bestselling Authors Tour

UPDATES AVAILABLE AT
WWW.ELLORASCAVE.COM

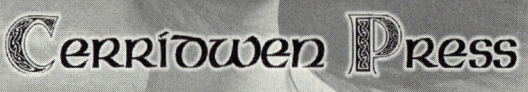

Cerridwen Press
Monthly Newsletter

News
Author Appearances
Book Signings
New Releases
Contests
Author Profiles
Feature Articles

Available online at
www.CerridwenPress.com

Cerridwen, the Celtic Goddess of wisdom, was the muse who brought inspiration to storytellers and those in the creative arts. Cerridwen Press encompasses the best and most innovative stories in all genres of today's fiction. Visit our site and discover the newest titles by talented authors who still get inspired - much like the ancient storytellers did, once upon a time.

Cerridwen Press

www.cerridwenpress.com

Discover for yourself why readers can't get enough of the multiple award-winning publisher

Ellora's Cave.

Whether you prefer e-books or paperbacks,

be sure to visit EC on the web at
www.ellorascave.com

for an erotic reading experience that will leave you breathless.